The Burning Desire Dupe

james blakley

the Burning Desire Dupe

THE POWERS THAT BE
PUBLISHING

Publisher: The Powers That Be Publishing

Paperback ISBN 978-1-7362537-6-2
eBook ISBN 978-1-7362537-7-9

1 3 5 7 9 10 8 6 4 2

Thanks to God for everything. First, for giving me a wonderful, hardworking family who raised me, supported me when I was nothing, and encouraged me to achieve my first feat of fiction. For the blessing of tremendously talented teachers, professors, friends, and colleagues who helped broaden my mind. For the flair for fiction and for the guts to go where I've had to in order to help make it grow. And finally, for three great states among the fabulous fifty: Missouri (where I learned what I know); Kansas (where I've used it to survive); and Oregon (where Anno Domini Creative Services' top-notch production design assistance to The Powers That Be Publishing has given me the opportunity to thrive).

"The more things are forbidden, the more popular they become."

—Mark Twain

"All art is quite useless."

—Oscar Wilde (preface of The *Portrait of Dorian Gray*)

Il faut souffrir pour être belle (To be beautiful, one must suffer).

—French saying

"These trials will show that your faith is genuine. It is being tested as fire tests and purifies gold…"

—I Peter 1:7 (New Living Translation Bible)

Contents

Prologue

The rays of the rising June sun ripped back the brisk black cover of night, exposing The Western Cherokee Nation and Oklahoma, in which it lay, to what was guaranteed to be a scorching summer day. But with it came the certainty of another kind of cruelty. One that criminals fret and sweat about and is known as 'the heat' or, in Indian Country, the marshals.

A squadron of drones sniffed out something suspicious, burrowed in Indian Country, and Cherokee Marshal Service cruisers made a beeline for it from the capital in Tahlequah. One by one the cruisers finally stopped; law enforcers then poured out and awaited word from Roberta "Billie" Cosh: The hard as a baton lead officer.

Cosh found a beat-up moving truck in an apartment complex parking lot. She knocked on the back of it three times, causing the door to rise just enough for her to crawl inside and see a concealed man sitting in front of computer screens. "Well?" Cosh queried.

Kenwood Comms turned his attention away from controlling the high-flying surveillance swarm to his superior. "The drones picked up a lot of heat patterns," he reported.

"Human?" Cosh wanted to know.

"They are a bit high but could mean people are inside. If so and they're jumpy, worries can easily drive up body temperatures," Comms replied. "The curtains didn't help readings though. If the tenants were smart enough to put mylar behind them, it messes with the drones' infrared sensors bigtime. And even though we're here early, the forecast still calls for a high of 104. With that kind of heat, their infrared cameras will probably have trouble telling the difference between human body temperature and the summer heat. And if they killed the air conditioning, it will be like an oven inside."

"So we may already be getting false positives," Cosh concluded.

"Could be," Comms answered. "But there's another reason for high temp readings. The drones may be picking up explosives."

Cosh knew this was no longer her call. She left the truck for her cruiser. "Tahlequah Control, this is Command," she radioed from inside.

"Go ahead, Command," the disembodied voice of authority replied.

"Surveillance picked up heat patterns within the

probability range of being human inside the target but can't be sure."

After 10 minutes of deliberation, the orders finally came down.

Cosh returned to Comms. "Break out the EVD, we're going in," she told him.

The technical officer unloaded the Explosives Vapor Detector (EVD); then, donned a helmet and body armor; and finally left the hive for the front-line. The other marshals received their orders and also took up arms. Cosh finally motioned them forward and led a sprint through the apartment complex to the target: A two-bedroom bottom floor unit.

Once there, Cosh issued the customary loud knock on the front door followed by saying, "Mister Casper Duppy, this is the Cherokee Marshal Service. We have a warrant for your arrest. Open the door, please."

There was no answer. Cosh repeated the order. But the only ones to come out were innocent tenants to see what the commotion was about. Cosh drew her 9 MM pistol and waved another marshal to the front. He arrived with a battering ram. Everyone readied their weapons and Comms the EVD, as the oblong steel bar broke through the wooden entrance with one demolishing swing.

BOOM! The marshals barged into a living room full of life, electronic life that is. Tables of abandoned laptops and burner phones greeted them. As they fanned out into other rooms, only leftovers of a past life were found (abandoned sleeping bags and wastepaper baskets crammed with snack food wrappers and crumpled beer cans).

"*Well?*" Cosh asked Comms.

"No explosives detected by the EVD, but its abilities are limited," the tech officer responded. "I wouldn't turn anything on until the bomb techs and Hazmat arrive with heavy duty detection, in case of timers or delayed triggers."

"Thanks. Other than the weather, what caused the false positives?"

"EMI."

"*EMI?*"

"Electromagnetic interference," Comms explained. "The computer hookups to Wi-Fi probably spiked temperatures, along with the dark colored curtains and no air conditioning. Add to that heat released by top floor occupants and their stuff and that's what duped the drones. Speaking of "occupants," Deputy Marshal Cosh, I recommend contacting apartment management or the landlord to evacuate the premises until we get the all clear."

Cosh ordered her team out and holstered her handgun. She looked back over the empty apartment. "Casper, you've ghosted us...*for now*," Cosh muttered, as she left."

Wit's end

"On behalf of The Principal Chief, thanks for use of the thermal drones and EVD equipment. We owe you one, Molly." After the Attorney General for the Western Cherokee Nation thanked his Osage Nation counterpart for the equipment loan, he hung up the phone and reared back in his leather chair. With eyes closed, he recalled what should have been enviable law enforcement progress. "We doubled the number of victims' services advocates, granted three million to support victims of crimes and their families, dedicated another thirty-five worth of investments to develop our legal system, and finally built our own penitentiary,"

"Don't forget the addition of a dozen more marshals to police the 14 counites," Deputy Attorney General John Whittier Writ mentioned from the other side of the desk.

That expenditure, however, brought the A.G.

back to the present. "Money for more marshals...
who couldn't bring in Casper Duppy!" he moaned at
another missed opportunity that the press didn't
fail to publicize and criticize the Principal Chief for.

"That's not exactly *all* we hired them to do, sir.
They did their best, but they're not crack computer
techs. We are dealing with some crafty devils who, incidentally, fooled the Osage's drone tech you praised."

"Not "praised," but gave thanks for," The Attorney
General explained the call to the Osage A.G..

"All we know for sure about computers is that we're
only as smart as our last system update," Writ said.

"I still don't know RAM from ROM and CGI
from AI. Do you?" Before Writ could answer, his
boss recognized his youth and grunted, "Of course,
you do." The aging Attorney General stood, trudged
over to the window of his office, and peeked through
the blinds, wondering where Duppy might be. Was
he even still in Indian Country?

"I hate to say it, sir, but maybe it's time to invite
the Feds in," Writ recommended. "If for no other
reason than to maybe have them go over what data
is on Duppy's computers and phones."

"*No!*" the Attorney General stubbornly objected.
"*McGirt v. Oklahoma* gave us the right to prosecute
criminal cases involving tribal members on tribal
lands. Now, especially with the headline-grabbing
Casper Duppy case hanging in the balance, everyone's watching to see how well we do. Actually,

watching with hungry eyes to snatch it away from us under the Major Crimes Act and give it to some U.S. Attorney who will claim having more resources and experience to get the job done. I don't want to give them that chance. Your thoughts on how to make my thoughts a reality, Writ."

"I have a way to keep this case in the family," Writ announced, hatching the plan he came up with during the A.G.'s rant. "Duppy probably thinks setting up shop in The Cherokee Nation is safe because the most he can get, if convicted of fraud, is three years. But by a quirk in that same law, we could stack three offenses and nail Duppy for almost ten years."

Hope shone in the Attorney General's eyes for the first time. "Good plan, if we can capture Duppy."

"I know of someone with a knack for spotting knockoffs and stopping scams."

"Being capable is one thing, but will they accept the risks that come with the job."

Writ's smile suggested the odds were great because, as he announced, "The nominee is a Cherokee."

CHAPTER 2

Exercise in Espionage

It was shaping up to be a late July morning that was stranger than most in a city famous for its oddities: San Francisco. Missing was the scenic, sudsy fog bank blanketing the bay and cool breezes brought in by the prevailing westerly wind. And for the waking masses, moving around in heavy, dull air that reeked of exhaust gas and sweat felt sticky and plain icky. It led one early riser to wonder, as she peeked outside her top floor hotel room window, *Is this The City by the Bay or L.A.?!* She would find out, as she drew the shades and prepared to start the day.

The out-of-towner was revived by a cold shower. She then slipped into a red, ribbed-knit tank top and black leggings; then laced up her 4D footwear; and tied her long hair into a ponytail. Last came the necklace which she looped around her neck and carefully centered the artificial onyx teardrop pendant mid-sternum.

When ready, the woman locked her room and rode the elevator down to the lobby. Outside, across the street, she spotted the plain gray sedan she was told would be waiting. Once traffic thinned, the woman approached the car and got in.

The driver turned her head and said, "Good morning, Ms. Nightcrow."

"Luna's fine," the passenger replied.

The sedan started and began the steep descent from Luna Nightcrow's hilly Hotel District digs into the valley of grittier street level life in "The City's" Crawdad District. In the shadows of its skyscrapers, shop after mom-and-pop shop, dives, and itinerants' tents passed by. Finally, a strip mall at the far end of Crawdad caught Luna's eye.

The driver told Luna the mall was one of the city's attempts to clean up the area's image. "*Gentrification*," she scoffed. "Imagine what would happen if New York City tried rehabbing Harlem's unique, inner city charm and culture or ..."

"Yeah," Luna idly replied to the anti-urban renewal ramblings. She was fixated on the mall's layout. Let's see, Luna took stock mentally, there's the plastics distributorship, hip seafood café, and ... *bingo*: *Cable Cardio Fitness Center!*

The driver parked across the street from the strip mall. Luna opened the passenger side door and left. Once inside Cable Cardio, she stretched and then spotted an empty treadmill. Luna walked up to the console, punched in the pace, and began the stationary race. *This is one way to keep your bod as fit as your fraud busting brain!* the insurance investigator laughed to herself.

It wasn't long before a deep voice stopped Luna's stride with the greeting, *"Hola, mamacita!"*

Normally, hearing that she is still *mamacita* material (or a 'hot momma' in Spanish) would be an ego boost for 50 year-old Luna. But she wasn't Hispanic nor, when she turned, was the man who admired her. Luna couldn't help but to drink in his dark roasted, upper body robustness; and then simulate an inviting smile. *"What up, bro?"* she finally voiced her interest.

The man grinned. "Isn't it obvious?" he asked.

Luna played along; her eyes obligingly hurried downhill this time, and back up. "I guess so. Biker shorts leave little to imagine," she chuckled.

The man looked Luna up and down too, though it lasted like a marathon. But when through he asked, "Are you new?"

Luna nodded. "From SoCal," she fibbed. *"And you?"*

"I am a NorCal homie from the crop of 1992, Miss..."

"My friends call me 'Chase,'" Luna continued to lie on the fly.

"Because you play hard to get, I bet," the man guessed.

"It's more like most guys find it hard to keep up with me, mentally not necessarily coitally."

"I guess that last word, whatever it means, shows you're right."

"Don't let that stop your attempt at a conquest, Mr..?"

"Steel, Ferris Steel."

Luna grinned. "Cute name to go with that swole frame."

"Shows I got a brain." Steel noticed Luna's necklace. "That chain is straight fire, by the way," he said.

Luna stopped him from touching it, suggesting instead, "Maybe we could cool off with a protein shake sometime."

That did the trick, as Steel's attention turned to Luna's taste. "Do you like chocolate, Chase."

She nodded. "As long as you're down with caramel, too."

Steel beamed. "*Straight up!* I can stretch it to two."

"Sounds fun. But if you'll pardon me," Luna said, starting up the treadmill, "I have to run. Catch you later?"

Steel grinned but told himself, It was fun while it lasted, but she's out of my class.

Luna resumed the motions of a serious treadmill training. Suddenly, out of the corner of her eye, she spotted Ferris Steel heading for the weightroom. *Finally!* Luna exhaled and took the chance to leave. She jogged back across the street to the ambiguity of the gray car. Inside though, she was met with one clear question from Caitlyn "Cait" Ashbury (the bookish junior insurance fraud investigator who was stuck behind the wheel because she knew the streets but didn't have Luna's all around appeal). *"Was it him?!"* Cait pressed her colleague for the rundown.

"Let's see," Luna suggested, reaching into the backseat. She recovered a laptop and turned it on. Luna then undid her necklace (whose pendant was the lens of a hidden camera and DVR) and plugged its "chain," really a USB cord, into the connecting port. After typing in keyboard commands, the results of her encounter replayed for Cait.

Luna also wanted to verify the identity. *"So..?"* she asked her partner who had the only photo to date of the man who called himself "Ferris Steel."

Cait compared her black-and-white security camera shot to Luna's footage. "Looks like our man to me: Casper Duppy," she replied.

Luna let out a sigh of relief and fatigue, as she grabbed a few napkins from the glovebox to wipe her glistening brow clean. Meanwhile, Cait gazed at the necklace camera. *"This is lit, Luna!"* the thirty-something marveled. "Who is your jeweler?"

"The Osage Nation's skunkworks branch back home," Luna confided to her colleague. "They cook up all kinds of cool fieldwork tech. They wanted to hook me up with one of their superfly mini drones, but I didn't want too much automation to put me out of a job."

"Don't worry, Luna. California has some pretty strict rules about civilian drone and GPS surveillance. So I think the up close and personal approach slayed it."

"Thanks. I overdid the treadmill gimmick though. I feel like I stepped out of a sauna."

"Me too, after your Cardio innuendos with Casper. *Damn, girl!*"

Luna grinned. "You liked my little cam show?"

"Is that your side hustle?" Cait wanted to know.

Luna suddenly saw something. "Feast your webcam on who's coming out," she told her partner.

It was Cait's first time seeing him in the flesh. "Casper Duppy," she reaffirmed.

"Are you up for a little exercise in espionage?" Luna asked.

"Lift, point, and click? Copy that," Cait answered back, raising her Digital Single Lens Reflex camera to her eye. Feverishly, she snapped fresh photographs of Casper strutting to his car but not just any car.

Luna identified it as, "The white, turbo-charged model. It has to be the car that pissed off poster tipped the crime catcher chatroom about."

"Yeah, the apple of Casper's eye," Cait agreed.

Then, Luna seethed. "Bought through his ghost brokerage scheme. Forty thousand conned out of Tribal Trust Transportation Protection customers back home."

"And another fifteen hundred from my people, the Muwekma Ohlone," Cait added.

"Without whose help I couldn't have tracked him here. Thanks again, girlfriend."

Casper's con involved applying for real auto policies in others' names, pocketing the premium payments, and then quickly cancelling the policies without their knowing, until filing a claim. Through advertising cheap "insurance" on a slew of social media sites and messaging apps set up in the rural Oklahoma apartment, Casper and his cronies tricked shoppers for lower rates into leaving personal information on the application process. And because each Internet, phone app, and other gateway didn't share records, tracking the crime was slow. But The Western Cherokee Nation Attorney General's Office tasked Luna with the job.

After relentlessly tracking social media, collating and separating its hard facts from hearsay, and file carving clues from Casper's confiscated but wiped computers, Luna's best guess was that the hoodlums headed west. Nevada boasted a high number of car insurance scams. But when nothing turned up there, Luna hopped a jet for The Golden State next door.

The scammers' high level computer habit and

appetite for American Indian prey made California ideal new digs. And when a single joint auto policy with the same phone number and address for dozens of the Muwekma Ohlone, a small Bay Area tribe, was created, Luna was certain Casper Duppy did it. She was thrilled that he apparently didn't know the Muwekma Ohlone weren't federally recognized. So Oklahoma's McGirt law didn't apply and allowed the state and local police to act without tribal jurisdictional authority. However, they needed more evidence for a warrant, as the scam was so far a largely low dollar insurance matter.

Cait gave a tip of the cap to Duppy. "Nice car."

"Crooks never learn, do they?" Luna grunted. "Like moths to a flame, they're attracted to the flashiest things."

"Maybe it's a smart choice," Cait replied. "That car would be like hell on wheels to catch up to, with a V12 that can reach nearly 200 miles per hour before redline. And that chassis will let her still turn on a dime. *Whew!*"

"It sounds like you're really hot and bothered," Luna chuckled. "Turn on the AC for us both."

Cait laughed and prepared to start the air condition for her perspiring partner.

As Luna watched Casper unlock his car, she muttered, "If all else fails, maybe we can bust him for a car that sounds like it breaks California emissions standards."

As Casper got settled in, there was a flash. Then morning shot from 80 to 1,000 degrees Fahrenheit with a … *WHAM!* A jolting explosion blew out the front plate glass windows of the Cable Cardio Fitness Center. Rockets of roaring orange flame shot into the sky and billowing black smoke blanketed the next-door businesses.

Luna and Cait peeked over the dash from duck-and-cover to see chaos outside. Panicked people rushed for their cars or scurried for any safety. Luna thought Casper triggered a car bomb, until his white model appeared undamaged and pulling out in too leisurely a manner.

Cait felt it too. "Do we go with what we've got?" she asked.

Luna worried that "it might not be enough."

"Shall we then?" Cait asked.

Luna nodded and gave the battle cry, *"Charge, girlfriend!"*

CHAPTER 3

Crosstown Traffic

Cait turned the key and stepped on the gas. But the car accelerated too fast. Casper must have detected she was on his tail and also sped up. Cait eased off a bit since Casper's white paintjob wouldn't be hard to miss in the flow of darker cars.

With the Cable Cardio inferno a rearview memory, both cars left The Crawdad District and entered increasing crosstown traffic that was congested by an onslaught of stoplights. At first, both Casper and Cait went with the flow. But when the light turned green at Fourth and Gold, things quickly changed.

Whether Casper thought he could lose Cait and Luna or they thought they would lose him someone panicked. And shadowing's disciplined pace suddenly turned into a stock car race. Casper turned sharply into the right lane. Cait followed a bit late but with some skill squeezed in too. Another traffic light appeared ahead. This time, though, Casper ignored its yellow flash and dashed through the intersection. Cait raced after him on red, narrowly missing motorists entering from the other direction. Casper pulled into another line of traffic a minute later. Unfortunately, it was on a narrow one-way street which slowed his roll.

When Casper checked the driver's side mirror, the gray car was still in tow. And with sidewalks to the left and right, both cars were hemmed in. No place to go...*or was there?* Casper's criminal mind measured the sidewalks' size. One was a perfect fit, to his surprise, although it had more storefronts behind it. Casper made up his mind. As soon as the car in front inched forward enough, the turbo-charged sportscar tore from the clogged line, jumped onto the just-right walkway, and barreled headlong. Cait wouldn't be outdone; when her break came, she wheeled up onto the sidewalk and continued hot pursuit. Terrified pedestrians leaped for their lives, as the 2 cars continued their dangerous drive.

"Damn, girl!" Luna swore. "I thought you were for keeping up the inner city image, not destroying it!"

"This isn't Crawdad," Cait told her passenger. "Just bringing a bit of it to another district."

Suddenly, the white sportscar ripped a snack bar awning off. It hit the trailing gray car's windshield and snagged on the wiper blades, flapping like a flag and blocking Cait's view. Luna reached out the window and yanked it and a blade off, returning clear vision. Both cars banged off the corner curb and roared into another intersection, narrowly avoiding collisions with law-abiding drivers who could only honk their horns in protest.

For five more minutes, even though it felt like forever to Luna, both cars weaved in and out of traffic, flying from street to street. Casper finally had enough and whipped around a corner at 20 miles an hour. The low-riding sportscar fishtailed into the opposite lane but quickly straightened and zoomed away. Cait forgot she wasn't driving a sportscar, until her high-speed turn sent the gray car into a dangerous spin out. Cait jammed the brakes and just avoided hitting a telephone pole. The car came to rest 180 degrees the other way. Oncoming vehicles screeched to halts, allowing the gray car back into the correct line of traffic.

Cait banged the steering wheel in disgust at what felt like defeat. *"Dammit, he got away!"*

Luna dangled her necklace camera in the air. "Not for long," she announced. "The game is still on."

CHAPTER 4

Cooler Climes

The white sportscar made the Highway 101 turnoff and coasted into the far away safety of South San Francisco. The man who appeared to be Casper Duppy eventually parked near his destination and took out a small flip phone styled cellphone. On cue, it rang. Alias Casper lifted it to his ear and answered, "The job's done. I had a blast," he laughed.

The voice on the other end sounded worried but not about Casper's amusement. "We didn't expect so much collateral damage," it told him.

Casper shrugged and reminded the caller that, "Shit happens. You are lucky it all went down in a crappy part of town. Besides, you came to me; you knew what might happen. I went through, and your upfront pay is true. So, keep your head and stay cool."

"I hear you."

"You got alibis, right?"

"It's taken care of. And you?"

"Likewise," Casper confirmed. "Still looking forward to the rest of the pay."

"We'll call after we hear from the insurance company," the caller promised.

"Solid. And remember to keep your head or you might end up ... dead."

"All right, all right!"

"Peace, out."

Casper hung up, reached into his gym bag, and retrieved an engraved wooden totem pole ornament from his contact in town. He unscrewed the crowning raven's head. The hollowed out inside hid papers. Casper pulled them out and discovered that one piece contained an offer to commit his crimes in cooler climes. The second piece was his ticket there.

Casper left the car, pulled out the flip phone cellphone, and placed it tightly under the front tire. He got back in and started up. The car rolled forward, crushing the device to bits as it continued on course for the private airport terminal.

The man Luna and Cait thought was Casper Duppy still wondered to himself, *Who were those chicks chasing me...Freddie Burns?!*

CHAPTER 5

Taken for a Ride

It wasn't too long before Luna was called to the district attorney's office. *Maybe this is the big break in the Casper Duppy case!* she hoped.

Luna cut short her around-the-clock Internet quest for Casper Duppy. She showered, dressed, locked the door, and caught a ride on the BART (Bay Area Rapid Transit). An hour later, the insurance investigator sat in the office of one of the assistant district attorneys. It was a small, oak-paneled place with shelves of golden law manuals that seemed like props in the age of easy online research. Its current occupant was the Assistant District Attorney for Fraud Investigation Golda Gates: A lanky Jew of sixty-two whose round spectacles and dark hair tied into a bun made her look like a law school dean.

During their initial pleasantries, Luna discovered that Gates once worked as a barista to help put herself through Berkley; and Gates, when offering her guest a drink, found that Luna's particular poison was espresso. So she brewed a cup, added ice, and was pleased (from her guest's purr) that it was done to perfection.

"Someday, a revived coffeeshop career awaits," Luna cajoled Gates.

"Glad I haven't lost my touch," the A.D.A. replied. Finally, the women got down to business. "Your strip mall intel proved valuable," Gates revealed, "if not in the way that The Western Cherokee and Muwekma Ohlone Nations might hope for. The man you "tracked," shall we say, through town was not Casper Duppy."

It sounded like the operation wasn't a total failure; Luna and Cait did something right. So Luna wanted to know, "Then who did we capture ... on film, anyway?"

"As you know from police reports, Cable Cardio wasn't the source of the explosion," Gates said.

"Right. Ground zero was the plastics distributorship next door. It sounds like you're going to tell me the fire wasn't an act of god or caused by some careless chemical imbalance."

"Those were the first thoughts of the fire department. What hasn't been released yet, Ms. Nightcrow, is that arson caused the explosion. A fire investigator made the determination, after which one of the distributorship's partners caved during police questioning and confessed it was done to stave off bankruptcy. For what it's worth, he also decided to confess because of the many injuries caused."

"Did his partner or partners ask forgiveness, too?" Luna inquired.

"If the police can find them, they will no doubt ask," Gates answered. "The man they hired, though, seems beyond contrition; arson is his life's mission. No flash in the pan antics for Mr. Freddie Burns: Aka Flaming Freddie, The Pyre of Desire, Freddie Wildfire, Fredrico Fuego, and half a dozen other street names. He is the man from your Cable Cardio surveillance footage."

Luna sighed, "It figures we'd be taken for a ride, fooled as it were. Our fitness center fieldwork came about from a tip about the purchase of a white sportscar by our target, Casper Duppy. But it was this Burns guy who splurged on the hotrod instead."

Gates handed Luna a manila folder filled with black-and-white photographs. "A special investi-gator with our office contacted the car dealer and obtained additional camera footage. As it turns out, Ms. Nightcrow, your Mr. Duppy only looked at the car but didn't buy it. Instead, it was Mr. Burns who came along later and bought it with cash and a false ID with the name C. Dupree.

"The meager surveillance evidence you received didn't show the actual purchase by Mr. Burns. According to the dealer, he extensively photographs browsers milling about for evidence of shoplifting or any other suspicious activity."

After leafing through the photos, Luna handed the folder back to Gates; then, took another sip of espresso. "I guess it would be easy to remember a customer putting down cold, hard cash for a car and engaging in the old-fashioned handshake to seal the deal," she admitted. "Afterward, the dealer could recycle old camera tape that didn't reveal anything unusual."

Gates took another album from her desk, removed the photos, and arranged them on top. "Although both men are bald African Americans, Mr. Burns obviously developed a more muscular build and shaved or lost his hair naturally since the last known image of him years ago."

Luna leaned in for a closer look. "So that explains the weightlifting: To change his appearance," she assumed.

"Mister Duppy, on the other hand, is older and taller if it's him, that is. We have only your Internet dossiers to go by."

Luna added, "Our Oklahoma hunt was spurred by informant reports. One common observation is that Mr. Duppy is believed to be a Freedman."

"I know the term well, given California's high number of Native American residents," Gates replied. "Freedmen, as it applies here, are descendants of African Americans who were originally enslaved by

The Cherokee and some other indigenous tribes but later set free."

"The U.S. District Court granted them full Cherokee citizenship rights before the pandemic," Luna added. "Which explains why our tribal authorities want to prosecute Duppy; it doesn't automatically involve Sooner State oversight or that of the Feds."

"Mister Burns, on the other hand, is not a Freedman," Gates said. "Although we do have solid evidence of his existence from not only your new footage, but issuance of a longstanding John Doe warrant."

"*A John Doe warrant?*" Luna asked.

"It is an arrest warrant that has—like your dossier for Mr. Duppy, for example—lots of detailed information about a suspect that usually doesn't include a real name or identity, hence "John Doe." The California Supreme Court recognizes their importance, allowing law enforcement to use detailed physical attributes of skin, eye, hair color, weight, tattoos, and even DNA to help arrest a suspect. The wanted party also doesn't have to know they are wanted for it to be legally binding. Furthermore, John Doe warrants can be out-of-state warrants for suspects in a state different than their own."

"So where do we go from here, Ms. Gates?"

"*We* don't go anywhere," she replied sharply.

Luna nodded knowingly. *The damned car chase!* she groaned silently.

"We have plenty from you already," was the

reason given by Gates for relieving her guest from further Casper Duppy duty. "With the club footage, photographs, and your dossier, we can ask a judge to issue a John Doe warrant for Mr. Duppy. Plus, the Golden State Fraud Department believes that the use of a fake ID with a name similar to Casper Duppy could mean that the 2 men were working together or they perhaps travelled in the same criminal circles. They also think that if they identify the tipster that led you to the white sportscar at Club Cardio, it can help them craft a better method of closing down the ghost brokerage scheme. So, Ms. Nightcrow, your hard work wasn't wasted."

"I understand. I've been wrong about tips before," Luna finally conceded. "Sometimes, it's the insurer's fault; they give me a wrong lead to follow or automatically mistake a claimant's motives for fraud. This slipup was on me, though, for believing too much of what I found on the Internet to be true."

"I think it's reasonable to assume that we've all been guilty of that," Gates agreed. "As for your tailing Burns through town..."

Uh oh! Luna braced for the impact of the book she knew was going to be thrown at her. She hoped to soften the blow by apologizing for authorizing Cait Ashbury to go through with the car chase.

"You are a civilian here, not law enforcement," Gates firmly reminded Luna. "And verily I say unto you, from California Code of Pursuit Conduct,

Chapter 1, Paragraph 2: 'Vehicles not equipped with emergency lighting and siren(s) are commonly barred from beginning or participating in any pursuit.' Given the time of day, no one was hurt but a lot of nerves were frayed."

"Along with an awning," Luna added, "which I don't mind paying to replace."

"It's been covered," Gates told her. "But don't take the law into your own hands, Ms. Nightcrow. Even in what we'll call an attempted citizen's arrest like this, there are serious consequences when not done properly. I won't take any more of your time. Please enjoy the rest of your stay *as a tourist* of The City By the Bay."

"Point taken, Ms. Gates. Thanks for the warning," Luna said, finishing off her iced espresso. Blowing our original car insurance case but looking like geniuses for discovering an arsonist because of it—*what a world!* At least I'm not in hot water here anymore, Luna said to herself.

As she left and closed the door, Luna suddenly thought, *Damn!* What grilling will The Cherokee Attorney General's Office have in store?

CHAPTER 6

Out of the Frying Pan

Luna returned to her hotel and phoned The Office of The Attorney General of the Western Cherokee Nation back home. Deputy A.G. John Whittier Writ, her handler, answered. Although Luna was a contract agent, he didn't consider himself her covert operations puppet master. It was more in the boxing sense of being a handler. He was managing a prize-fighter's drive in Luna: A woman who took down many criminals in a career that was far from done, despite what she reported as "a setback in San Fran."

"At least you scored the John Doe warrant to expand the search for Casper Duppy, Luna. And no one got killed in the process," was Writ's way of forgiving the insurance investigator's removal from the case.

Whew! Luna breathed a second sigh of relief as her lucky streak continued. "Thank you, sir," she said.

"It would have been nice to have Duppy as the inaugural inmate of the new Western Cherokee Nation Penitentiary, but…"

"Don't give up hope, sir. There's nothing keeping me from continuing with private online shadowing and adding what I find to the dossier. And there is a sizeable Cherokee population out here that may have pointers. As for my fee, please donate it to the Muwekma Ohlone. May they get federal recognition as a tribe."

"Done. And I know I dragged you into all of this, Luna, but think about taking a breather. Bill us your vacation expenses."

"Now I have been served two take a rest warrants," the insurance investigator jested.

She then heard Writ laugh, "It is only legal advice, Luna."

"So do my next deep dive from a beach into the Pacific, right?"

"You are a passionate swimmer, I hear. So it shouldn't be difficult," Writ responded. "Well, on behalf of The Attorney General and The Principal Chief, we appreciate your enduring loyalty to The Cherokee People and charity to the betterment of our indigenous brothers and sisters nationally. And good beach hunting."

The cellphone line dropped, and Luna plopped down on her bed.

··◆··

Ninety-degree days weren't selling points for vacationing in normally mild San Francisco. Nonetheless that's what Luna was forced into. So she humored herself: Who is to blame for the temperature bait and switch? Her probing brain settled on...*Mark Twain!*

Luna wasn't a fan of Mark Twain's fiction but appreciated his sarcasm. She remembered he was to have said, "The coldest winter I spent was a summer in San Francisco." So, it came as a surprise when she discovered that the author never gave the famous weather report. But when Luna thought about it, Mark Twain wasn't his real name nor was he a weatherman. She couldn't turn Twain in for fraud. Pen names and hyperbole weren't attempts to mislead; just tools of the literary trade that Luna had to admit Samuel Clemens skillfully used to create a few classics indeed.

Now it was time for Luna to get serious and start sightseeing, as per legal counsel. In less than a week, the popular city sites circuit ended at the harbor. There, Luna considered the sizes and shapes of the many seagoing vessels. Among them were cruise ships.

"Where do the cruises go?" Luna wondered aloud. A check of her smartphone showed stops up and down the Pacific Coast and passenger reviews of the ships' accommodations. That gave Luna the sudden idea to go somewhere guaranteed to be cool: Alaska. She eagerly bought a ticket.

Once packed, Luna boarded the triple-decker cruise ship *The Glacier Goddess*. She bid the Golden Gate Bridge and the last day of July good-bye, as both sailed past, then set sights on what would hopefully be a carefree, month-long getaway to Alaska: "The Last Frontier State."

CHAPTER 7

Into the Fire

The orange skies just above the timberline seemed to be just another pretty sunset over the 500-mile long seaside expanse known as The Alaskan Panhandle. And why not? The summer sun only powernaps just below the skyline for a few hours before returning to prominence. But there was something different in this sunset show; it flickered instead of glowed. Was it stadium lights that allowed packed pleasure seekers to hear every single note of a concert or see each critical play of a sporting event? Or to a tourist, was it just the famous Arora Borealis awakening?

It was neither.

Instead, sunset looked more like a rushed sunrise, as the orange glare climbed higher into the sky. And as it mixed with a menacing gray haze, it became clear that this wasn't the normal Northern Light show but was a four-alarm fire all aglow!

Fire engines flew to a burning structure along the banks of a channel on the far end of downtown Juneau, Alaska. Once there, firefighters rapidly unrolled hoses and began another fight against their arch enemy. Strong and steady streams of water shot out. And soon, the fire crew won the bout. But for all their fight, one fireman turned to another and said, "You know, this is one I can say I'm happy to see go."

CHAPTER 8

Dinner Date Damper

"You play a mean volleyball match, Luna."

"Are you talking about 'mean,' as in average?" she asked Dr. Adonis Healy to explain his analysis of her earlier performance.

"No, as in, well, "commanding" is the best word I can think of," he clarified his comment. "Where did you derive such competitive drive yet display it so gracefully?"

Volleyball didn't exactly fit Luna's idea of stimulating conversation over a luxurious dinner aboard *The Glacier Goddess*, as the sea green glow of the aurora borealis beckoned beyond. But neither did her favorite iced espresso, though served in gold-rimmed Martini glasses, fit the gourmet lobster and shrimp fettuccini main course either. It was probably as awkward as ordering red wine, instead of white, with fish.

Nevertheless, Luna couldn't help but blush from the cascade of compliments coming from her Indigenous dinner date: A dashing Canadian Cree physician. After a bite of lobster, she chewed over his question and said, "Stickball."

Adonis looked puzzled. *"Stickball?"* he asked.

"The stick-to-itiveness: That's where it comes from," Luna replied.

The doctor sat his glass aside and leaned closer. "I'd love to hear more."

"To many Cherokee, stickball, or *anejodi* as it's called, inspired lacrosse."

"We have a couple of professional lacrosse teams back home in Saskatoon."

"No such luck in my neck of the woods, Adonis. Besides being just another game, *anejodi* was used among my people to settle tribal disputes in olden times."

Adonis chuckled, "Don't go to war, let a stickball match settle your score, eh?"

Luna nodded. "Back then, of course, mostly men played. It is still played competitively today by both men and women in many regional tribes like the Choctaw, Chickasaw, and mine. Stickball is played on a field with two facing goal posts that are 12 feet high on each end of the field. Two teams line up to play each other."

"It sounds more like American and Canadian football," Adonis said.

"Yes, but that is where the similarity ends because stickball rules are different, depending on the tribe. Some Cherokee stickball rules call for no protective gear. I played once against a barefoot girls team! Tackling at any time is legal, not like in football. And you can't catch the lobbed ball or pick it up from the ground with your hands. Only after a player uses their 2 wooden sticks with a cup-shaped net on the end to lift the ball above their knees can they move the ball to their hands. To score a point, players must toss the ball and hit the opponent's wooden pole. You can score 1 to 3 points, depending on where the ball hits the pole. First team to score 12 points wins. There are no timeouts between the 8-minute quarters, although I've been in tournaments where the quarters are 15 minutes each."

"And judging from today's dinks and dives, I would say you were one of the best stickballers, Luna."

"*Hardly!*" she laughed. "I was rough and tumble and loved the constant rule changes. Shoeless one week then wearing them the next. Women couldn't use sticks just our hands, historically, but now we can. Ten players per team then 20 the next on different sized fields. *So exciting!*"

Adonis asked, "Who controls such organized uncertainty?"

"Drivers," Luna answered, "and each team brings

their own. Drivers cooperate to set the rules for the game. Once decided, like any other referees, they enforce them. What burned me out though was that it was just a game at the end of the day. There weren't any tribal politics to settle, just who got a trophy and silly bragging rights that you have to look in old record books to find."

"So why put so much energy into that volleyball match if it was for bragging rights too?"

"Oh, I don't know. Reliving old memories, I guess. Anyway, it wasn't for not; the match netted you."

Adonis's chestnut brown eyes sparkled with delight in the candlelight. *"Fascinating!"* he said.

Luna smiled and twirled her shrimp fettuccine dreamily. "What's charming is your interest in me," she replied. "Aren't the rules of the dinner date game that I get you to talk about yourself, too?"

"What's to know? All I do is run tests, read dull medical texts, and prescribe, prescribe, prescribe."

Luna smiled and planted her chin on her palm, while the red fingernail of her other hand traced a path along the linen tablecloth to the back of Adonis's hand. "So, doc, what is your prognosis for just how far we can go?"

Adonis answered, *"The ship?* At least to Juneau."

Luna giggled, "No, silly: "We," as in you and me?"

Before Adonis could answer, Luna heard something she hadn't heard in over a week: The buzz of her smartphone. "Sorry," she told Adonis, plucking the electronic intruder from her handbag. When she read the screen, a familiar number appeared. It reminded Luna that she was still an insurance investigator, even when on vacation. So, she pulled herself away to answer the call in the hall.

The caller responded with, "*Osiyo*. Did I get it right, Luna?"

"*Kelly, it's been forever!*" Luna squealed. "Bingo, by the way, on pronouncing the Cherokee greeting correctly."

"How is your view from the freelance side of fraud investigations?" the caller named Kelly asked. "Making lots of the long green, I bet. And I'm not talking celery."

"Still fraud busting fulltime and on the road about 45 out of 52 weeks while clocking at least 60 hours per. This time, though, you caught me on an Alaskan cruise."

"*A vacation?*" Kelly asked.

Luna glanced back into the dining room. "It's beginning to feel like one," she answered.

"Spending it alone?" Kelly continued.

"Not exactly. I hooked a great date, with lobster, candlelight..."

"*Wait!* Have you gotten to the burning cake yet?"

"*Baked Alaskan!*" Luna chuckled. "No, not yet."

"Does the chef know how to handle the kitchen blowtorch that heats the meringue?"

"You are always on the job."

Kelly laughed, *"Look who's talking!* I bet your date's a person of interest."

"We'll see."

"Anyway, it's funny you're in Alaskan waters."

Uh oh! Luna thought. "What's so funny about it?" she asked anxiously.

"Because you're not too far from me. You see, I was called in on a plastics store arson down in …"

Luna rubbed her forehead and moaned, "I saw the explosion go down during a stakeout in a separate case. It caused a lot of collateral damage, injuring over a dozen people and gutting a fitness center next door. I even chased the suspect across town, thinking he was my target. Did he torch something else down there?"

"Further north," Kelly answered.

"Portland, Oregon?" Luna hoped.

"Getting warmer."

Luna prayed it would stop with her next guess. *"Seattle, Washington?"* she asked.

"The insurer's headquarters are there, but not the fire."

There was only one state left. "Please don't tell me…"

"Sorry, Luna, but the Panhandle portion of Alaska – about ten percent of its population—is hot under the collar about a houseboat blaze early this morning. The local fire marshal says there are sightings of a man fitting Freddie Burns' description in the Juneau area," Kelly reported.

"*Seriously?!*" Luna groaned.

"Not too many of my people, blacks that is, live in Juneau," Kelly said. "Maybe some yokels confused innocent African American residents for Burns, which makes me worry they'll think I'm Burns in drag."

After Luna stopped laughing, she asked, "So how do I fit in, Kelly? You're the hotshot fire investigator, not me."

"The houseboat's insurer heard I was on the west coast and hired me to have a looksee. They know that in hot button cases like this—one full of Burns warnings and with the houseboat doubling as a strip club owned by a controversial character called Bernie "Sparky" Sparks—locals may not have the expertise or can rush to conclusions. The insurer wants a thorough investigation that can hold up in court, if necessary," Kelly said.

"But calling in an outsider almost always looks like the locals can't take care of business themselves," Luna warned. "Their conclusions almost always butt heads with a freelancer's, somewhere down the line."

"Don't worry, Luna. Some of it's for show: To give the press something to cover or to prove the fire team's worth. Remember when we first worked together: Bringing you in didn't affect our relationship, did it?

I think the Juneau fire marshal has the same kind of confidence; after all, she the one asking me for my two cents."

"The Northern Lights can mess with cellphone reception. So maybe you didn't hear me: How do I fit in, Kelly?"

The fire investigator laughed and said, "You were a good luck charm in the San Francisco case, according to the A.D.A., She recommended contacting you for more insights."

"*Good luck charm?!* Was this the same A.D.A. who criticized my case management skills?"

"Okay, okay: So I added the 'good luck charm' part, Luna. Since Gates said you weren't working that car insurance case anymore…"

"And you're already in Juneau, Kelly?"

"Roger that. I landed about 2 hours ago. We had to circle because of high winds. All that turbulence felt like riding a jet ski! I still live in Detroit and could have driven through Canada. But even so, I wouldn't have been able to drive into Juneau; there's no direct highway in or out. It's only reachable by boat or plane."

And the ads said Juneau is the perfect place to get away from it all! Luna berated another bait and switch. *When I want to be on the job, I can't. And now that I don't, I am…damn!*

"When will you put into port, Luna?"

"Tomorrow."

"Good! Even with 15 hours of sunlight, I haven't had a chance to inspect the site of the fire; just read a lot of reports and then got a hotel. And since there aren't many, we'll probably be at the same place."

"Great."

"Lovely! I'll see you soon, and sorry about the damper this put on your dinner date," Kelly issued an apology. "Oh, damper reminds me: It's rainy up here most of the year. I hope that love boat sells raingear."

How Luna longed for Adonis. "I hoped to buy rubbers after tonight, but not for my feet," she lamented.

"How's that, Luna?"

"Uh, nothing Kelly. Later."

CHAPTER 9

Backwater Backstory

The *Glacier Goddess* entered the busy Gastineau Channel the next afternoon, signaling Luna's arrival in Juneau. From a downtown of largely low-rises dwarfed by cruise and cargo ship girths to residences that snuck up and snuggled into the surrounding evergreen slopes of misty Mounts Juneau and Roberts, yes: The capital city of Alaska looked as quaint as advertised.

The lingering gray from yesterday's rain slowly gave way to partly cloudy skies, as Luna came ashore. Even if the caller who washed out her dinner date hadn't made her presence known with an enthusiastic wave, Luna easily picked fire investigator Kelly Day from the largely Caucasian crowd. The women greeted each other with a hug and then proceeded to the parking lot.

Kelly popped the rental car trunk and helped Luna load her suitcase and duffel bag. "Nice trench coat," Kelly commented on Luna's choice of wet weather wear.

"Thanks," Luna replied. "You wouldn't believe the stuff you can buy on a cruise ship. Anyway, where's the rain you forecasted?"

"Give it time. If it doesn't arrive, then buy a fedora and you'll look like the classic private eye."

Once in the car, Luna said, "I love what you've done with your hair. The peppy curls, bright rosy lips, and jeans give you a kind of relaxed look."

Kelly started the car and clearing up how the style came about. "Thanks. I hoped you'd notice how much leaner I look. But at fifty something, I'll take kind words when I can it get them."

"I always assumed you were lithe, Kelly."

"Lithe, Luna?"

"Sorry. I meant athletically slim. It didn't show back then because of your uniform and a gun and pounds of other gear around your waist."

"Thanks. I admit I'm a little late to the freelance dance and probably behind the times. Now there are mentorships, even though women are still only a tiny part of the fire investigator field. When I started out, being book smart wasn't enough; you had to show a little thigh to get a leg up. So the hair and the whole getup."

"So true," Luna sympathized. "Although women

outnumber men as insurance investigators, most of the CEOs and head honchos are still males. But with style changing drastically during the pandemic, I don't worry about its impact as much."

"When we uncovered that scam that saved the taxpayers millions and cost the complicit council-woman her job, Luna, you weren't just in control of the facts and figures but had almost everyone eating out of your hand with your fashion, too."

"Come on, Kelly, don't sell yourself short. You were the fire marshal for Detroit: The 10th largest city in America. Fashion be damned, once a woman has that kind of command."

"Motown has slipped from 10th on the charts to 26th biggest," Kelly sighed.

Luna laughed, "See what happened when you're not around!"

"Thanks for the memories," Kelly replied.

A stoplight appeared and turned red. While waiting, Luna suddenly thought, This is why Kelly recruited me: As gratitude for getting her independent investigator career off the ground. But Luna's skeptical side whispered other ideas. Maybe Kelly's feeling sorry for me, after getting kicked off the auto insurance job. Or it could be she's jealous of me gushing over Adonis and it's a scheme to share the drudgery of another fraud inquiry? Luna laughed off the last notion.

The light turned green, and Kelly finally started

filling Luna in on the case. "According to the National Fire Incident Reporting System (NFIRS) report, the fire broke out aboard a 65-foot houseboat called *The Burning Desire* early yesterday morning around 2 a.m. or a couple of hours after it closed. It launched a few years ago, as the COVID pandemic faded, and is Juneau's first gentleman's club to operate full-time since the 1950s. It held 26 people tops but luckily no one was onboard during the fire. The fire department saved it from sinking, but it's a total loss."

"What about its owner, Bernie Sparks?" Luna asked.

"From what online prep I did inflight, many locals blame him—nicknamed "Sparky"—for prostitution, bootlegging, and now, arson. He allegedly kept shady company in places known for their casinos, clubs, and nightlife: Namely, Las Vegas and Reno. He beat a Vegas pandering charge in the late 70's when the police went beyond the limits of their search warrant and used excessive force to gain evidence. That may have caused Sparky to move to Juneau. Although, some locals claim it's a cover for a witness protection deal. But maybe it's as simple as no state income and sales taxes to pay."

"Or because of that state payment of over three thousand dollars every fall just for being a resident," Luna offered an alternate, but still appealing, explanation.

"I heard about that," Kelly added. "As long as

you're not jailed or have certain kinds of convictions, it's pretty much pass go for the dough. That probably helps residents pay the state's high property taxes."

"Have the Juneau cops or DA actually charged Sparky with anything?" Luna asked.

Kelly said no. "Haters say the club is a front for prostitution but have no proof so far. Others complained the liquor tasted watered down or "fishy," leading to claims that Sparky served bootleg booze in a state with strict alcohol laws. As for fears about guns on the property? This is a mostly rural red state; nothing stuck. The police did, though, have to warn a few customers to turn down their hi-fis and broke up a drunken scuffle or two in the parking lot but without any serious injuries."

Luna's first thought on the matter was that, "Sparky sounds only guilty of running a strip club in a small town that isn't used to the problems that go with it."

"Not just any small town; Juneau is also the state capital. So some of the haters probably want to maintain that dignified state of mind," Kelly cautioned.

"These strip club opponents: Are they the usual religious nitpickers and such?" Luna asked.

"If you think religion is only about finding others' faults, then yes."

"Sorry if I offended thee, Kelly."

"Nah. It's more of a personal connection for me, Luna."

"Right, you're more spiritual than religious."

"In a way. I see literal fire and brimstone every day and am "preaching" against it in some way. And it gets me thinking about how hell awaits the unapologetic for eternity. So more than anything, it's reassuring to know that there is a higher power—God, if you will—who can save me from that fire that can't be extinguished."

"Noble thought," Luna commented.

"But yes," Kelly said, "some of the houseboat's most vocal critics are deeply religious, like the Reverend Sebastian Herald and his 200 followers of the Sect of the Sanctified Pier. Trespassing laws kept them a reasonable distance from *The Burning Desire*, but still plenty close to picket and be a nuisance. Their hatred for ships doesn't stop there, though; they also blame cruise ships and tourists for corrupting and overcrowding Juneau."

Luna reviewed photos of *The Burning Desire* before it burned. It was a white, two story affair with deck chairs, an outside spiral staircase, and what looked like a porch on the roof. "This doesn't look like any strip club I've seen," she stated. "If you put a paddlewheel behind, it would almost look like a smaller version one of those old-fashioned Mississippi riverboats."

"I didn't know you were a connoisseur," Kelly commented.

"Of riverboats or strip clubs?" Luna asked unfazed.

Kelly laughed and continued dishing out details. "Now for those residents who supported *The Burning Desire*: It gave them something different to do and some of the comforts of big sister city Anchorage, who they forever feel like bridesmaids to. And financial reports ranked it fourth in tourist hotspots and tops in nightlife, bypassing the local museum circuit in post pandemic tourist dollars. Only the Mendenhall Glacier, a tram that goes up and down one of the mountains, and nature trips beat *The Burning Desire*."

After all that, Luna said, "Thanks for the backwater backstory. But there's still something you're not telling me."

CHAPTER 10

Deal Me In

"Right, right," Kelly said. "You want to know the division of labor. Who carries the biggest bags?"

"And what's in them," Luna added. "I know you'll be busy with the fire marshal, going over debris and then issuing arson findings and conclusions. And since Juneau's the capital, a few suits will probably show up."

"A fair assessment, although I'm not strictly an arson investigator," Kelly said. "I am looking for what caused the blaze, not necessarily arson. If it leads to that, lovely. But if not—say it's an accident instead—then..."

"Then there may be some angry residents who won't believe it and insist that it's another fast one Bernie Sparks pulled on them," Luna replied.

"Maybe not just angry but fed up enough to take the law into their own hands," Kelly warned.

"Vigilantes, you mean," Luna dared utter the word that some tar and feathered her with in San Francisco.

Kelly nodded. "And if this "Sparky" is as shady as they say, I need someone who can take care of herself and still have the smarts to look into his finances, interview associates, and—well, you know the routine."

Luna understood. "You need someone with brawn and brains. And now for those "bags" you mentioned: How much money is in mine?"

"Ten thousand dollars," Kelly announced. "My take is five grand from the houseboat insurer; another five for consulting on the fire; and ten thousand from the San Francisco job. Twenty thousand split fifty-fifty is a cool ten grand for us both."

"Ten thousand," Luna reveled in her cut. "Enough to pay my liability, errors and omissions coverage and car insurance for a long time. *Deal me in!* Although you sold me with the brawn and brains bit."

CHAPTER 11

Point of Origin

Luna and Kelly motored along a remote stretch of downtown waterfront that snaked towards *The Burning Desire*, or what was left of it. The blackened houseboat frame remained, along with exterior metal railing, and what was probably once deck furniture although now distorted into less recognizable mounds of melted plastic. All of it was still cordoned off by yellow barrier tape that read the obvious: "Fire Line Do Not Cross."

The police were long gone, leaving only the fire marshal to sift through the wreckage. She emerged from the lower deck, alerted by tires crunching the gravel turnoff that led into the parking lot. Kelly parked close to a Fire/EMS sport utility vehicle. Luna and she got out and were soon greeted by Fire Marshal Bernila Lluvia: A broad-shouldered Filipina with a warm smile. She wore the full firewoman's suit but was happy to remove her helmet to let her long hair breathe in what was now refreshing, rather than chilly, air.

"Bernila, this is my partner, Luna Nightcrow. Luna, Fire Marshal Bernila Lluvia," Kelly introduced the pair.

The women shook hands.

"Nice to meet you, Ms. Nightcrow."

"Luna is fine."

"Luna it is. So how long have you been in the fire investigation game?"

"Not long. I am an insurance fraud investigator, actually. I just got here."

"From the way you're dressed, I should have guessed," Lluvia said. "I doubt you'll find this case to be glamorous though. I know a cleaners who could use your business after you get covered in dust and soot."

"They will top my list of sights to see," Luna promised.

"I will give you their—oh, you both will need one of these." Lluvia waved Kelly and Luna over to the sport utility vehicle where she opened the trunk. "Hard hats," the fire marshal announced, tossing each investigator one. "The white color will go with anything, Luna. But most of all, it should be easy to see if rubble falls on you and we have to dig you out."

Luna supplied a laugh, if nervously. "Uh, thanks," she said.

"Just letting you know what you're getting into," Lluvia replied.

"Don't worry about gloves and goggles," Kelly told her, "I have plenty on hand."

Luna and Kelly adjusted the headband straps inside until their headgear fit securely.

"Anyway, as for the nitty-gritty on *The Burning Desire* herself," Lluvia continued, "she was one of over 100 houseboats berthed in Juneau and definitely one of the largest. This town has some of the highest property values in the state; it's not unusual for an average family to pay over a quarter of a mill for a small home. So instead, some opt to live on a houseboat.

"As long as the houseboats are mobile and the owners agree to pay about five bucks per foot a month mooring fee, plus a little extra for utilities, they can stay. Juneau's Department of The Harbor supplies power, water, latrines and a sewage pump to some of them. To make it easier to understand, a houseboat is more like a recreational vehicle than a house. You can drive around or stop at a RV park and hook up for power; likewise, you can sail the houseboat or dock it at a harbor. Sparky fired up the engines and had a harbor pilot move her around when we did our inspection last year; so, it's not just a house on the water setup."

"Did anybody actually live aboard *The Burning Desire*?" Luna asked.

"*Sparky?* No, he lives uptown in the hills. The

houseboat was just for business. Although he spent so much time here that his wife, the poor woman, probably thought it was his home," Lluvia answered. "What a piece of work, that Sparky!"

"Still no idea how the fire started?" Kelly asked.

"Not yet," Lluvia said. "There wasn't any gasoline/ diesel fuel aboard, but plenty of alcohol at the bar."

"How about *where* it started?"

"I am working with a special agent from the state fire marshal's office on it. And as far as we can tell, it started along what's left of the far wall near what would have been the stairs leading up to the upper deck, or the VIP section of the club."

"*V-I-P?*"

"You know, Kelly: Where Very Important People, or customers who paid more, got, *ahem*, "private dances," special treatment..,"

Luna winked at Kelly and said, "In other words, more bang for their buck...*perhaps.*"

"I underestimated you, Luna. It sounds like you have been around," Lluvia chuckled. "I'll let you gals dig in. If you need anything else, give a shout."

Kelly turned to Luna with a shocked look. "*More bang for their buck?*" she whispered.

"*...perhaps,*" Luna said advisedly, "until we get all the facts."

"Want to change into your platform heels and tube dress, too, before we start?!"

"Who said that you have to show a little thigh to get a leg up?"

Kelly grinned. "You got me," she plead guilty.

Luna reminded her, "Like Bernila said, this isn't going to be glamorous."

Instead of Luna's suitcase, Kelly retrieved a camera, toolkit, safety gloves, and glasses from the trunk. She instructed Luna to carry some paint cans. Then, the investigators set out to start the task of picking through the debris for clues.

Kelly led Luna to and through what was once the lower deck doorway. Most of the upper deck collapsed onto the spacious lower, but some steps leading up the stairs remained. Luna let Kelly do most of the serious snooping while she nosed around for anything of size that might look interesting.

"*Luna!* " Kelly hollered.

The insurance investigator stepped carefully over the rubble to reach her colleague. "What did you find?"

"The classic V-shaped pattern along the lower wall," Kelly replied. "It's produced by something flammable and is a clue that maybe the blaze started down here and moved upstairs."

"*Maybe?*" Luna asked.

"Yeah, because what looks like the area with the most damage isn't always the point of origin, or where the fire started," Kelly explained. "You see, most people would guess that the bar over there would be the place where the fire started because of all the alcohol. And it's true that alcohol is a great accelerant, or stuff used to start a fire. But this was a club; and with other alcohol-based products like hairspray, nail polish remover, and perfumes, maybe it started in a dressing room. The alcohol out here is just one of many ignitable liquids that, once the fire started, contributed to the burning but wasn't the accelerant nor the point of origin. Knowing where the fire started will give me a good idea of how it started."

"I know it's too early to tell, Kelly, but what do you think happened?"

"My gut tells me this isn't as simple as Sparky hiring Freddie to burn down the houseboat," she answered. "What do you think, Luna?"

After a moment, she sighed, "The heat is on for an arson conviction, for sure. And if we don't find it among the ashes and intrigue, Juneau will blow its top."

CHAPTER 12

Fresh Findings

Kelly shot interior and exterior photos of *The Burning Desire* while Luna helped can samples of remains in critical portions of the club. Once finished, Kelly talked briefly with Bernila Lluvia and then drove Luna to what looked like the most modern building so far. Its dome seemed like a conditional surrender to space-age elegance and crowned what residents informally called "The Big C": The Hotel Chichagof.

"We will have separate rooms," Kelly told Luna, as she pulled into the parking lot.

Luna was surprised, at first, that Tight Ship rolled out the red carpet. "On second thought," she said, "this is the capital and a high profile case."

Kelly instead said, "I like to think that it's special perks for special people. Besides, I thought you might like some privacy for downtime with that dinner date."

Luna cribbed a line from the 80s song, asking, "Keeping our love warm?" *How I wish!* was what she really thought, resigned to having lost the opportunity.

Kelly picked up on Luna's skepticism. "You exchanged numbers, right?"

Luna forgot they did and said with renewed optimism, "You're right. Thanks for the reminder and the extra space."

··◆··

The women entered the hotel's bustling grand lobby: A marbled affair with polished wood and golden highlights that indicated an upscale experience awaited. They made their way to the reception desk where Kelly was personally greeted. "Welcome back to The Chichagof, Ms. Day. I hope you're still enjoying your stay," recited the young Chinese clerk.

"So much so that I actually recommended a friend check in," Kelly answered. "I just need to make the necessary arrangements. Pardon me, please."

To kill time while Kelly called Tight Ship Assurance in Seattle, Luna asked the source of the hotel's curious name.

Despite the corporate look of his blazer, the young desk clerk was the geeky type and happily told Luna, "It's named in honor of Chichagof Island, even though some tourists misspell it as 'Chicagof.'"

"Did you know it's the fifth largest island in the country?"

"I would never had guessed that," Luna remarked mildly.

"*Facts*, as they say. It is also cool that even if the hotel was named after Chicago, it would still fit," the clerk continued to blather.

"*Oh?*"

"Chicago's the third biggest U.S. city; we're the third biggest city in Alaska; and, Chicago is also called "The Windy City," which Juneau has a lot of, too."

Luna looked up and said, "Which explains why they capped this with a dome."

"*Wow, ma'am!* You know that domes' curvature allows wind to flow around them, reducing damage from gusts and microbursts."

"There's lots of wind where I'm from, but surprisingly not many domes."

"The dome makes The Chichagof the tallest building in town," the clerk continued. "At 253 feet, it beats the SOB."

"*SOB?*" Luna had to ask again for clarity.

"It is slang for the State Office Building, not a person," the clerk answered.

"I'm so glad there isn't someone that disgusting in stature," Luna laughed. But she remembered Bernie Sparks qualified in the minds of many. And his arson accusation prompted Luna to pull a photo from her shoulder bag. "Oh, by the way," she asked the clerk an important question, "ever see this guy around?"

After taking a look at the picture of Freddie Burns, the desk clerk shook his head and said, "No, but I will keep a look out. And I also have friends who can watch for him. What room will you be in for me to report anything I find out?"

Luna shrugged. "That's what I'm waiting to see."

The clerk blushed. *"Oh, silly me!* I should get you checked in, Ms..."

"Nightcrow, Luna Nightcrow. And thanks, Hui."

"How did you know my name?"

Luna tapped her breast, causing the clerk to look at his lapel where he recognized his nametag.

"Yes, Ms. Nightcrow. What I mean is how did you know to pronounce my last name correctly, as in "way" and not "hoo-wee," as in the Hawaiian way."

"We are closer to China than Hawaii; so, odds are Hui is pronounced 'way' rather than 'hoo-wee,'" Luna replied. "Besides, I've been to Hawaii before."

Hui had to pull himself away to continue his behind the desk duties which included getting payment from Kelly and giving each woman key cards.

Kelly pulled Luna aside. "See why I wanted you along? Already in town and you've made a contact," she whispered.

"Only if I decide to become a contestant on

Jeopardy! and need trivia tutelage," Luna dismissed Hui's value to the case.

Luna finally moved into a suite across from Kelly's. The mocha-colored motif of the walls and carpet was instantly inviting, although the king-sized bed and marbled bathroom were a bit much. And any old TV would do, even though she had a wall-mounted flatscreen. But Luna liked the presence of a large coffee table in the living room (for workspace) and the big sofa with plenty of pillows. And when she opened the curtains, the steep mountainside view beyond the window was certainly inspiring.

Bernila Lluvia was right about Luna getting dirty. She changed into a robe and gathered the clothes for the cleaners. Then, the insurance investigator's phone buzzed. The caller ID revealed Tight Ship Assurance. It was specifically their chief financial officer, wanting to review the terms of participation and compensation. Luna explained the deal she Kelly reached, and the CFO gladly agreed. A few minutes later, another call beckoned. Reflexively, Luma's thought turned to Adonis.

"Want to grab dinner?" Kelly asked instead.

Luna looked at her watch and returned to reality. "Four o'clock is a little early for me."

"Hui told me Alaska has two time zones. Around here, in the summer, four o'clock is seven Central Time. But a lot of places stay open later for the tourists."

"I forgot about the time zone difference. What did you have in mind, Kelly?"

"Nothing fancy, but I'd like to see a little of the town."

"I think we've seen most of it, haven't we?" Luna laughed. "I agree though: Getting a feel for the people, the culture helps."

"Lovely. See you soon, Luna."

"Later then."

Luna showered. Afterwards, she barely got her jeans zipped when there was a knock on the door. She threw on a T-shirt and answered, thinking it was Kelly. Instead it was...

"Hui, hello," Luna said with a welcoming smile.

"Hello, Ms. Nightcrow," he nervously replied. "I am Hui Zhen, Chichagof Front Desk. I am surprised you remember me; I'm off duty and don't look the same in civies. Or, I mean, don't feel the same."

"How can I forget the man who got us checked in and knows more about Alaska than anyone I have met so far? As for your jeans and tennis shoes, don't worry. I am dressing down, too."

Hui noticed and was relieved. "Thanks. You said to let you know if anyone saw that guy in the picture, remember?"

Now it was Luna's turn to be tense. *"What did you find out?!"*

"A friend saw him about four blocks away 5

minutes ago. While on the phone, she said he's shopping where she works."

"Great!" Luna rushed across the hall and pounded on Kelly's door.

Expecting to see Luna, Kelly answered in only a bath towel. "I'm not quite ...*oops!"* Kelly closed the door to a crack at the sight of Hui alongside Luna.

"Thow on anything. Hui's contact just spotted Freddie four blocks away!"

Kelly took mental note of the address from Hui. *"Don't wait for me, go ahead!* I will catch up," she told the two, then slammed the door to get dressed.

Luna and Hui didn't waste time waiting for the elevator, but made a mad dash down the service stairs instead. Quickly, they headed straight from the hotel on foot, saving the time it would take to drive. Five minutes later, both raced inside the preppy downtown convenience store Fresh Findings. Luna doublechecked each aisle for Freddie Burns and didn't think twice about barging into the men's restroom. But they were too late: The elusive arsonist appeared to have escaped.

Hui took Luna to his contact Jun, the store manager. Luna flashed her insurance investigator credentials along with Burns's photo; and then, through Hui's Mandarin translation, asked Jun for information. She idenitifed the man as Freddie Burns. "Hui said it was imporatant you find him. So I tried to stall for time, by letting him flirt with me at the checkout," she said.

"Good thinking," Luna replied, harking back to her San Francisco face-to-face strategy. Like then, however, Burns's Juneau sweet nothings to Jun didn't reveal his intentions or whereabouts.

Jun did notice that, "The man did not appear to have a car because he walked from the store and out of the parking lot."

"Then he can't be too far away," Hui said.

"Unless he walked to a car in another spot, caught the bus, or maybe a cab. If so, he could be miles away," Luna replied. She pushed forward with questions, this time asking what Burns bought.

Jun unfurled a receipt and read, "Some expensive whisky, cans of sardines, boxes of crackers, and fresh fruit."

"How did he pay?" Luna asked.

"In cash and with small bills which, I must say, I always welcome," Jun answered.

Kelly finally arrived on the scene. Luna filled her in, including about the grocery list. "Remember that line from the *Sesame Street* ditty: 'One of these things is not like the other?'" Kelly asked her partner.

"I was thinking the same thing," Luna replied. "Freddie is a health nut. The fruit and fish make sense, but the whisky? At forty dollars a bottle, it smells like a bribe."

"Or accelerant for another job," Kelly warned.

"On the whisky sale: Did he show you his identification?"

"Yes, as it is the law. The name is not the one Luna said. Yet, the picture looked the same," Jun answered Kelly through translation.

"Looked the same … *uh, oh!*" Luna worried.

Kelly sensed Luna's concerns of mistaken identity. "Do you remember the name on the card?" she asked.

After careful thought, Jun gave 2 names: Cheat and grass.

"Cheatgrass," Kelly connected the two and then told Luna, "an alias and a flammable plant he used as accelerant on a job once. Despite the fake ID, this sounds like a real sighting."

To which Hui, who was stoked with excitement, gasped, *"Wow! This guy sounds like bad news!"*

Luna quickly tried to downplay the danger in what they were doing. "We just want to talk to him," she said. Luna then thanked Jun for her help, but her fifty dollar tip was declined.

"I am still a bit old-fashioned," Jun explained. "When I came along, tipping was seen by many as a handout, rather than appreciation, in China."

"Sorry, Jun," Luna apologized.

Jun nodded and said, "I trust you will be in town for a while, searching for this man. Stop in again to shop for more than information."

Luna agreed and gave Jun her business card. She

then turned to her colleagues and said, "Well, let's get cracking."

With Hui at the wheel, Kelly armed with her camera, and Luna possessing the sharpened savvy of who to photograph, a block-by-block manhunt began. Hui threaded them along the narrow downtown streets and into an occasional dim back alley for an inkling of the arsonist. And while none of the Juneau roads led out of town, except to the airport or waterfront to buy passage, there were still many residences and the vast wilderness for Burns to lay low in.

As shops and stores began closing their doors, Luna looked at her watch. "It's almost 8 pm, everyone. Looks like it was close but not quite for tonight."

Hui was still raring to go, like most young men. "This is only twilight and will provide enough light to see well into midnight. It could work to our advantage."

"More light or not, we still need rest," Luna let Hui know.

"...and food; Luna and I have been on the go since breakfast," Kelly added.

Hui hung his head and said, "I understand. Where you come from, it is almost midnight."

"Right. So where can we grab a bite?" Luna asked.

"The hotel restaurant doesn't close until 9 pm. You will both probably want room service, although the dining experience is 5-star quality. I've not eaten there but would love to some day."

"Well, that day has come," Luna said. "Want to join us there for dnner?"

"Our treat, for all your hard work," Kelly added.

Hui's eyes became as big as dinner plates at the prospect of a threesome dinner date. Most guys struggle to get one woman in Alaska, with its ratio of 111 men to 100 women, Hui thought. But I will have two, and not just any two. It will be a pair of cougars who act like secret agents; *and one of them I saw in a towel!* My co-workers will think I'm such a player.

Hui came to and told his passengers, *"I'm game!* Jun may be traditionalist when it comes to refusing tips, but not me. Besides, this is the land of plenty."

I hope that means "plenty" more cracks at catching Freddie Burns, Luna wished.

CHAPTER 13

Shipshape?

The next day was inescapably gray, but Luna was in sparkling, all pro insurance fraud investigator mode. She first contacted The Juneau Police Department and learned they already questioned employees of *The Burning Desire* and Bernie Sparks about the fire but without learning the cause. Luna then shared the alleged Fresh Findings sighting of Burns and asked about others mentioned. The police gave her the names of the eyewitnesses and Luna promptly set up interviews.

Of the ten eyewitnesses she contacted, 8 changed their stories after getting a good look at Luna's photos of Burns. They mistook other African American tourists or residents who looked like him. But the 2 remaining, one of whom was African American, stuck to their sightings. Luna checked the locations where the sightings went down. Both, however, were claims to have seen Burns walking through the vicinity but not entering any specific property.

One was a residential street: *Good luck with that!* Luna laughed, as there were many houses on either side that stretched for several blocks into the distance. So she tried the second location instead: The Mother Lode Motor Lodge. It was the only business for half a mainly wooded mile. While not a flophouse, its isolated setting radiated lay low vibes. And the feeling intensified when the jittery clerk wouldn't release the names and number of guests. Of course, Luna couldn't force him to. And in the time it takes to get a warrant, Burns will be gone, she said to herself.

Rather than make a fuss, Luna left and simply waited for a few tenants to appear. She approached them for information but the inducement of tips, sadly, got no Burns confirmations. And after a couple of hours staking out the motel from across the road, Luna didn't see Burns come or go.

As Luna canvassed the rest of the capital, she saw a sizeable crowd congregating a ways from a docked cruise ship. It wasn't a tour group nor passengers coming ashore. From some carrying picket signs, it looked like a demonstration about to begin.

Luna parked, got out, and cautiously moved towards about 70 assorted Alaskans. They huddled around an angular, olive-skinned man of mixed descent—probably an Alaska Creole, Luna guessed—with a high forehead, slicked back hair, and bushy beard. He radiated confidence, with eyes wide and glistening, and a resonance that kept the crowd listening to what turned out to be God's marching orders for the day: To try and turn another cruise ship away. The multitude shouted, "Amen," then took up posters and signs.

As the crowd cleared, Luna decided to make her move. She approached the speaker. *"Reverend Herald!"* Luna called.

The tall man turned and smiled warmly. "Salutations," he said. "And you are?"

Luna extended a hand in friendship. "A mere Luna," she answered.

Herald shook Luna's hand. "You are more than just ordinary; in the eyes of the creator, we are each precious vessels ready to filled and used for our intended purpose in the grand design."

"And what is your *purpose* and that of your friends?" Luna asked.

Herald lifted his arms. "To turn Juneau from a lightning rod that attracts the wrath of the creator into a shining display of divine excellence on Earth" he proclaimed.

"I see. But what makes God so angry with Juneau, Reverend?"

"Cruise ships: Their excess from the depths will forever ruin the frontier."

"So you plan to preach to the passengers and make their souls shipshape again?"

"Yes, Sister Luna. Maybe what we impart here will be a seed they will carry with them. And when the time is right—when they realize what *is* right— the creator's message will bear fruit elsewhere and make the world, if not Juneau, a better place."

"Makes sense: The Johnny Appleseed principle," Luna said.

Herald recalled the good old days. "I was born and raised when Juneau was testimony to progress and wilderness working together, when one ship and maybe two hundred or so visitors didn't ruin creation. Now, the docks swarm with cruise ships that carry as many as five thousand outsiders. Forests of once thriving yellow cedar trees whose hardy wood the Tlingit, Haida and Tsimshian used to carve totem poles and canoes are suffocating, as travelers consume both town and country like locusts."

Luna shuddered at the thought that the guy made some sense. "Like overfishing, over drilling, it's too much of a good thing," she surmised.

"I heard a cruise ship's size and stabilizing gear eliminate the feeling of floating. People pretending to walk on water when sacred scripture commands that we should marvel in the original purpose," Herald continued to preach. Then, as if snapping out of a trance, he turned his attention back to Luna. "So you are an Indigenous Alaskan? A visiting Athabascan from the interior perhaps, considering your questions?"

Uh oh, Luna thought, *He's looking to shepherd me into the flock!* Having heard enough, she came clean. "I am a Native American but not Athabascan ... Cherokee, instead. And yes, I am visiting."

"Which means..?" Herald asked nervously.

"I came by way of cruise ship." Luna reached into her purse and produced her investigator's license. With it came the big reveal. "I am Luna Nightcrow, insurance investigator," she announced.

Herald began to walk away, but with head still held high as he approached his true believers. Luna caught up with him. "Reverend, I am not here as a tourist or on behalf of a cruise line."

"Then you must be here to peddle the false hopes of your profession. For insurance is not assurance of the creator's eternal happiness."

Luna pushed back a bit. "So you have no insurance to cover your earthly church and other private property in the meantime?"

"Render unto authority that which is authority's to ask for but nothing more," Herald replied.

"Name, rank, and serial number ... *I get it!* Like I said, though, I'm here on business but not to look into your business."

Herald finally stopped and turned. *"Oh?* Then whose?"

"I am looking into *The Burning Desire* fire," Luna replied.

Herald's smile returned. "The creator works in ways unbeknown to us sometimes. Perhaps you are sent to prevent the resurrection of Bernie Sparks, that disciple of the despicable."

"If that's where the evidence leads," Luna remarked more objectively.

"So you are willing to give him the benefit of the doubt or, as Saint Augustine said, '…vice an easy bed in which to lay?'"

"For good or ill, we all have free will. So if someone freely committed arson, Reverend, shouldn't they face the judgement of man and the creator?"

"Not necessarily in that order, but yes," Herald agreed.

"And are arsonists condemned forever? Can't they be given another chance to do good if, in your eyes perhaps, only by the creator?"

"I see that you are truly heaven-sent, Sister Luna!" Herald declared.

Luna turned her sudden godsend status to her advantage. "Did you burn the houseboat, Reverend?"

"As the creator is my witness, no," he solemnly swore. "I was preaching the night of the fire. And 200 plus strong followers of the faith can also attest to it."

"Could any of your followers have burned the boat or asked someone else to?"

"The only entity we would ask is the creator. And as you said, it would be to save Bernie Sparks from drowning in wickedness and set him on course towards true enlightenment, Luna."

"You are your brother and sister's keepers. But try as you might, you can't be their collective conscience," Luna said.

She didn't get an argument from Herald. "Exactly. Only the creator can," he replied.

"So, it is possible that one of your followers—like Judas, if you want—could have turned and burned the houseboat."

"Honestly, we all stray from the path intended for us to follow by the creator. So, someone could have abused one its most divine powers, fire, to smote the houseboat."

"May I please ask your followers about their intentions and feelings about the houseboat?"

"Please do," Herald granted Luna permission. "For I am convinced that from a multitude of tongues comes the truth; that being we never destroyed *The Burning Desire*."

··◆··

By 6 pm., Luna finished interviewing the followers of the Sect of the Sanctified Pier but without much effect. Although none of them saw Freddie Burns,

Luna picked up on perhaps another person of interest. Many of the followers thought they saw "an angel" in the midst of their meetings and protests: A well-built Caucasian with a long beard and blazing blue eyes. The man appeared to be watching but not really participating. Luna didn't recall seeing such a person during the most recent demonstration. Nonetheless, she thanked what could be her biggest informer score yet with a generous tithe.

·· ◆ ··

Back at the hotel, Luna briefed Kelly with the bad news first. "No new credible sightings of Burns," she said. Then came the good news. "I encountered Reverend Herald's crowd. They are the reverse of the Cargo Cults in the Pacific."

"Cargo cults?" Kelly queried.

In World War Two a group of Melanesian islanders met Allied military and found particularly American technology and culture incredible. *And who wouldn't?!* But after the war, we pulled out, leaving the people in shock. They became so obsessed with bringing back the prosperity lost that it turned into a religion. The people actually built wooden planes and runways and prayed these symbols would bring back the divine deliveryman, a god called "John Frum," who in reality was the GIs who gave the gifts.

"The Sect of the Sanctified Pier, however, is the

opposite. They pray for "the creator" to keep the cruise ships with their cargoes of corrupting ideas and pollution away. Herald even went so far as to blame tourists for what is, according to climatological reports I'm reading, beetle infestation and wind damage that causes some forests to naturally die off."

"One of those tourists, at one time, was Bernie Sparks who then stayed and, to them, became the avatar of original sin in Juneau," Kelly replied. "Did any of them confess to burning the houseboat at the stake?"

"No," Luna chuckled. "Like Reverend Herald, none of the flock I met admitted to arson. After questioning, they returned to their "sanctuary" on one of the remote islands in the area. The other 100 or so either stayed there or were protesting "dens of sin" somewhere else in town."

"Do you think they are hiding Freddie Burns on their island?" Kelly asked.

"None of them recognized the photo I passed around. Frankly though, if Freddie burned the houseboat, he's probably cleared out of town by now. They did mention the presence of a shaggy-bearded, blue-eyed "angel." Maybe they are hiding *his* involvement," Luna mentioned.

"Or maybe he's a deep cover agent, assigned by the cops or Feds to keep an eye on them," Kelly suggested. "If so, then we won't have to worry about questioning the remaining followers."

"Herald has no doubt told them about me and how to answer," Luna replied. "With cults, you usually get the goods on them when someone escapes and is deprogrammed."

"I won't hold my breath for that," Kelly laughed. "Besides, we still have a lot more to cover in town."

"And for me, that means finally stepping into the octagon with Bernie Sparks," Luna said, picking up her smartphone to schedule a time.

CHAPTER 14

Call From the Wild

The cellphone rang. "Yeah?" the man answered, bolting up wide-eyed in the dark.

"Cheatgrass?" the caller asked.

The mention of another in his long string of street names brought a mixed feeling of fear and expectation. *"Who's this?!"* Freddie Burns asked again, though more forcefully.

"It is another call from the wild, seeking the warmth of your company."

"If you want warmth, sorry: I'm chillin'."

"Yes, now that a certain abode is no longer burning."

Freddie feared staying on the line too long. "So let's talk now, not then. My company don't come free. How much?" he cut to the bottom line.

The caller was persuasive. "More than before."

The prospect of another job already (one that sounded like it would pay more than that which brought him to town) made Freddie giddy. But he played it cool. "Where do we meet that won't bring the local heat?"

The caller gave the time and location.

Freddie agreed to meet but had to ask, "How will I know you?"

"Just look for a bearded man that is as physically striking as you, only with blazing eyes of blue," the caller directed.

The line dropped. Freddie returned to his cargo hold hiding spot, pleased that his trip wasn't for nothing since hopes of doing in *The Burning Desire* were already done.

CHAPTER 15

Too Many Irons

The next morning was cloudy and cool again, accompanied by what always seemed like a chance of rain. Nevertheless, Luna sent her trench coat and slacks to the cleaners and power-dressed for the big meeting with Bernie Sparks in her double breasted blazer dress. She went through the rental car routine and then, for lunch, ate the seafood burrito and drank the now lukewarm iced espresso that were supposed to be breakfast.

Afterwards, Luna skimmed Hui's Alaskan culture notes from their late supper; then, dialed up GPS directions; and started on a trip from paved downtown streets to gravelly rural roads in the hills. Finally, a small, log cabin-styled lodge appeared. Luna pulled into the driveway, parked, walked to the door, and knocked. When the front door opened, so did the mouth of the man who appeared in the doorway.

"Connie, hi," he stammered at the sight of a Native

American woman he thought he knew. "You didn't have to dress so formally. How did you not get wind of the club burning down? Were you out of town?"

Luna was confused. *"Connie?"* she asked.

The man pounded his forehead with the palm of his hand. "Sorry, Miss, I mixed you up with somebody at the club," he apologized. "Working in a nightclub so much can throw your daylight eyesight out of kilter. You and Connie are a spittin' image though; both in tip-top shape and with good fashion sense. Although the closer I look, you're more like Gina Lollobrigida, only taller. Maybe it's your thigh-high boots? Are you Italian, Miss..?"

"Nightcrow, Luna Nightcrow, and no, I'm not," she finally answered, handing the man her business card to refresh his memory and end what felt like endless objectification.

"Oh, yeah," he finally realized, "you're that insurance rep from Tight Ship who wanted to chit-chat."

"I take it you're Mr. Bernie Sparks?" Luna still needed to ask.

"Yeah, I'm Bernie Sparks or "Sparky," as most know me around here. Come on in."

Bernie Sparks was a jowly white man in his early 70s who probably blow-dried his silvery hair back into youthful thickness. His flannel shirt and suspenders gave him a lumberjack air that fit The Last Frontier atmosphere. Although the accent and homespun style gave away definite down-home heritage. Sparky offered Luna a seat in the living room beside an empty fireplace. "Thanks," she said, sitting in a pink, hardback chair.

"So," Sparky began to ask, plopping down in his recliner, "any news on the houseboat barbecue that went askew?"

"Not yet," Luna answered. "I am working with your insurer to find out. As part of the job, I read news reports and talked to some residents. It seems not too many are sad to see what happened to your houseboat."

Sparky disagreed. "You must have missed the decent number of folks who told me off the record, mind you, that it was a crying shame what happened."

Luna took out her notepad and pencil. "What exactly would you say happened to *The Burning Desire*, Sparky?"

"I don't know. It caught fire one way or another after quitting time. I am aching to know what you and the fire department think before I have my final say."

"Understandable," Luna remarked.

"I won't pussyfoot around, Ms. Nightcrow. You know that I take a lot of flak around here. Truth be told, a lot of it is jealousy. Been here damned near 30 years, but I'm still from "The Outside." That's what they call out-of-towners. I am an electrician, by trade, and helped get Vegas, Reno, and Tahoe plugged into the grid. A lot of stars called me when their own stuff went on the fritz. Frankie, Sammy..."

"Everybody who was anybody," Luna cut in, in order to condense the conceit.

"Yeah, and they swore I did right by them too. If you wanted lights, camera, action, Sparky was the man."

"Why move here then?"

"One, I was getting too old for journeyman work in mainly a desert. Climbing poles and stairs, toting around tools, and digging in attics, basements, and yards in 90 plus degrees during the day and aching cold at night was getting the best of me. Then, I had to stay up on building codes to guarantee the electrical work would pass inspections. And as Vegas and Reno grew, the younguns who could weld and do concrete work got the contracts to lay pipes and install boxes, leaving me the odd man out. Hell, I was never going to be a master electrician anyway. So I hit the bricks."

"You mean you learned masonry to be more competitive?" Luna asked.

Sparky chuckled at her confusion. "I mean I left, hit the road," he explained. "It was close to 2000, too. The end of the world was near, remember?"

Luna nodded. "Oh, yes," she replied. "Y2K: A lot of worry about how computers and power grids all over the world would go down because of years of neglecting to update old code."

"Did you buy it, Ms. Nightcrow."

"No. I knew enough about computers to realize the problem could be fixed."

"Smart bird," Sparky praised Luna's awareness, then continued chronicling his own. "If the end was near, though, one of the things on my bucket list was to see Alaska. So I took one of those cruises. And when I saw all the wild county—the bush, they call it—and how folks need a lot of power to live in it, I figured that with my knowhow, I could jumpstart my career here by getting things running again, if Y2K was just a hiccup instead of a heart attack. Turned out it wasn't even a burp, so I set up shop for reasonably priced electronics upkeep. I took up electronics as a hobby in Nevada. A lot of folks down there had CBs and ham and shortwave radios that went on the fritz, and I cut my teeth on fixing them."

"So the gamble to move paid off, so to speak," Luna replied.

"Yeah. And because of Y2K, I wasn't spooked by talk of COVID-19 doing us in. I already had my ducks in a row and made a lot of dough when supply chain issues made folks hold on to stuff, and they brought it to me to fix."

"Is that how you bought the houseboat, Sparky?"

"Pretty much, but with a little of the usual financing that folks get to help. It was an investment because I knew that once the virus was licked, folks would be back to buying cheap TVs, computers, microwaves, and the chips that go in them from foreign parts. Business slowed, like I thought, but not my bills. But I knew how to pay them.

"I saw all those quarantined folks pouring out of their basements after lockdown was lifted, hankering for something new to do. And that reminded me of Vegas. Back in the day, you were shit-out-of-luck if you wanted something else to do besides play slots and the tables. And Juneau's a one trick pony, too. Unless you like watching nature or roughing it, there ain't much to do. But what if I gave them something new to do *indoors* not outdoors?"

Luna was confused. "Kind of odd, isn't it: People finally get the okay to go out only to go back in?"

"But the key is "new to do indoors," Ms. Nightcrow. Fun times: Like the ones when they opened up Vegas for the whole family with all kinds of indoor goings-on. They got Hollywood style floor shows, magic acts, circuses, and even pro sports teams now."

"So, you bought the houseboat and turned it into a strip—pardon me, a gentleman's—club," Luna concluded.

"Which makes it something new to do, as the Panhandle hadn't such a place in damn near a century. And that "strip" slip of the tongue only tells part of the story; it isn't like getting butt naked in a brothel. Anyway, what goes on in most folks' bedrooms is way dirtier than what some wet blankets here accuse me of providing."

"You're giving them a chance to live out their fantasies in a *gentlemanly* fashion. Is that it?"

"Now you're seeing the light, Ms. Nightcrow. And besides, there's a mess of fellas up here who can't find a woman because y'all are in short number."

Luna remembered the unequal number of men to women Hui spoke of. "Is that the men to women ratio? I heard the problem is mostly a bush country concern; in the Aleutians, for example, I'm told it's over 180 men for every 100 women."

Sparky shook his head and mourned for, "All those boys eking it out alone, in the bush, with nothing but pent-up feelings for women. And Juneau might as well be bush; it's hard getting in and out of here unless you're a fish or bird, and we have to bring in damn near all our food nowadays at the cost of an arm and a leg. And even though we still got a little gold up in the mines, it's hard getting miners because cheap housing is as scarce as hen's teeth and there ain't a hell of a lot to do after quitting time except drink.

"So in a way, Ms. Nightcrow, I did the community a service with *The Burning Desire*. Hell, Nome, Fairbanks, and The Big A are getting with the times and setting up red-light districts or having dancers come in from time to time to satisfy folks' needs. That's what I was aiming to do down here."

Luna changed subjects. "What does Mrs. Sparks

think of *The Burning Desire* and it requiring you to interact with its alluring staff on a nightly basis?"

"If "alluring" means the same as half naked, not all my staff are. I got a woman bartender and a woman disc jockey; both no longer spring chickens and are clothed. As for my wife, Tanis, she's an Alaska Native and 15 years my junior. That stirs up a hornet's nest of trouble right there: You know, mixed marriage and all? But it takes a heap of work to keep two businesses afloat, especially when one's a houseboat. I'm not here much. But I reckon Tanis thinks like any woman with her head screwed on straight would about this: That I'm a lying bastard who conjured this up as a way to cheat on her. And to add injury to insult, her folks don't think much of me and the club either.

"But no one's forcing those ladies to perform nor making anybody stop by. Like I said, I'm providing the community another kind of entertainment and the chance to branch out its job openings. You know, Ms. Nightcrow, not all of us can sail a ship, log, drill, or work behind a desk."

"So if Mrs. Sparks and her parents don't approve of *The Burning Desire* could ...?"

"Could they have struck a match?" Sparky finished the question. He then shrugged. "It's hard to tell. Hell, Bigfoot could've done it out of spite for me not having a lady Bigfoot dancer. I'd lay odds though that if it's arson, you're not just here to figure a way for the insurance not to pay, but to also see how I might like my jail cell fixed up, right?"

"I am just gathering information, Sparky. Do you know of any other helpful people to interview?"

"You are a smart bird, Ms. Nightcrow; you'll come up with more."

"Do you have any black employees or customers at the club?"

"As in kind of tan-looking like you, or…?"

"As in African Americans, not me. I'm Native American, Cherokee specifically."

Sparky thought for a moment. "No dancers, yet. As for customers, I suppose we had some. Not many, but I suppose."

Luna wanted to be sure. "But some definitely?" she asked.

Sparky repeated, "Like I said: I'm a fair-minded kind of guy."

"Just show you the money and you'll show anyone a good time?"

"Hey, that would be a dandy sales pitch, if I ever get back in the adult entertainment business."

"It's all yours, Sparky." Luna then reached into her shoulder bag, removed several photos of Freddie Burns, and handed them to her guest. "Ever see this man inside or maybe waiting outside the club?"

Sparky cleared his coffee table and spread the photos over it for a better look. "A brawny fella for sure—an oil rigger from upstate, right?"

"Just a person I'd like to interview, if you've seen him around," Luna replied.

"Hell, if I had seen him, I would have offered him a job as a bouncer or maybe a dancer. You know, some women here got unmet needs for men, though you would think they wouldn't have trouble finding one with so many unhitched."

"Maybe that saying up here sums it up: The odds are good, but the goods are odd," Luna offered a reason.

Sparky grinned.

"Who is your doorwoman, Sparky? Maybe she saw this man come in."

"You mean *doorman*, Ms. Nightcrow, since it was me. You can't get past me with a fake ID! And no: In that part of my job, I still never saw this fella."

Luna nodded, recovered the photos, and asked, "Do you mind if I talk to some of your employees?"

Sparky threw up his hands. "Talk their ears off if they still want to listen," he said. "Cops already grilled us all like salmon. I had 10 dancers: Five starters and 5 on the bench who were ready to go in if one called in sick or quit. Some ladies try to come down here from the Big A, but I give Panhandle gals first dibs because Anchorage has its own clubs. Still, most just dance for enough to pay a few months' rent and quit. I don't have many professionals. And nowadays even they work during the day. I can't fault them too much though. You got to have more than one iron in the fire. I thank my lucky stars for a second business."

"Sometimes, it's best to have only one; too many irons cool the fire and heat none," Luna cautioned.

The front door suddenly banged open. Luna turned to see a bony brunette wearing a tight dress and enough makeup for 2 women. She lugged plastic bags and rasped, *"Sparky? Aren't you going to help…"* The woman's bloodshot eyes spotted Luna.

Sparky hurried over to help with what looked like groceries. He took the bags and forced a smile. "Tanis, this is…"

Luna stood. "I'm Nightcrow, Luna Nightcrow," she said, offering her hand to shake.

The woman walked up and extended hers too. But she quickly reared back and landed a hard slap across Luna's face. The woman named Tanis then roared at Sparky, *"How dare you drag one of your whores into this house!"*

"She is from the insurance company, Tanis, asking about the fire!" Sparky tried to tell his wife.

"You are such a liar, Sparky! She's too good-looking to be an insurance agent. If you want to know about the boat, whoever you are, it got what it deserved. And you will too if I catch you around my husband again! *Now get out!"*

Luna rubbed her cheek and brushed past Spark's wife, catching a whiff of booze and the name of the grocery store on the bags as she headed for the open front door. After bidding The Sparks Family farewell from afar, Luna returned to her car, put her head on the steering wheel, and cried. It was more about her vacation being ruined by another fraud investigation. Ten thousand dollars couldn't replace the priceless *Glacier Goddess* dinner date with the Canadian doctor and the wasted chance for it to develop into so much more. Instead, Luna was slapped and mistaken for a whore.

CHAPTER 16

Here and There

Luna regained her composure and returned to work, stopping by Juneau City Hall before heading back to the hotel. It was nearly 6 pm when Kelly responded to the knock on her hotel room door. When it opened, she was stunned at the condition of the visitor.

But Luna managed a stoic grin to put her at ease. "This isn't going to be glamorous, remember?"

"*il faut souffrir pour être belle,*" Kelly remarked.

"*Huh?*"

""To be beautiful, one must suffer," or so the French say."

Luna grinned. "As they say, 'a thousand Frenchman can't be wrong,' if they meant enduring high heels and underwire bras. I didn't know you spoke French, by the way."

"When you live close to Canada, you hear stuff

come across that might come in handy," Kelly joked. "Come on in."

Luna saw Kelly's suite had just about everything hers did except for the picturesque view. She waited while her hostess went to the kitchenette. Kelly finally returned with an icebag. "Thanks," Luna said, applying it to her cheek.

After learning what happened, Kelly asked, "Aren't you going to press charges?"

"The only thing I wanted to "press" was my smartphone stun gun against her face," Luna replied.

Kelly asked, *"Smartphone stun gun?!"*

Luna went to her purse, took out her smartphone, and pushed the protector's lower side button. Two stainless steel pincers popped out of the top portion and crackled to life with intense blue arcs of electricity. "Meet the Stinger smartphone protector stun gun, Ms. Day. Sixty-thousand volts of concealed power."

Kelly was amazed. *"Stunning!"* she said. "Does it affect your phone though?"

"Relax: I can still shoot the breeze with it, not just people," Luna reassured her colleague. "Besides, stun guns shoot in pulses that greatly lower the current. Sixty thousand volts sounds deadly, but it's not the same continuous flow of the electric chair."

Kelly breathed a sigh of relief. "I get it: Ohms Law and all," she said. "Because electrical shock also depends on the current you're exposed to. And human skin has some resistance to shock, although it lowers the wetter you are. That's why a lot of people get shocked in kitchens and especially in bathrooms."

"But Tanis was so sloshed that she'd have felt the full shock even in the living room where she slapped me," Luna remarked.

"Besides fantasizing about frying her, what are you really going to do, Luna?"

Luna removed the icebag, then went into the bathroom. She checked her puffy reflection in the mirror and called out, "Nothing. No bones broken… just Tanis's heart. You're paying me ten grand to put up with this kind of crap, remember?"

"If you still need information, why not do an online call or return to those thrilling days of yester-year and phone her next time?"

"Dust off my social distancing skills, huh?"

"Just a thought, Luna."

"All right," the insurance investigator sighed. "But I picked up some things from visiting the house in person. Tanis lugged some grocery bags from the same store Burns was seen in. I couldn't see what was in them, just the name. And she was obviously drunk."

Kelly asked if Mrs. Sparks was employed.

Luna finally joined her colleague in the living room and took a seat. "She has a drinking problem that pretty much confines her to housekeeping and temporary gigs."

"Has she always been an alcoholic?" Kelly asked.

Luna shrugged. "If not, it's not hard to see how the club probably led her to it," she guessed.

"That puts a lot of pressure on Sparky," Kelly said.

Luna laughed, "Speak of the devil, he's from Lovelady, Texas, or so says more online sleuthing, and sounds every bit Southern."

"So Sparky probably wasn't as well-connected with Sin City celebrities as he says?" Kelly asked.

"Probably not. Many of the big names either left Vegas by the time he arrived or arrived after Sparky left," Luna replied. "But I believe him saying he was burned out as a journeyman electrician and came to Alaska for a vacation. Once here, Sparky liked it, saw the need for electronics repair, and set up a mom-and-pop shop during the Y2K scare. It did pretty good during the pandemic but is going broke now."

"It is probably losing to online tech trouble-shooters and people buying cheap replacements," Kelly replied.

"If anything should be incinerated, Kelly, I would have expected it to be the repair shop, not *The Burning Desire*."

"A hundred percent, Luna."

"Also, City Hall and The Department for Permits told me that they can't ban gentleman's clubs but can decide where they will operate. They apparently let *The Burning Desire* drop anchor downtown, although along that remote section of shoreline.

Sparky didn't put up a fight when they asked him to pay normal docking fees as if he were in the harbor itself and got his liquor license with no trouble."

Kelly asked about Sparky's houseboat's insurance.

"A lot of states don't require it," Luna replied. "But without houseboat insurance, your travel and choice of docking locations are limited. Sparky's financing *The Burning Desire*; he needed proof of insurance to run it out of storage. The Juneau Harbor requires houseboats to be suitably insured in order to drop anchor and to also help protect their property. Tight Ship Assurance charged Sparky less because he reduced travel in the houseboat to local waterways and a passed a boating safety course."

"Did you get an appraisal of the houseboat?" Kelly asked.

"Yes," Luna confirmed. "They are called marine surveys and check current value, condition, and sea-worthiness. *The Burning Desire* was mobile, with two H-600 inboard engines and cruising speed of between eight and ten knots. But I don't think Sparky plans to sail it anywhere. I will e-mail you the PDF."

"Roger that," Kelly said.

"I also found out that Sparky doesn't just pro-mote *The Burning Desire* as entertainment for mostly horny guys but also as some kind of equal rights cru-sade to increase the number of available women in Alaska."

"Oh yeah: Hui told us about the shortage of eligible

women," Kelly recalled. "But unless Sparky's hiring dancers in greater number or importing them, then…"

"Then," Luna interrupted, "as that sage Alfred P. Neuman once said, 'Political speeches are like steer horns: A point here, a point there and a lot of bull in between.'" Which means that I agree that some business-minded girls can make a lot as dancers when they make themselves what men want. Even those who can't have a good shot because '…all the girls get prettier at closing time,' or so the song goes. So desperate customers probably lower their standards just to be satisfied.

"But where Sparky is full of it is that more women are moving to Alaska. That shrinks the men to women gap. And those men jonesing for bachelorettes are mostly in remote areas, not the cities and towns."

"But that does show a big motive for arson: To buy a bigger boat with the insurance payout and make more money in showbusiness. The kind, I might add, that cities like Anchorage and Fairbanks make with their clubs," Kelly cautioned.

"I will check out the houseboat market for any calls from Sparky or possibly Tanis; then, start calling up dancers and staff for information they may have kept from the police," Luna added. "Economics and demographics aside, have you made any headway on the figuring out how the fire started, Kelly?"

CHAPTER 17

Burning Questions

"What caused the fire is a burning question fueled by speculation," Kelly responded. "Many ignitable substances, from acrylic to alcohol, no doubt sped up the fire. Sparky sailed the houseboat to prove it was mobile, but Bernila didn't find any diesel gasoline containers in the debris. So was the accelerant something as tiny as a spark from an overheated appliance or, with rumors of crimes being committed, was it as big as a bomb?"

Luna nodded. "Makes sense," she said.

"Anyway, it will take time for the GC/MS tests I submitted earlier to come back."

"And GC/MS is…?"

"Sorry, Luna. Gas Chromatography/Mass Spectrometry is a combination of gas chromatography and mass spectrometry. It has been around since the

1950's and is handy in determining what causes a fire. I sent samples of all that debris we collected to be analyzed for hydrocarbon accelerants by a local lab and then for independent testing in Seattle. They will remove and look for the amount of usual suspect accelerants from the debris and report their findings.

"That GC/MS is the tool they use. The gas chromatograph separates the debris into small parts and sends them to the mass spectrometer. The mass spectrometer breaks the molecules into particles and documents the spectrum that shows up. The spectrum readings are a reliable way to identify what compound was ultimately used."

"How long did it take the results to come back from the San Francisco fire?"

"Not long because one of the business owners copped to paying Burns to blow it up. But with all the lawsuits and appeals that could come out of this case, especially if it's handled wrong, I'm going over the diagrams of the houseboat and meeting with Bernila to compare notes in a day or two. Maybe she turned up something I missed like a faulty appliance that survived."

"If this is arson, Kelly, would it fit Freddie Burns's MO (modus operandi)?"

"There is an "MO," as in m-o-n-e-y. Freddie is an expert, not some sicko pyromaniac who gets off on seeing things burn. He is paid to make fires look like accidents or, if not, confuse fire investigators about their cause."

"Looks like he's going the confusion route, in order to give his client a shot in court if any claim is rejected," Luna commented.

Kelly agreed. "Outside of Michigan, where Detroit kicked off the end of the pandemic with four hundred seventy-seven arsons in 2023 alone, California ranks high in arsons committed, particularly in Northern California. Freddie is linked to multi-millions of dollars of damage to properties in Chico, Merced, and Eureka. The San Fran inferno is the first time someone confessed to hiring him; and from your evidence, the only time anyone's caught him in the area of a fire."

Luna asked, "What is the going rate for an arson these days?"

"For someone like Freddie, about ten grand a pop. He gets half upfront, the other half after the fire is set, and a percentage of any insurance money that the client collects," Kelly answered.

"The plastics owners paid up, right?"

"Five thousand upfront that went up in smoke because the claim will be rejected."

"But I don't get the California connection, Kelly. With arsonists in every state, why not hit up a fellow Alaskan?"

"There are lots of fraud and fire investigators in every state, too. But if you want the best, you won't settle for less. Same goes for arsonists. If the buyer is a cheapskate, they will hire amateurs or rookies. But with a total state population about the size of, well, San Francisco, the chances of a hometown arsonist's methods being tracked and him or her being found out are greater than a buyer drawing one from among some forty million Californians over two thousand miles away."

It began making sense. "I get it," Luna acknowledged. "Plus, there are enough corrupt charter plane pilots or shady ship captains with mouths watering at the opportunity to smuggle him home. If they stick it to him for half of his ten grand take to escape, Burns will just up the percentage of his cut of the insurance payout to recover the loss."

"Exactly," Kelly said. "And with the ongoing hunt for him down south, maybe Freddie wanted to take a job in the last place most people would imagine. Although Anchorage once ranked 49th out of 100 cities in arsons. So it's not unusual nor, by the way, is being an African American in Alaska necessarily a disadvantage. As of this year, 2027, there are about five hundred black residents in Juneau. Not many, but enough to make up a little more than one percent of Juneau's thirty thousand residents."

"And that helps explain why 80 percent of the small sample size of Freddie Burns eyewitnesses changed their stories when I followed up with them and 2 others simply didn't pan out. A tourist or someone they've never seen causes suspicion."

"Or maybe with additional questions coming at them, Luna, they changed their stories for fear of being mixed up in something bigger or called racists. Freddie loves that kind of confusion; someone else gets profiled and blamed while he gets away."

"So, Kelly, let's look at the other side of the ledger: Those who hated the houseboat and may have paid to destroy it. Juneau has over a thousand millionaires and is one of the wealthiest parts of the state per capita. So someone here could afford to pay Burns's going rate."

"Yes, but there are also many here who aren't rich but just as eager for the houseboat to burn. String enough of them together and they could afford Freddie's rate, too. So I wouldn't just limit it to millionaires, Luna."

"I won't. I just meant having many millions carries with it a baked in kind of status that not only could finance an arson but, if necessary, cover it up. Still, let's consider some middle and lower income suspects. How about … Tanis Sparks, for example?"

Luna's face may have remained straight, but not Kelly's. "How convenient," she laughed. "You got bopped by Sparky's ball and chain and now …"

"Revenge aside," Luna cut in, "Tanis does have a legit motive: Burn the houseboat for the love it cost, not the money it made."

CHAPTER 18

A Cute Trick

It was 9 am when the phone rang. "Luna Nightcrow speaking," the insurance investigator answered in formal fashion after seeing the name on the caller ID wasn't a friend.

"Ms. Nightcrow, hello," Sparky greeted her. "Look, I sure hope you will forgive Tanis."

"Turn the other cheek so she can slap it too?" Luna snorted.

"Okay, I'm mighty sorry for how she acted. But you can see why. I mean, I reckon I haven't been the most understanding fella, by running a strip club. And because of it, you got hurt."

"So what do you want, Sparky?"

"I want to ask you not to file charges against Tanis...*please?* I mean, you see what shape she's in and all."

There was a long silence before Luna agreed. But

it was on one condition. "Can you ask Tanis to talk to me about *The Burning Desire*?"

"*Done!* Ask her whatever you want to. I won't be around to coach her up about what to say. But you might want to talk to her over the phone next time."

Luna went along with Sparky's suggestion and hung up. About 2 hours later, her smartphone rang again. And as promised, it was Tanis. Although Luna was subjected to more of a rant than conversation.

"*Sparky is a whoremonger!*" Tanis slurred her words.

"Then why stay with him?" Luna dared to ask.

"Because he—he knows what would happen if I left. See, I have some control over him, and I don't mean with threatening a divorce either."

"Do you mean *threatening* him with what you know about *The Burning Desire*?"

Tanis gave Luna an answer, but not to the question she asked. "He's nothing without me. I run this house. And no one sits in my chair but me."

"So I deserved to be slapped for not knowing, Mrs. Sparks?"

"Sparky didn't tell me someone from the insurance company was coming over. So, a lawyer could say I was defending myself against an intruder. Anyway, I said you're too pretty to sell insurance; doesn't that get me off the hook?"

"You know what they say about women: We tend to fall in love with our ears, not eyes," Luna replied.

"So telling me more about *The Burning Desire* fire might convince me not to press charges."

With that, Luna detected a bit more remorse in Tanis's tone when she said, "It's too bad all Sparky's strippers are out of work but them's the breaks. Besides, they're young enough to latch on someplace else or even get real jobs. But not shedding a tear over what happened doesn't make me an arsonist—what woman in my position would? Anyway, I was never aboard the whore by the shore. You know, that would have been a better name than what Sparky came up with."

Luna wasn't going to get anywhere with Tanis, and finally said, "Thank you, Mrs. Sparks. Try to enjoy your day."

"Don't you worry about that," Tanis assured her. "Sparky may be a skirt chaser, but he has his good points. Like today: He sprang for a nice bottle of North of the Border Blend for calling you up."

"Then cheers," Luna revised her goodbye accordingly. *Cute trick, Sparky!* Get your wife liquored up and angered about you being everything but an arsonist.

CHAPTER 19

Fiery Art Form

The forecast called for cloudy skies, no surprise, but with a temperature of 72 degrees (practically a heatwave for The Panhandle). After the call with Tanis, Luna decided to do a bit of sightseeing instead of what felt like bounty hunting. She dressed casually, had a bagel with salmon spread and espresso for brunch, and left her suite.

In the daytime, the downtown historic district reminded Luna of photos of Swiss Alpine villages, with old-fashioned monuments and shops of every color offering goods and services as best as could be found and the entrancing majesty of the misty mountains all around. One particular building's banner-style sign with a red and orange design that resembled flames when it rippled caught Luna's eye. It invited the curious to "Come and see Pyrography."

Luna recalled Kelly talking about those who enjoyed setting fires, or "pyromaniacs." Some fiery form of art must be on display, but in what way? she wondered. Luna decided to find out and entered what turned out to be a center for the arts.

A crowd of spectators gathered on the main showroom floor, absorbed in a host of coffee-colored portraits of people, places, and things. Luna joined them. Upon closer inspection, she noticed the canvases were wooden. And instead of paint, their pictures looked as though they were branded or etched by the artists.

A voice sprang up, the curator's, and explained to the audience, "Simply put, pyrography is decorating a variety of substance with heat. The word comes from the Greek words *pur*, or fire, and *graphos*, meaning writing. And thus, it means 'writing with fire.'"

"In its civilized form, pyrography likely began in Ancient Egypt but samples can be found as far abroad as Great Britain and among the Nazca People of Peru. Back then, hot pokers were used to burn pictures into, among other things, wood. The exhibits here fit that category of pyrography. But now, by using special heated pens or metal tools called nibs or even lasers, these artists "burned" pictures into soft wood like Juneau's abundant pine. By changing the kind of nibs, the temperature, or the angle used on the wood, these pyrographers created detailed portraits, landscapes, and other designs. After the drawing is burnt in, some artists chose to also color the wooden objects. But many left them in their seared state."

After the tour ended, Luna approached the Caucasian curator and homed in on her nametag. Eleanor Fjord, PhD, it read. She then gave her a passing grade for adopting the "smart casual" look of jeans, even if designer; a houndstooth blazer and pearls that embodied business sense; and finally, caramel-colored ankle boots that enhanced an already statuesque bearing. The women walked as they talked during which Luna learned Fjord was a fellow Generation Xer, although slightly younger, and also the arts center director.

"I am delighted you found the pyrography exhibit appealing, Ms. Nightcrow, The art form, however, isn't without inherent risks. Burning wood produces fumes and requires proper ventilation, in order to reduce the risk of fire or injury to the artist," Fjord said, her elocution shameless in showing she wasn't just a pretty face. That there was a first class intellect at the controls.

"Any local talent on display?" Luna asked.

"Not in this exhibit, I'm afraid. But other works by local prodigies are available. For instance, a Juneau graphics artist designed the pyrography banner outside."

"Very imaginative," Luna lauded the artist.

"I will certainly tell him that he has acquired national admiration," Fjord promised.

Luna grinned. "By way of Oklahoma, in case he wants to know where his newfound fanbase is."

"I apologize if I blew your cover, so to speak, but people know one another or of each other in small communities such as this. When I moved here from Greenwich, a town of comparable size in Connecticut, I initially faced the same scrutiny."

"No harm done, Dr. Fjord. What originally brought you to Alaska?"

"I followed my beau, an Army captain in the 10th Mountain Division, when he was transferred some years ago from Fort Drum, New York to what is now Joint Base Elmendorf-Richardson upstate. Tragically, though, he succumbed to the virus."

Luna issued the compulsory, "I'm sorry."

Fjord accepted her sympathies with an accomplished smile. "Had it not happened, perhaps I would not have followed my passion: Art."

"Since the cat's out of the bag, I'm also a visiting insurance fraud investigator."

"An essential job, to revive COVID era nomenclature," Fjord said.

"Yes," Luna agreed. "How we all worried whether our jobs were "essential" or "non-essential." If essential, you risked infection by reporting for duty, unless you could work from home. Non-essential meant you were laid off indefinitely or fired."

"So, Ms. Nightcrow, you are in Juneau on business?" Fjord asked.

Luna answered, "Yes. During which I got a door slammed in my face, you might say, therefore the bruised cheek. It's an occupational hazard that comes with poking around."

"But usually associated with "poking" into controversial matters. Is what you're investigating contentious, Ms. Nightcrow?"

"In this part of Alaska, yes. I am looking into a houseboat fire."

"Of which Juneau has plenty. Of houseboats, that is, not necessarily fires or frauds."

"The houseboat of interest has become quite the tourist attraction: *The Burning Desire*."

Fjord nodded. "It has—pardon me, "had," given its decommission of sorts—managed to build itself a lucrative, if perhaps lewd, reputation."

"Lucrative, absolutely," Luna echoed Fjord. "I understand it recently surpassed the museum circuit, in terms of tourist attractions. But is "lewd" your moral view of it?"

Fjord then stopped and looked Luna directly in the eye. "Now I understand why you have paid a visit: To find suspects in *The Burning Desire* fire."

"Did I say that, Dr. Fjord?"

"No. But you wouldn't be doing your job if you didn't examine every possibility, including me."

Luna tried to simmer things down. "Look, I'm only an insurance investigator, not the police. I was sightseeing and happened across the curious sign outside. This is not an undercover sting. You can frisk me for a wire, if you want," she offered.

"With all the innovations in secret communications, the absence of a microphone on one's person is no guarantee of not being recorded. Investigators' power of recollection, for instance, is often remarkable."

"Okay, then lobotomize me."

Fjord laughed for the first time. "No, no, Ms. Nightcrow," she declined the offer. "Please forgive me for casting such unpleasant accusations. Everyone yearns for relaxation. I should be pleased that you chose the arts to fill that need."

"I am sorry for the bad vibes," Luna apologized.

"Since you mentioned *The Burning Desire's* rise in popularity, I will share my feelings about it. First, I am well aware that dance is considered an art form. And some believe that, given a chance, striptease might evolve into a respected style."

"Or return to its burlesque roots that were once respected, a la the 1907 Ziegfeld Follies," Luna added.

"I agree that what qualifies as art is ultimately in the eye of the beholder. But unlike some cities in Alaska, the arts sector contributes significantly to Juneau's economy; nearly $80 million a year. So as both curator and director, I must judge not only aesthetics but anticipate the political and social impact of displays on the community. With that in mind, I have developed a policy of selective sensitivity."

"Pardon me, but that phrase sounds like one in the same."

"Then please allow me to explain the difference, Ms. Nightcrow."

"By all means, doctor."

"The color blue, for instance, was once reserved for royalty because of its scarcity. Plants like indigo and woad and stones like lapis lazuli were prized commodities in the ancient world. But after centuries, as the process for making artificial blue dyes became normal, it found its way into everyday articles like jeans and even our state flag design. In art, blue retains a psychologically cooling and stabilizing effect in works that depict water and sky. And in our largely rural state, such themes are most valued by our patrons.

"When blue is applied to movies, humor, and dance, it can evoke pornographic imagery or racy oration, which are attributed to blue state values by many of our patrons. Hence the formation of blue laws in colonial times that still exist today: To curb such activities, particularly on Sundays."

Luna nodded. "I get it: You simply have a discriminating taste in art," she summarized.

"A fair approximation, if that helps you grasp the policy."

"Vis-à-vis your "policy," doctor, I guess you don't have Michelangelo's statue "David" or Botticelli's "The Birth of Venus" painting, as they might be viewed as sexual objects by the likes of the Sect of the Sanctified Pier."

"More suspects, Ms. Nightcrow?"

"Just members of the community whose display of challenging norms I found thought provoking on the docks the other day."

"And practically every day, Ms. Nightcrow. It is likely that some of its members, though not its leader, have visited. Although sans their signature placards, I couldn't identify their parishioners individually, as my devout agnosticism prohibits membership. How impressive, by the way, that you know of the artists Michelangelo and Botticelli's other works."

"Chalk it up to an old case where I helped recover a stolen artifact of great cultural and insured value back home. It required a lot of art history research."

"Thank you for your service to the arts, Ms. Nightcrow. It is reassuring that Oscar Wilde was wrong in his declaration, 'All art is useless.'"

"One art form is useless, doctor: Con artistry. It doesn't pay in the end."

"Do you always 'get your man,' as is said of the Canadian police?"

"As I'm not Canadian, no. But I get your meaning and like to think I'm good at my job stateside."

"I see," Fjord said. "Continuing with David and Venus, I realize some consider me a hypocrite for choosing among portrayals to display. But the aforementioned are classic depictions of adults in their natural states that are often held in high esteem worldwide, We once had a marvelous gypsum bust of David on traveling display from Khabarovsk, for example."

"Khabarovsk sounds Russian."

"It is, Ms. Nightcrow. It is a city three times the size of Anchorage that borders China. It was the first Russian district to begin a "sister-state" arrangement with a U.S. state, Alaska, as the Cold War ended under the Soviet policy of *glasnost* or "openness" with the West."

"Then it's sort of a cultural exchange program, doctor?"

"On a grander scale but essentially correct. Over the last 40 years, many Alaskans, from politicians to entrepreneurs, visited or conducted business there and vice versa. But with recent world events, that has obviously declined. Nevertheless, we were honored to have hosted David's bust, if not his entire body. It placed us head and shoulders above other museums in the region."

So she has a sense of humor after all, Luna thought, then chuckled aloud, "Nice one, doctor."

"Thank you, Ms. Nightcrow. We have similar au naturel representations of the human physique that might interest devotees, while upholding community standards and expectations."

"And they are..?"

"The traveling cedar paddle exhibit by Tlingit

artist Ms. Alison Marks offers a unique perspective of the actor Burt Reynolds's nude 1972 "Cosmopolitan Magazine" pose on a bearskin rug," Fjord answered.

Before Luna could get directions to the display, her smartphone rang. *Rhys Yéil: Who's that?!* was Luna's response to the caller ID. But upon answering the phone, his reason for calling put her back in her insurance investigating depth. "I'll stop by another day to see that nude paddle display," Luna said.

"When you return, I would relish your opinion of whether or not the display adequately represents the modern state of undress, as it relates to our selective but sensitive policy."

Luna promised an assessment.

Fjord extended her hand. "It's been a pleasure speaking with you, Ms. Nightcrow."

Luna shook her hand. "Likewise, Dr. Fjord," she said. "And I'd be as interested if you have any other thoughts on *The Burning Desire* matter."

Fjord accepted Luna's business card. "Indeed," she replied.

After sharing routine smiles, the women departed amicably.

CHAPTER 20

Hard to Face

Mr. Rhys Yéil and Mrs. Nita Yéil, the parents of Mrs. Tanis Sparks, wanted to speak to Luna. After changing into business attire, it was about 3 p.m. when she crossed the Douglas-Juneau Bridge to Douglas Island where the modest Yéil Family home was. The only thing that enlivened the premises was the presence of an ornate totem pole.

Mister Yéil was shorter than Luna but taller than his wife. Luna was taller than both Yéils to their amazement. After tea, The Yéils began to give Luna the niceties of their daughter's involvement with *The Buring Desire*.

"Tanis, whose Tlingit name is Khutxh.ayanahá, is not well," Mr. Yéil told Luna.

"She called us," Mrs. Yéil added, "crying that Sparky is having another affair. She claims it's with you, Ms. Nightcrow. And while she is right, in that you are lovely, we heard you are only here to investigate the houseboat fire."

Luna nodded. "That's why I didn't go to the police after she slapped me."

"Thank you," both parents said.

"You're welcome. When I spoke with Sparky, he said that your daughter and both of you don't like *The Burning Desire*. Is that true?"

"Yes," Mrs. Yéil sighed, "but perhaps not for the reasons others think. For our people, the Tlingit, the abundance of alcohol aboard Sparky's boat is a problem. It affects people in different ways but has enslaved our daughter."

"We are a modern Alaskan people, Ms. Nightcrow: Keeping our traditional culture alive, but also succeeding in tourism, education, and even government in not just Alaska, but throughout the West Coast. My wife was a school counselor; and I, a craftsman," Mr. Yéil added.

"Did you carve the *Kootéeyaa* outside?" Luna asked.

"Thank you for appreciating the proper name for what many simply call a "totem pole," Ms. Nightcrow. But no, I didn't carve it. Ours is a doorway *Kootéeyaa* that describes our family and tribal history. I designed it but a master carver in Ketchikan crafted it out of red cedar for almost six thousand dollars."

"I'm sorry to say that the world's largest concrete *Kootéeyaa* isn't too far from where I live in The Lower 48."

"*An eyesore, Ms. Nightcrow!* I prefer the over one hundred seventy feet tall authentic wooden article from the Kwakwaka'wakw People down in British Columbia at Alert Bay. Some others say that *Kootéeyaas* in California and Washington State are the best constructed."

"I am also Native American, a member of the Western Band Cherokee of Oklahoma. So I understand your pride in tribal customs," Luna told the couple.

"You certainly came a long way!" Mrs. Yéil laughed.

"I'm glad I did; you have a beautiful town," Luna replied.

"Except for *The Burning Desire* part of it. The corruption draws people like a porchlight draws flies," Mr. Yéil grumbled.

Mrs. Yéil tried to explain. "Many of our people believe that drunkenness is like being controlled by an evil spirit that causes you to lose your own identity. You become a means to someone else's end."

"Like a pawn in chess," Luna guessed.

Mrs. Yéil nodded. "But we also believe that you have the will to resist others' control. You must be of firm will, though, like a mountain. Nothing has moved these mountains. We can only build so far into them or around them, but we can't move them."

"Our daughter, Tanis, wasn't strong enough to resist the sway of Bernie Sparks," Mr. Yéil sighed.

"She wanted to be an actress and go to Hollywood," Mrs. Yéil added.

"Something many women want to do," Luna said.

"Yes, but most grow out of it. Tanis didn't," Mrs. Yéil replied. "She was attracted to anyone who looked rich, bragged, and promised her the stars. Sparky was such a man, forever touting his time in Las Vegas and how famous people sought his services when it was more like him currying their favor. But when *The Burning Desire* opened, Sparky poured all of his time into making other women feel like stars. He is evil and cares nothing about our daughter nor probably for anybody but himself."

Luna finally asked, "So do you think your daughter could have destroyed *The Burning Desire*, as a way to maybe escape or even save her marriage?"

"Tanis is beginning to realize the mistake she made in marrying Sparky," Mr. Yéil answered. "He is an electrician who could still patch up wiring in planes, boats, cars, and houses. So maybe Tanis thought that burning the houseboat wasn't a risk but a way to regain her identity and free will. I don't approve of arson, Ms. Nightcrow; there are other ways to leave Sparky. But I can understand why Tanis could have done it."

Mrs. Yéil didn't agree with her husband. "Rhys, this is a throwaway world. Most people don't fix broken electronics; they just buy new ones. My understanding too is that because someone is an electrician doesn't mean he's an electronics genius. Maybe back in the 60s and 70s when we didn't have personal computers. But today, they seem like different fields.

"Besides, few people want to be connected with Sparky because of all the bad publicity. Tanis knows this and couldn't have destroyed the houseboat because it makes Sparky more money than his repair shop. And she is seen as a disgrace by many of our people and couldn't remarry."

Mister Yéil huffed, *"Such a mess!"*

"On that we can all agree," Luna said tactfully.

But then Mister Yéil dumped diplomacy. "I think that if I catch Sparky with another woman, it would be hard for me not to kill him. Actually, not many people could blame me if I did!"

Ms. Yéil's intentions for the hypothetical other woman took a more feminine, if still confrontational, approach. "I would definitely have it out with her, wouldn't you Ms. Nightcrow?"

Suddenly, Luna's smartphone rang. She excused herself to answer it in the foyer. It was Kelly.

"Luna, did I catch you in the middle of something?"

"Finding out about a fiery form of art, and now how to dispose of unwelcome lovers," she murmured. "What's up? Did you find Freddie?"

"The police did, not me," Kelly told Luna.

"That's great! Did he confess to starting the houseboat fire?"

"If so, it's only to his maker. He's dead," Kelly said.

CHAPTER 21

How It Ends

Luna followed Kelly's directions back downtown to a bar where the body was found. Kelly was already on site after hearing the first news report about the death of a "well-built, young African American male." Both investigators finally met but like the crowd of other onlookers, neither were immediately allowed into the crime scene.

Kelly stared across the way at the body shrouded in white. "You know," she told Luna, "for some reason, I'm reminded of that poem about death. The one that goes, 'This is how [it] ends.., not with a bang but with a whimper.'"

Luna knew the elegy well. "It's called 'The Hollow Men,'" she told Kelly. "Were you thinking Burns would go out in a blaze of glory instead? Maybe both of you at one another's throats like Sherlock Holmes and his sworn enemy Moriarity, as you fell from a burning building?"

"I never knew Holmes's fate was suicide. *That's not for me!*"

"Sorry. But ever the smartass, I added the burning building bit. Actually, they jumped from a waterfall, giving author Sir Arthur Conan Doyle a way of reviving Holmes. He swam away to solve many more mysteries."

"I can live with that. Thanks. Any bright ideas on who might be responsible for this?"

"Until we know how he died, it could be anything or anyone for any reason. The big question: Is it related to *The Burning Desire?*" Luna answered.

Once the police secured the area for the crime scene team and gave statements to media outlets, Luna and Kelly finally introduced themselves (Kelly, for the first time). Despite identifying the dead man as Freddie Burns, Luna offered to provide The Juneau Police with surveillance footage from the botched Casper Duppy sting and the John Doe warrant from the San Francisco A.D.A. meeting, as part of the confirmation process.

CHAPTER 22

Smorgasbord of Research

After police questioning, Luna and Kelly returned to the hotel. Kelly informed several California fire investigation contacts of the day's events. Meanwhile, Luna returned to her suite. Let's see if plasma screen beats my laptop LCD, she said, clicking the flatscreen on for the first time.

Luna caught the opening of the local evening news. It didn't lead with Freddie Burns's death, but instead with breaking coverage of a roof collapse that trapped some transient Juneau tenants on the other side of the channel. The tease of the "discovery of an as yet unknown body in the alley of a local downtown bar" came after the quarter past commercial break. And its reporting was lackluster; just another death without a cause given, and the presence of a homicide detective explained as standard practice. Luna's spirits lifted a bit when she realized no autopsy was performed nor had the cops a chance to vet her documentation. *Calm down! The case is just starting,* she told herself.

The broadcast then switched to weather—a waste, considering 19 of August's days were scheduled for rain. And highlights of the windup of the Alaskan Baseball League season proved that at least the flatscreen was better for watching sports. Luna clicked it off, as coverage switched to medical news from the interior villages.

The bathroom was Luna's next stop for a steamy shower that was cleansing but not relaxing. Room service then delivered dinner that she nibbled and sipped from but wasn't filled by. Luna was still wrapped up in the events of the day, preferring to gorge on a smorgasbord of research, thoughts, and notes. But then, an unexpected knock on the door pulled her away from her laptop. Luna walked to the peephole. When she saw who was on the other side, the door opened freely.

Kelly Day stated her business as, "Just stopping by to find out how to dispose of lovers with a fiery dart, or something like that."

"*Fiery art,*" Luna clarified. "I think you better come in; it might take a while."

Kelly walked in, sat on the couch, and was soon immersed in her associate's latest developments. "So you've sized up Sparky's wife, his in-laws, and a museum owner for prison apparel too?" Kelly asked.

The insurance investigator nodded. "Tanis's parents hate Sparky and the insult to Tlingit customs the strip club represents. They told me how they would deal with any lover they suspected Sparky of having an affair with when you called."

"And it wasn't going to be a fireside chat, right?"

"Only if it meant throwing the other woman in afterwards. They also appear to have the money to hire Freddie Burns, as Mr. Yéil bought a custom-made totem pole for the house that cost almost six thousand dollars. And to cover their tracks and leave Sparky as the obvious arson suspect, one or both could have had Burns killed."

"That's definitely food for thought," Kelly admitted. "Which reminds me: What's for dinner?"

Luna looked over her barely touched room service fare and pushed a plate across the living room table towards Kelly. "You tell me."

Kelly devoured the shrimp cocktail and asked, "Now what about this fire art?"

"Pyrography," Luna kindly gave its proper name and handed Kelly a brochure. "An exhibition caught my eye while touring."

"*Wow!* Some fire burning pens are wrapped in leather because the tips that cut the wood can get as hot as nine hundred degrees Fahrenheit," Kelly read from the flyer. "And it's recommended that the artist use a respirator, as smoke inhalation from normal woodburning has been linked to cancer. All that trouble to have a picture appear in an art gallery."

"I am sure that if an artist promotes their work or finds a patron of the arts who will sponsor them, there are more ways than just an art gallery to make money, Kelly."

"And I guess being on the cruise ship route ups the chances of sales and worldwide publicity. Now what about the owner of the arts center?"

"Eleanor Fjord is an elitist from back east and quite aware of things. She picked up on who I was and assumed I was there to haul her off to jail for arson."

"*So why didn't you, Luna?!* We could be on a boat or plane out of here."

"I didn't remember finding woodcutting lasers or nibs in the debris, Kelly. Anyway, her place ran a pre-pandemic profit margin of fifteen percent that, after I looked into it more online, dropped to nine percent from hemorrhaging tourist dollars to *The Burning Desire*."

"How did she ever survive the pandemic shut-downs then?"

"In addition to everything else, Fjord's quite the capitalist. I read online where she basically took the show on the World Wide Web road rather than just close shop. Fjord created webinars, virtual tours, creative arts courses to keep the kiddies busy, and hawked the usual merch. She charged a lower ticket price to access everything online."

"She didn't ask for any of those Paycheck Protection Program loans to keep the art gallery going?" Kelly asked.

"None that I could find. She furloughed or laid off staff who didn't want to learn the online process, eventually making her the go-to gal for the arts in this part of the state—a virtual one woman show," Luna replied. "But once the pandemic ended, people looked for the hottest thing to do. Enter *The Burning Desire* and its troupe."

Kelly pulled up Fjord's bio on her smartphone to do her own truth-or-trash trawling. "Is she really 'a model and actress,' too?"

Luna nodded. "Memorizing all those tours and doing online and TV interviews requires good acting chops. As for modeling, just look at her."

Kelly did. "Yeah," she accepted the fact, "it would take something as fascinating as pyrography to tear most eyes away from that hair, bod, and smile."

"The hair and bod were on full display, but not much smiling," Luna replied.

"I can see The Yéils' flesh and blood connection to the club leading them to go to extremes to protect their daughter. But Fjord getting incensed over a slow business cycle to the point of risking losing everything?"

"While the Yéils may be losing their daughter, Fjord may feel she's losing her baby, so to speak, with all she puts into the center," Luna answered.

"But maybe you're right. An Ivy Leaguer like Fjord might get back at Sparky by simply allowing a Tlingit paddle with a naked Burt Reynolds illustration to be displayed."

Kelly's jaw dropped. *"What in heaven's..!"*

Luna chuckled, "I didn't get a chance to see it, but it probably can't hold a candle to the original article."

"And what did you get from Tanis Sparks?" Kelly asked.

"Just a drunken rant about Sparky's alleged adultery. Otherwise, nothing useful—wait, I like the name she had for the houseboat: *The Whore by the Shore.*"

Kelly chuckled, "Maybe once she's dried out you can get something more valuable."

"Nah," Luna disagreed. "It will take bribing Tanis with a better brand of booze than Sparky."

New Developments

Lightning flickered across the bedroom window of Luna's suite, and a clap of thunder jolted her out of a feverish night's dream about discoing with Dr. Adonis aboard *The Glacier Goddess* to the reality of rain. It began to pour and continued for a better part of the morning. As room service cleared last night's dishes and delivered new towels, Luna's smartphone rang.

"Luna Nightcrow speaking," she answered, after the maid left.

"Good morning, Ms. Nightcrow, this is Detective Sergeant Garrett Fisher, Juneau PD Robbery/ Homicide."

Luna recalled the gravelly voice of the country strong Caucasian cop at the scene. "Good morning, Detective Sergent," she replied.

"Thanks for the information on the victim. You were right: It was Mr. Freddie Burns. As it turns out, it was a homicide; he was shot to death. We haven't released his identity to the press yet, as an autopsy is pending. So we ask for your discretion and that of your partner, Ms. Day, before going to the media with additional information."

"You are welcome, Detective Sergeant, and our lips are sealed."

"I also called with new information that might help your fraud investigation."

Luna jumped up from the couch. *"I'm all ears!"* she said.

Fisher reported, "The bartender said he saw Mrs. Tanis Sparks, wife of *The Burning Desire's* owner, talking to Mr. Burns at length the day before yesterday. He didn't know who Mr. Burns was but he entered with the lunchtime crowd that included a few minorities and sat in a back booth. He ordered two alcoholic beverages, whiskeys, that he didn't drink. It was a signal to the bartender that Mr. Burns was probably waiting for someone. And about five minutes later, Mrs. Sparks joined him."

"Because of the crowd, I don't suppose the bartender heard what they talked about?" Luna asked.

"No," Fisher replied. "He only noticed that Mrs. Sparks seemed nervous, wearing her sunglasses inside, and that the drinks were probably to calm her nerves. We called her in for questioning and understand that you subjected The Sparks couple to the same."

"Yes, Detective Sergeant. Both were cooperative, but Mrs. Sparks didn't want to be interviewed the same day as her husband. For what it's worth, she also smelled of liquor the day I visited the home. When I spoke to Mrs. Sparks later by phone, I found out that she claimed not to have visited *The Burning Desire*, nor seemed to care what happened to its employees, and repeated her joy that it burned down."

"And you dropped by the Sparks's residence when, Ms. Nightcrow?"

"On my third day in town. Mrs. Sparks carried grocery bags inside. I didn't get a peek in them but caught the name of the store on the outside: Fresh Findings. It was the same store whose manager tipped my partner and I that she saw and spoke with Burns during checkout."

"Yes, you reported that earlier, including a pricey bottle of Canadian whisky as one of the cash items purchased by Mr. Burns. Since Mrs. Sparks and he were in the bar drinking and you noticed shopping bags from Fresh Findings, did you, by chance, see evidence of Mr. Burns outside or inside the Sparks's residence?" Fisher asked.

"No," Luna answered, "I was only in the living room and hallway; so from those areas, I didn't see anyone other than the couple inside. And I didn't see any sign of Burns when coming and going."

"Okay. Thank you, Ms. Nightcrow."

"You're welcome. Will you continue updating my partner and I of any new developments, Detective Sergeant?"

"As they relate to your case, certainly."

The two bid their good-byes. Luna then phoned Kelly with the latest news before preparing to call the various employees of *The Burning Desire* for interviews.

CHAPTER 24

Paying Customer

After lunch, Luna met a wall of resistance to her requests for ex-employee interviews. From hang ups to *'leave me alone!'* to 'talk to Sparky,' most were tired of the houseboat mess. But persistence paid off when, at about 4 p.m., Luna caught a break.

"Thanks for at least listening to me, Ember," Luna said to the caller.

"I will tell you though, Luna, I would rather talk more in public. That way if Sparky tries something, there will be witnesses," the caller named Ember said.

"Why would he 'try something?'"

"You looked into his background; you know what he's capable of, right?"

"Makes sense. So where do you want to meet?"

"The Mount Roberts tram on Saturday when I'm off. I work up top in the restaurant weekdays. And there are woods behind it where we can talk. I am so sick of all this and just want out."

"Thanks, Ember."

"Oh, Luna, I hate to ask but things are kind of tight, moneywise. Could you…"

Luna sensed Ember's need. "I am a paying customer if I like what I hear."

"Don't worry. I won't dance around your questions," Ember promised.

Luna chuckled, "Okay. See you Saturday."

Balancing Act

It wasn't until the end of the week that Kelly finally met with Fire Marshal Bernila Lluvia at her office to compare notes about the findings at *The Burning Desire* site. And they weren't alone; a Japanese man in a blue dress shirt and red tie and a Hispanic man in a sharkskin blazer in pored over paperwork when she entered the conference room. The suits, Kelly thought. No surprise, being this is the capital city.

Lluvia introduced the Japanese man as, "… Akashi Hono: Special Agent with The Office of The State Fire Marshal."

Hono stood and shook Kelly's hand. "It is a pleasure, Kelly, you come highly recommended. Welcome to the team," he said.

"Thanks, I hope I live up to the hype," Kelly replied.

Lluvia presented the Hispanic man as, "…Alvaro Armas, Certified Fire Investigator from The Bureau Field Office in Anchorage."

"The Bureau of Alcohol, Tobacco, and Firearms, or BATF. Not The Federal Bureau of Investigation nor Bureau of Labor Statistics," Armas explained.

"My bad, Alvaro," Lluvia apologized.

"Not at all. Just didn't want another organization getting recognition for whatever we turn up in the way of a capture."

"But if we *capture* the wrong person?" Kelly wondered.

"Then I'm with the FBI or Labor Statistics."

Kelly laughed and then took a seat.

"Sorry we had to cancel meetings with you, Kelly," Lluvia apologized. "Alvaro just got in last night from Anchorage; then, the roof fell in on that homeless shelter on the other side of the bridge."

"Luckily, everyone was rescued," Kelly said.

"Agreed," Hono added. "If nothing else, it's great publicity for Juneau's fire and EMS first responders."

Lluvia chucked, "Spoken like a true P.R. guy. Akashi was in public relations for a stretch."

"I even dressed up as Smokey Bear once for that preventing forest fires campaign," Hono said. "I thought I was going to have a heatstroke inside the costume!"

That got a few laughs. Afterwards, the meeting officially began.

"There was plenty for me to do while waiting to meet. I see that you've reached at a pretty definite conclusion since calling me in. That being that this is a slam dunk case of arson with suspects whose strong expertise in the crime or motives for approving it make up for a clear cause of the fire," Kelly said.

"I cop to it being circumstantial. But circumstantial cases can still lead to a conviction," Lluvia said.

"And are often preferred by prosecutors with tight budgets and trouble getting juries to put too many puzzles pieces into one solid picture," Kelly added.

Hono strengthened Lluvia's position. "The case for arson gets stronger when you consider that before the pandemic, Juneau had sixteen such fires; and Anchorage, ninety-three. One of the arsons was even done by a pre-teen, if you can believe it. So there is a modest market for it.

"We also found no problems with The Department of the Harbor's electrical lines that fed power to the houseboat. The fire's point of origin appears to be within the houseboat itself and not outside. It's only a matter of time until we identify how arson was committed."

"Now you, Kelly, on the other hand, are angling for direct evidence of arson and without it, can't say that the sightings of Freddie Burns and the suspect financial motives of Sparky mean as much as scientific proof," Lluvia summarized Kelly's position.

Armas saw the logic in Kelly's approach. "It makes for a stronger case than inferring that the presence of an arsonist means arson was committed," he said.

"The National Fire Protection Association's 921 guide recommends we use the scientific method to find cause. So, here's where it comes in," Kelly defended her case. "There were lots of ignitable liquids concentrated on the lower deck in the form of alcoholic beverages at the bar and alcohol-based hair spray, perfumes, etc. in the dressing room. But.."

"But," Hono cut in, "we all found the textbook "V" pattern nearest those ignitable liquids. That's pretty strong evidence of the point of the fire's origin."

"Only if you buy totally into the theory that the "V" pattern automatically equals the point of origin," Kelly contested the assumption. "Ignitable liquids are the main source of energy in a fire and are consumed during burning. Accelerants, on the other hand, are used to start or speed up the rate of a fire. When I looked at the diagrams of the houseboat, its age required a lot of upgrades to pass inspections and be certified for business operation. Every single outlet and wire needed to be check for wear and tear because there's always power available for a fire to start, even if nothing is plugged up. So do you see why I'm not convinced of arson yet? There are other ways this could have happened and other motives."

"Good points," Hono gave Kelly credit.

"Getting back to the houseboat inspection: Did it pass?" Armas asked Kelly.

"My partner, independent insurance fraud investigator Luna Nightcrow, checked with The Department of Permits and found, among other information, that *The Burning Desire* passed. It also passed a marine survey," Kelly confirmed. "But I wonder how much Mr. Sparks actually put into keeping the houseboat up to code on a regular basis. If he didn't, that fire could have started in any number of places aboard. And when you consider that he does run another business…"

"An electronics repair shop that itself is short circuiting," Lluvia specified, thumbing through a financial report, "The money from an accident insurance payout on the houseboat would be enough to retire from fixing mostly disposable appliances like microwaves and outdated tech like shortwaves."

"I am not convinced Mr. Sparks wants to retire," Kelly said. "In addition to money, adult entertainment made him important and lots of friends."

"And enemies," Hono warned.

"Yes, you certainly have lived up to your billing. That's one thought-provoking theory all right," Lluvia commended Kelly. "But with Freddie Burns around, it's clear to me that arson was on somebody's mind."

"But was it on Mr. Sparks's mind? Even if this all turns out to be a garden variety arson, could those enemies Akashi mentioned have done it instead?" Kelly asked.

"It's amazing that I might be defending a guy

like Sparky against one of them when all's said and done."

Kelly then asked bluntly, "You don't like Sparky do you, Bernila?"

"If we're going to lay our cards on the table," she began to say, "a guy like that, who puts women in a bad light when we have too many rapes and batteries up here as it is, is…" Lluvia then stopped herself. "I know this is an investigation. But no, I don't like Sparky."

"Mister Sparks isn't someone I would care to entertain an evening with nor have my daughter make friends with," Hono made his feelings known. "But you must have similar feelings towards Freddie Burns for the damage he caused in the Lower 48, Kelly."

"Touché," she admitted. "But I've always followed the evidence where it leads, not where my heart wants it to. Not always easy to do."

"That is also The Bureau's position: An objective investigation is ideal," Armas said. "The Bureau knows that in Alaska, arson investigations are mainly run by the state fire marshal and local fire departments, with help from their law enforcement counterparts when needed. The Bureau gets involved in cases with federal interests; hence my presence as an interested observer because of all the calls from residents alleging Mr. Sparks is guilty of or that he is being framed for other crimes that led to the fire."

Lluvia nodded. "And that's exactly why I wanted Kelly to come," she said. "It may sound like we are locking horns over this. But, we'll get not only expert input from around here but from out of state, too. Whatever caused the fire, no one can say we didn't turn over every rock to find it."

"Well, Luna and I are technically hired by Sparky's insurer but he hasn't filed a claim yet. So for now, we are consulting on the cause of the fire. So we do have skin in the game, as they say, but will stay open minded," Kelly answered.

Armas looked over a report. "The Juneau PD didn't get anything from Mr. Sparks and his employees about the fire. Typical, I guess; they were probably afraid of what would happen if they talk too much. So has your independent approach gotten something from them about the fire or any criminal activities that could have led to it, Kelly?" he asked.

"Luna is handling most of the interviews, including checking the used and new houseboat market, from Anchorage to San Diego, for any feelers from Mr. Sparks for another houseboat. If this is arson, it could have been done with the idea in mind of buying a new houseboat to increase future strip club revenues."

"The Bureau will be very interested in what Ms. Nightcrow finds and the results of your tests. Keep us abreast," Armas advised.

Kelly nodded and promised to keep everyone

updated. *Whew!* she breathed a silent sigh of relief. Having the feds, with their massive resources ready to go if needed, is great. But then she realized that their tailwinds of support for an objective investigation could easily turn into a hurricane-force hinderance, if it fit political needs.

CHAPTER 26

Peacekeeping Kill

America never ceases to amaze me! Brutus Chekoff amused himself with the ignorance of the average citizen. *Despite what most of them think, I am near their second largest city of Juneau not Los Angeles. And I am not too far, by ferry, from their largest city: Sitka!*

It wasn't population that made Sitka and Juneau the first and second largest U.S. cities, but instead the enormous size of their counties (boroughs): Thousands of square miles of mostly rugged terrain made inaccessible by mother nature's avalanches, landslides, forests, and rain. It was the perfect camp of operations—camp, not base, because of no homesteading allowed. Every 14 days, Brutus pulled up stakes and found new ground so as not to have forest ranger flyovers snooping around.

I like nomadic life, Brutus thought, *but not being as alone as a Siberian tiger.* He was never too far from a village that needed labor, which provided income, but was far enough not to intrude on his privacy. Only the eagles, deer, and mountain goats cast a curious eye over his camp. But they stayed away, sensing his presence and every action had behind it an intent to kill.

I am no heartless killer! Brutus believed. Or maybe that's what years of training and authorization to kill taught him to think. I am a peacemaker: I help good people sleep as free of worry as can be. That is my code of honor. It is like that of the American Paladin of "Have Gun: Will Travel." I am free to set what price I choose to give good people peace of mind.

The last two weeks put Brutus near Juneau, where he learned of *The Burning Desire* situation through reading, listening, and infiltration. So when his satellite phone buzzed again, Brutus was reminded of which side he was allied. *"Yes?"* the hatchet man answered, pretending not to know the caller hiding behind the flimsy cloak of "unknown" on the Caller ID.

"The outside light that burned twice as bright burns no more," the voice told Brutus. "But some still play with matches."

Brutus understood and was pleased by a job well done, and even more at the prospect of continued employment. He then asked, "How many are there?"

"One," the voice counted. "The others saw the light and have no *desire* to be burned."

"But what of this "one" without wisdom?"

"It is just an ember but could burn many things."

Brutus knew what had to be done. "Must it be put out?" he pretended not to know.

The voice calmly confirmed it: "Only you can prevent fires."

The line dropped. Brutus picked up his rifle and then launched the satellite phone high into the air. He swung his rifle around and blasted it to pieces before it hit the ground. After gathering water from a nearby stream, Brutus followed the path he'd cleared to his makeshift lean-to. He pulled back the tarped entrance and entered.

Brutus sat his rifle and kettle aside. He left to pull a couple of logs from the pile, went back in, and fed them to his camp stove. Brutus filtered his water while waiting. And once the stovetop heated up, Brutus dipped some water and boiled a cup of coffee. After shoving in two more logs, the stove was satisfied and released enough heat to make lean-to's interior toasty. Brutus took off his shirt, revealing a lean, lustrous figure whose stomach demanded its dinner. So he slapped a slab of game on the stove, seared it to perfection, and finally sated his hunger.

Afterwards, Brutus dipped his hands into the kettle and splashed some of the now lukewarm mountain water on his face. Once the rest settled, he had a makeshift mirror and cast an icy-blue eye on his bearded reflection. What if someone saw my face like this before? I must now change, Brutus told himself. He unsheathed and sharpened his Bowie knife to shave and then prepared for his next peacekeeping kill.

CHAPTER 27

Rainforest Reflections

Luna's first weekend in Juneau began with clouds aplenty and a 70 percent chance of rain throughout. She arrived a few minutes early at the Mount Roberts Goldbelt Tram Station parking lot on the waterfront docks. Luna watched the cruise ships and envied their passengers filing off for adventure and fun while her shore leave involved of another fraud investigation that had to be done. Luckily, she didn't have long to lament; the rumble of an approaching motorcycle put Luna back in investigator gear.

On schedule, the rider parked and then carefully approached Luna's car. The automatic driver's side window parted, allowing Luna to feel her out before getting out. Quite the biker bunny, was her first thought about the shapely rider with a heart-shaped face and head of layered, sun-kissed hair.

"I am Ember from *The Burning Desire*. But I prefer Sunny," the rider said.

Sunny Ignacio, Luna took note of her full name on the Alaska driver's license she was given. "Sunny it is," Luna confirmed, handing the ID back.

Now it was Luna's turn to pass inspection, as the leather-clad Latina took her business card. After a long look, Sunny seemed satisfied that she was speaking to the same woman who called her earlier: "Luna Nightcrow."

Luna finally left her car. "Nice bike, by the way," she told Sunny. "A mid-century dual-sport model that probably flaunts that four modes selection system, for on-and-off road travel, and agile suspension (for a smooth feel and handling)."

Sunny was pleasantly surprised. "*Wow!* You know your bikes. Do you ride?"

"Now and then," Luna replied. "Knowing things like that is just part of the job."

"Juneau is too small for a car and the price for gas is higher than the mountains," Sunny explained.

"As for mountains, the tram ride is on me," Luna said.

"Thanks. By the way, can I leave this in your car until we get back, Luna?" Sunny opened her purse and drew a snub nosed .22 caliber revolver. She saw

Luna's concern. "Don't worry. I'm not an outlaw biker or anything," Sunny promised.

It still made Luna question, "Is capital city crime sky high too?"

"It's getting there, with that outsider shot," Sunny warned, "and could go higher after what I have to tell you."

After locking the handgun in the trunk, both women departed for the tram. Once on board and the long gondola lurched forward, they calmed each other's nerves. Sunny assured Luna that the six-minute, 1,800 feet climb through the dense rain forest was safe. And Luna pointed out safety in the number of passengers to witnesses and stop any attack on Sunny. Luckily, there were no problems; the passengers and tram behaved themselves and arrived at the visitor compound atop Mount Roberts.

Once outside again, Luna looked up and said, "No rain yet. Let's take that walk we talked about."

Sunny led Luna along a nature trail behind the tourist compound that wound its way into the misty, mossy rainforest. "I love to take my lunch break back here. The tourists don't come this far because they worry about bears. But most of them are way over on Admiralty Island. So all of this is perfect for relaxing, reflecting, and inspiration. Out here, no one knows me and there's nothing to fear."

Fear. The word gave Luna the opening to return

to *The Buring Desire* case. "You worry about Sparky so much that you need to carry a gun?"

The dancer sighed, "Sparky's not really the problem, I guess, but it's what I got myself into by working for him. When I started, I thought he was just some old guy who framed deepfake pictures of himself palling around with a few stars from the 60's who those true crime podcasts say had mob connections. They're dead and we're in the middle of nowhere; so who was going to really complain or sue if wasn't true? Anyhow, nobody but cheating husbands and lonely hearts from the interior came in. So it seemed like the whole OG (original gangster) thing was probably Sparky just trying to build the club's brand."

"So when did things cross the line into regret and fear, Sunny?"

"I didn't think a strip club was a big deal. It wasn't like any of us were totally naked and we weren't sleeping with Sparky or banging him, or at least I wasn't anyway. But things changed when the cops got called in for stuff going on outside in the parking lot because you know they're looking around for other things that they can arrest you for. And when some real ex-cons came in for drinks or dances, I started stressing about everything.

"Sparky's not some OG hiding out in Juneau. But he might be holding down some thugs' turf or be caping for fat cats in The Lower 48. Or worse, he could be fronting for one of those Russian bosses since Alaska's not far from there."

That pretty much summed up everything Luna was briefed on, all rolled up into one frightened and confused young woman. "How much did you make dancing?" Luna asked.

"Around eight hundred a week and it was that much some nights in the winter. But I would only take home about four hundred because Sparky took nearly half of whatever I got for 'using the club,' he called it. If you want to think of it like sports, he was sort of our agent, and we supplied our own uniforms: The skimpy dresses that would come down to our navels anyway if we got paid enough. I didn't get roughed up like a football player, but the emotional hits—well, you know how that is, Luna, being a woman."

Luna nodded. "How much per twirl, twerk, and topless show?"

"Nothing for the dancing itself onstage; that was kind of a tease. If the guy wanted an offstage twerk and twirl or to pay us to just sit and socialize, it was twenty bucks. We'd talk for maybe five or ten minutes before asking the guy if he wanted to go upstairs to the VIP lounge. If they said yes, then we'd do a lap dance, or rub up against them topless while they sat, for seventy-five bucks per song played. Sometimes, the guys would tip the DJ to play a really slow song so they could get the most out of just one lap dance."

Luna grinned at the customers' creativity. "It figures," she sighed. "How many times did you dance to "Hotel California," then?"

"Lots. But believe me, it was easier than trying to boogie for five minutes to 'Rocky Mountain High.'"

It was Luna's turn to laugh.

"The houseboat was big but still too small for a large stage like you see in the movies. So Sparky put up two small platforms with what they call footlights and stripper poles downstairs. Most of us spun around them as we danced in front of guys and the rare gal. Since there could only be about eighteen customers at a time, though, Sparky had a one hour stay without pay rule.

"It doesn't sound like most bars, where you can just stay and get drunk all night," Luna said.

"Getting drunk makes the customers spend freely," Sunny revealed. "But if you held your liquor or didn't drink and weren't spending money on dances, you had to leave after an hour and make room for the next group."

Luna nodded.

Sunny explained that, "Dancing was a side gig: A way for most of us to pay a few months' rent ahead. Some girls squirreled away enough for plane or boat tickets to Anchorage during the winter, when the cruise ships leave and Juneau's like a ghost town. Most of us had other jobs; mine was up here and as an artist."

Luna was curious. "Are you a painter, sculptor, illustrator...?"

"Pyrography," Sunny answered. "That's where..."

"*Really?!* I visited a pyrography exhibition at Juneau's biggest private arts center recently but didn't remember seeing your name," Luna interrupted. "Do you have a doing business as or stage name as an artist, too?"

"No DBA name. But the reason you didn't see me or my artwork is because that la-di-da Dr. Fjord said she didn't want the face of the exhibit to be a naked dancer's," Sunny grumbled.

That explains Fjord's disposition, Luna thought, and told Sunny, "So Fjord just wanted the art of burning wood not desire."

That made Sunny laugh. "Fjord may own the place but she couldn't paint, sculpt, or take photographs to save her life! She doesn't care that I'm a starving hometown artist with talent who can't catch a break. It's all about how a cheap side hustle looks."

"You're a very brave girl, Sunny."

"Thanks, Luna. I wish I knew before I started that dancing for hire is like playing with fire. It's all becoming too much. The cops dragged us dancers in and questioned us about not just the fire, but whether there were other things going on: Any drugs, prostitution, gambling.., you know? Then, I got anonymous phone calls telling me to keep my mouth shut about the fire."

"*Calls?!* What did the caller sound like? Young, old, male, or female? An American or foreigner?"

"It was a young-sounding guy with bit of an accent but not like from Europe. Maybe Canada; we're close to it, right?"

"Is that when you started carrying the gun?"

"Yeah, but I might need one of those mini machineguns, an Uzi, if Sparky's in with thugs. I really don't know who made the calls though. It was a man's voice, but not Sparky's," Sunny guessed. "I think other dancers got the same calls. When I mentioned mine, they said they didn't want to talk about it."

"I got the same rejections. You're the only entertainer who will talk to me," Luna said.

"I kept getting calls. So after a while, I told whoever it was to eff off."

"About the fire: Do you think Sparky could have set it, like some are saying?"

"Why would he, Luna, with all the money from drinks, snacks, parking, dances, cover charges, and user fees? And Sparky didn't have to buy ads because there aren't any competing clubs close by and horny guys spent crazy amounts of money to get here, especially in winter. He didn't give us costumes and what 'job training' we got boiled down to don't make the customers mad. I learned how to dance by online videos, which made me even more popular.

"So the fire was probably some kind of accident or something. But it sounds like everybody wants it to be arson. The caller might be one of them and was maybe telling me to shut up and agree. If it was one of Sparky's guys, though, he might have meant to remind me of who's the boss and not run my mouth about stuff that could cause bigger problems. I guess I'm damned if I do, damned if I don't, Luna."

Drizzle dappled the canopy of spruce and pine, signaling heavier rain was about to arrive. Luna and Sunny hiked back up the trail to the restaurant inside the tourist compound. Once inside, a couple of Sunny's coworkers saw her with Luna and immediately asked if she was the friend she always talked about. It led Sunny to come clean about another part of her life. "I'm a lesbian," she told Luna. "Sparky and the customers never knew."

Luna said, "That doesn't carry the shame it used to."

"Maybe not in everyday life. But on a boat full of mostly straight men, you have to be approachable to make money. That means pretending like you're an oversexed straight or at least bisexual gal," Sunny explained.

"Context is key," Luna sighed.

"Once this is over, I'm going to move in with Ursa, that's my "friend" to them, up in Anchorage.

The arts community will probably accept me up there, too."

After a light lunch of fish sticks and fries, Luna took photos of Freddie Burns from her purse and showed them to Sunny.

"That's the guy who got shot to death downtown! The news didn't say who he was, but I saw him in the club once," she claimed.

Luna couldn't reveal Burns's true identity yet but pushed for confirmation of the sighting. "You're sure you saw him, Sunny?" she asked urgently.

Sunny nodded. "We didn't get many black guys in the club. And this guy wasn't into dances when I asked if he wanted one. I thought he was maybe a dealer or a Fed from the way he sat alone in the corner looking around."

Luna remembered the V-shaped pattern Kelly found and asked, "In which corner?"

"The one next to the stairs, going up to the VIP lounge."

"If this guy was more than a regular customer, did you see him talk to Sparky?"

"No. But he did hang around longer than the 1 hour stay without pay limit. That also made me remember him. Do you think he's the one who made threatening phone calls?" Sunny wanted to know.

"I'm not sure," Luna said, "but did other dancers or maybe staff talk to him?"

Sunny shrugged. "It was a busy night; I had lots

of customers. So by the time I came down from VIP, he was gone. If Sparky wired the club with hidden cameras and microphones, they should show the guy, right?"

Luna hoped so.

Sunny leaned over the table and whispered, "Has this been helpful? Is this just to reject an insurance claim or proof for the cops to get him on something that will keep him from re-opening the club?"

"You have really shed a lot of light on things, Sunny," Luna let her know. She discreetly opened her purse and produced a plain white envelope and slipped it to Sunny under the table.

Sunny opened it as discreetly and saw $500 in cash. She couldn't help but shed tears. *"Thank you so much, Luna!"* Sunny gushed.

"If you could spread the word that I'm willing to also pay for your former co-workers' time to tell share their experiences on the houseboat, I wouldn't mind giving you a per capita finder's fee," Luna added.

CHAPTER 28

Here We Go Again!

The tram ride from on high glided downhill without a hitch.

"Luna," Sunny asked, "could I please stay with you, until this thing blows over?"

"Sorry, Sunny, but my hotel suite is also my office; I have lots of sensitive equipment and information there."

Sunny laughed, "Top secret stuff. I get it."

"But I will spring for your own room for as long as you need one."

"*Great!* Follow me to my apartment. It won't take all day. There isn't much there; I keep a lot in a storage unit. I just need to pick up some extra clothes, Luna."

··◆··

Brutus Chekoff, the roaming Paladin of the Panhandle, looked at himself in the mirror of the old car he hotwired and stole late the night before from a rundown residence on the other side of the channel. His wild, mountain man beard was shaved off; and his brunette mane, trimmed. Nothing remarkable about him, not even his blue eyes. He could still blend in with the many other white residents and tourists in Juneau and get away clean. The only distinct thing about Brutus now was the high caliber "fire extinguisher" on his lap, ready to put out the threatening "ember" he was told about.

Luna and Sunny arrived at her apartment complex 10 minutes later. Luna parallel parked down from the door and didn't pay attention to the ordinary car positioned catty-corner behind. Sunny also didn't notice anything unusual, as she dismounted from her motorcycle. But Brutus stole a glance then returned to staring blankly head. *Perfect!* he told himself.

Brutus slipped on a surgical mask, as an added disguise. It would have looked suspicious before the pandemic but was now normal. Slowly, he manually cranked the window down. The long rifle barrel inched out; Brutus steadied the butt against his shoulder; and without delay, finally lined up Sunny without a scope. He was going to settle on a shot through the spine when...

Sunny suddenly remembered, "*Damn, I forgot my gun!* Hey, Luna, I..."

The moment Sunny turned from her front door it was into Brutus's direct line of fire. And he didn't miss. *POP!* Sunny never knew what hit her. The high-powered blast drilled through her forehead and blew out the back of her skull. Luna heard her call out earlier and had left the car to open the trunk. But now, she saw Sunny lying face up, eyes locked open and motionless. Someone, probably a tenant, came out of the main entrance. He apparently heard the shot and was pointing across the street as he tried attending to Sunny.

It took a minute for Brutus to retract the rifle, roll the window, and start the car. That was plenty of time for Luna to grab Sunny's .22 revolver and fire. Brutus ducked, as the first bullet cracked the windshield. Then he swerved away from the side-walk and sped off, but not without the car catching Luna's second gunshot that dented the back pas-senger side door. She wasn't in position to get a license plate number but spotted Sunny's keys on the ground. Luna ran to what were now 5 people grouped around the dancer. She pushed her way through, looked down, and noticed Sunny's keys and purse on the ground. Luna scooped up the keys.

"*HEY!*" a bystander objected.

"Who are you?!" another rightfully asked Luna.

"I am working with Juneau PD. I'm going after the shooter!" Luna told both, as she mounted the dancer's bike.

Brutus was still in view down the street, but no longer in firing range. Luna revved the motorcycle.

She remembered the San Francisco chase and groaned, *"Here we go again!"*

Brutus got the jump on Luna. *Bastard!* she cussed his luck. But then she thought, The motorcycle has better power to weight ratio, and I will have greater movability through Juneau's smaller streets. *You're still in it!*

But as the mountaintop drizzle became a steady light rain at sea level, Brutus gained another edge on Luna. *Yes!* he thought. Her motorcycle will skid on the wet streets. "Careless woman cyclist will kill herself!" Brutus laughed aloud.

Both motorists finally threw cautious calculations to the wind and increased their speeds through the side streets. Suddenly, they heard a familiar siren wail; a bicycle cop caught both fly by a stop sign and was now on their tail. All 3 zoomed into downtown. The police siren emptied the Franklin thoroughfare, as people and cars yielded the right of way..

As Brutus barreled for the waterfront docks, the gas gauge dropped nearly to "E." That was plenty for him to carry out his new plan. Brutus remembered the ferry. "I will board the boat and abandon the car. Then jump overboard, swim shore, and escape into the woods. *Yes!*" he convinced himself.

Luna turned sharply off the main street and onto the sidewalk, giving the bicycle cop a clearer line of vision. He apparently radioed ahead, as a cruiser was already in the area. It spun around to block the road leading out of the waterfront. Two officers jumped out. One drew his Glock 9 MM pistol; the other, her 12-gauge shotgun.

Brutus was so set on boarding the ferry that he missed the barricade ahead. But the buckshot from the policewoman's shotgun got his attention, as it peppered the windshield. Brutus bobbed to the right. Once upright, the assassin veered to avoid a collision, but there was one. Not with the police cruiser, but with the water instead. *SPLASH!* Brutus's car plunged 6 feet from the pier into the channel and sank into its icy depths.

CHAPTER 29

Lane Violation

Special Operations Officer Salmon Lunker (a burly, bespectacled Haida lieutenant in The Juneau Police Department) took his guest to task. "Some of the people on the scene said they heard you say you are Juneau PD."

"Well, they're wrong, sir. I said I was "working with Juneau PD," but didn't mean as a policewoman," the guest, Luna Nightcrow, tried to explain. "Usually, I give out my business card but couldn't, given the situation."

"But you had time to ride the victim's bike on a high speed chase?"

"If I hadn't, the man would be free to kill again."

"You are either incredibly lucky or clever in handling the situation the way you did. It is by far the most dangerous citizen's arrest case Juneau has seen."

"I apologize, sir, but it got our man."

"True, but it could have also injured or killed

innocent civilians in the process," Lunker argued. "However, Alaskan Statute AS 11.81.390 allows a private person to use deadly force when fairly certain it's needed to arrest or stop a suspected felon from escaping. And obviously the man, Brutus Chekoff, was escaping with a firearm used while committing a felony." But, Lunker didn't let Luna go lightly. "The department appreciates your help with *The Burning Desire* case, but remember something, Ms. Nightcrow: Your insurance investigator credentials aren't a substitute badge."

"Stay in my lane and signal when trying to enter yours; I understand, Lieutenant." Suddenly, something popped into Luna's mind. "Lieutenant," she asked, "what color are the killer's eyes?"

"Blue," Lunker replied. "Why?"

"Sir, you may have 200 possible witnesses or co-conspirators to question," Luna suggested. "I talked with some of Reverend Herald's followers; they reported the presence of a strange, blue-eyed man at some protests—angelic, they added."

"Anything more you picked up on Chekoff?"

"I was hoping he was an undercover officer keeping tabs on the Sect and didn't think anything else about it. But after today, obviously not."

"In the meantime, Ms. Nightcrow, do you need any counseling, support? After all, you did see someone killed and could have been killed yourself. I can arrange for our force psychologist or chaplain to..."

Luna stood. "Thanks, Lieutenant. But those are for cops. I'll be okay and around," she said, leaving the office.

CHAPTER 30

Torrent of Tears

Stormy weather socked Juneau outside and Luna got drenched, if by another mixed drink, inside. Ten hours after chasing down Chekoff and about seven since being dressed down by Juneau PD for doing it with impunity, Luna crawled into what she thought was the cocoon of the Chichagof bar. But it wasn't long before she had company.

"*Knock-knock,*" the visitor affected the customary request to enter.

Luna knew the guest, but muttered, "I thought I told you I want to be alone."

Kelly blamed Hui. "He saw you and said he was worried."

"*That snitch!*" Luna grunted.

"And of our making," Kelly replied. "But if you really wanted to be alone, then why come to a public place like this?"

Luna pointed to the bar.

"What are you having, Luna?"

"An espresso martini. I dreamed it up, I think." Alcohol's thickening pall made it hard to recall. "Three ounces of vodka, 1-and-a-half ounces of espresso, and half an ounce of Kahlua."

Kelly asked if it was any good.

"It tastes good," Luna confirmed.

"Which isn't good," Kelly sighed.

"Sit," Luna commanded. She then raised her empty glass. "In the immortal words of Shakespeare, 'Let us sit upon the ground and tell sad stories of the death of kings.'" The first drink was to drown lobster by candlelight one night with a man who showed promise—a doctor. But not responding to my texts in this hour of need is a terrible bedside manner indeed. *To hell with him!*" Luna sat that glass aside and raised a half empty second. "Now his one is for someone harder to forget. Sunny. Alive one minute, then—she had a lot of guts."

"I heard the news. I'm sorry," Kelly apologized softly.

Luna plunged into and swigged the second espresso martini. "All that talent...wasted. Wasted: That describes me, too."

"Luna..," Kelly tried to say.

But her colleague plowed forward. "I had to ID her in the morgue because someone swiped her purse and phone after the shooting. I guess I can't bitch about it: I took her gun, keys, and bike.

"At least the cops fished the killer out of the channel. They're supposed to tell me when he's ready to talk if he talks. I told them to watch out for a hit on the hitman, like when Harvey Lee got whacked by Jack Ruby. I had to make it rhyme: To show you Luna can hold her liquor any time."

Kelly finally stepped in. "Look," she said firmly, "I can pick up the slack. Take a couple of days off."

"And do what: Drink myself into more trouble? I'll be alright. Just please leave me alone tonight," Luna urged Kelly again.

Kelly stood and silently walked away. Luna then broke down into a torrent of tears like the rain outside.

Irrefutable Find

It was almost midnight when Kelly heard a knock on her door. She opened it and wasn't surprised who stood there.

"Okay, I'll take the night off," Luna groggily agreed.

Kelly smiled. "Sounds fine." She helped Luna inside where she promptly passed out on the bed.

There were no fits of drunken laughter or dancing on the tabletops to hide the pain. Just slumber that would result in a hangover once Luna came to eight hours later. It was the first she had in years and took four more hours to defeat with ice-cold showers and by forcing down toast and copious cups of coconut water.

Kelly was the first to see a semblance of her insurance investigator mentor return. "Back among the living?" she asked.

Luna nodded. "Thanks for everything, Kelly."

Kelly handed Luna a folder full of papers to

review and said, in her best boss's voice, *"Now get back to work!"*

"Lovely," Luna moaned.

Both women laughed, then Luna returned to her suite. There, she checked her smartphone and found, to her delight, that Sunny Ignacio's death didn't frighten *The Burning Desire* ex-employees into silence. Instead, it moved more of them to come forward with information. Luna invited Kelly to her hotel suite around 3 p.m. to share what new information they gave her.

"Well, three more "starter" dancers and the bartender came forward with stories about the shoddy condition of the houseboat in certain spots. I ran through your list of questions to ask them. The first one: Did the lights flicker in the business?"

"And?" Kelly asked.

"A few times," Luna replied. "I asked what the weather was like when they flickered. The dancers said it was usually during a storm. But the bartender said there was a flicker when the weather was clear."

"Storms causing power outages is normal, and the bartender may have seen a dying light bulb or two flickering. What about the question "did you ever notice a burning smell from an appliance or in a certain part of the business?""

"No one said they did," Luna said. "They also didn't say they got a minor electric shock when plugging in machines, and that electrical plugs stayed firmly in the outlet when they plugged them in. Nor could they remember seeing sparks when they plugged machines into outlets. And I'm afraid no one said they felt heat from the light switch when turning them on and off."

"Anything about what they may have plugged into the outlets?"

"One dancer said she plugged in a space heater in the dressing room, but that it wouldn't put out enough heat. I asked if she turned it up to the highest setting; she said yes, but "it didn't work.""

"We're getting warmer with that one."

"Not to throw water on the finding, Kelly, but who knows if that space heater was on the blink, or it was because of bad wiring? Again, no one saw lights flicker or saw sparks from outlets the night of the fire."

Kelly groaned. "Then please tell me there was an irrefutable find from the last question: "Was there flood or water damage aboard the houseboat?" she hoped.

Luna then pulled up a couple of smartphone photos and showed them to Kelly. "Two dancers sent pictures of the ceiling in VIP."

A smile stretched Kelly's face. "*Unbelievable, Luna, there's noticeable water damage!*" she gasped. "That transient housing accident a few days ago got me thinking about how rain affects property, especially something as old as *The Burning Desire.*

I already had some tests drawn up, but this should help move the needle away from everyone's assumption of arson to direct evidence against it. I will call the Panhandle School of Polytechnic Research and set up the tests."

"And I'll get cracking on checking houseboats new and used for calls from Sparky or..." Before Luna could make those calls, an incoming one buzzed her smartphone. Moments later, the call ended with Luna grinning from ear to ear. "That was Tanis Sparks's lawyer. He says she wants to meet!" she told Kelly.

Kelly was cautious. "Is *he* going to be with her?" she asked.

"Him and lots of others. The others will be armed to keep me unharmed."

"Tanis has become that dangerous?!"

"The cops must think so because "the others" are guards at the jail where Tanis is being held without bail," Luna revealed.

CHAPTER 32

Going Public

Kelly wouldn't let Luna drive just yet and instead took her to the Juneau Borough Jail to meet with Tanis Sparks. It was about 5 p.m. when the investigators pulled into the parking lot. Kelly waited in the car while Luna checked in with facility personnel for visitor credentials. She was then escorted by armed guards to the jail's private area. The metal door clanked open; Luna entered and saw jumpsuit-clad Tanis, looking much older and worn without makeup, sitting alongside her dapper African American defense attorney Johnnie Bench (flown in from Anchorage and one of the best).

Bench pulled out a chair for Luna and then returned to his. "Ms. Nightcrow, thank you for coming. You have met my client, Ms. Tanis Sparks," he said.

Luna shot Tanis a glare that, if looks alone were criminal, she'd be behind bars for too. "Yes, Mr.

Bench," Luna finally acknowledged their previous encounters.

"Mrs. Sparks says she has information to share regarding *The Burning Desire* matter," he announced.

"*Oh?* When last we spoke, if you can call it that, she told me she never visited *The Whore By The Shore*."

"Her husband coerced my client to call you," Bench replied.

Luna had to laugh. "*With a bottle of Northern Border Blend?!* Sounds more like motivation than coercion, counselor."

"He knows my client has an affinity for alcohol and used it against her. It probably affected her memory."

"Well, Mrs. Sparks, I hope whatever you have to say now is done with a clearer head than last time," Luna hoped.

"Obviously, it is. They don't serve booze in jail," Tanis scoffed. "And what I have to say is also about Freddie Burns and Sparky."

Luna asked, "Okay. What do you have to say?"

"Well first off, I didn't kill Freddie," Tanis insisted.

"But you're sitting in jail, even though the triggerman was caught. So the police must believe you're connected somehow," Luna replied.

"Oh, yeah: Sparky and me are "connected" alright, but not in the way the cops think. I know details about the houseboat Freddie was supposed to burn down."

Tanis caught Luna's eyebrow arch and asked, "Want to hear more, Nightcrow?"

Luna played it cool, crossed her arms, and leaned back in her chair. "Okay, I'll bite," she answered, although expecting more complaining than explaining.

"They say that going public when you commit a crime or know about one is the best protection. I don't want to end up like that stripper who got shot too. And after my parents were called in for questioning, I don't want them blamed for any of this either. So, I'm going to tell you what I know about the whole thing, Nightcrow," Tanis said. "There is a Tlingit community down in Santa Clara, south of San Francisco. They're small but tight-knit and help us out whenever we're in the Lower 48. Anyhow, Sparky was like a little boy begging for a toy. For him, it was a bigger houseboat. I got the feeling that he wanted to burn his but didn't know how to pull it off. San Francisco's big; somebody down there probably knew how to do it so the hicks up here couldn't figure it out. I didn't think they'd bring in somebody smart like you, Nightcrow, to look into it."

Luna snorted, "I hear Alaska imports many of its needs; so it's fitting I'm here, don't you think?"

Tanis wasn't discouraged. "So trying to be the good little wife who makes her man happy," she continued,

"I made some calls to The Gulf Coast, East Coast, and other spots with houseboats for sale."

"Did you call sellers on The West Coast where you're closest?"

"Sparky said it would "stir up a hornet's nest of suspicion.""

But Luna wanted to make sure that, "Mister Sparks told you or wrote down that he wanted a new houseboat and to check because he planned to set fire to *The Burning Desire,* Mrs. Sparks?"

For the first time, Tanis looked to Johnnie Bench for an answer. And, he didn't fail to provide Luna one. "There are still more records to go over before we answer that definitively, Ms. Nightcrow."

Luna didn't buy it. She stood. "When you find Mr. Sparks's verbal or written coercion of Mrs. Sparks to look for a new houseboat because he wanted to gut *The Burning Desire*, Mr. Bench, get back to me."

Tanis reached over the table. *"Wait, Nightcrow!"*

It worked! Luna congratulated herself. She turned and asked with dramatic flair, "I'm sorry, Mrs. Sparks, you wanted to say..?"

"There's more."

It better be good! Luna thought, taking a seat.

"That Tlingit community I told you about? I called them too," Tanis added. "My contact tipped Freddie that he could find business up here. I can tell you who tipped him off and maybe help out some people down there whose buildings got burned down."

"That would be helpful...*for the people down there*. But what about the houseboat here, Mrs. Sparks?"

"When Freddie came to town, we went to the bar. I guess I should have had him come to the house but—well, if Sparky can have his fun, why can't I? And it helped that Freddie was a hot, young guy who told me smooth things Sparky hasn't said to me in years."

Luna fidgeted in her chair. "I didn't come back to hear drippy daydreams."

Tanis apologized. "So, we finally got down to business. I told Freddie about the houseboat. He said he could 'match it,' burn it, for ten thousand dollars plus ten percent of the insurance money. I said that was out of our reach. So, he dropped the price to five thousand but jacked up the cut of insurance money to twenty percent. When it was all said and done, Freddie still had to talk to Sparky and see the houseboat himself."

"Did you ever actually tell Sparky that you hired Freddie?"

"No. As small as Juneau is, it wouldn't be too hard for them to meet and talk it over."

"Of course, if Mr. Sparks never met Freddie or maybe arranged a way not to meet him, that leaves you as the fall girl," Luna speculated.

"What do you mean by 'arranged?'" Tanis piped up.

"I said *if*. But really, Mrs. Sparks, you said it

yourself. With both Freddie and *The Burning Desire's* star dancer dead, you're next unless you go public. Question is, who's really gunning for you? Who has the most to lose if you snitch?"

Tanis's hands noticeably trembled. Then she gasped, "Sparky might try to..?"

"Okay, Ms. Nightcrow," Bench interrupted, "let's not confuse my client's husband's psychological manipulation with your insinuation of other crimes."

"Your client, not me, assumed that her husband is out to get her," Luna replied.

"And I suggested that you not "confuse" manipulation with murder. We wouldn't want what I'm sure is conjecture to turn into a defamation suit that could interfere with your investigation would we, Ms. Nightcrow?"

"Maybe Sparky is really going to whack me," Tanis worried. "Maybe he…"

Bench cut off his client. "The bottom line is this: Mrs. Sparks is willing to aid your ongoing arson investigation, by turning over her cellphone records and any other electronic resources. In addition, she is also willing to provide the name of the aforesaid Santa Clara contact who referred Mr. Freddie Burns to her. All this in hopes of your recommendation for leniency if a criminal referral is made."

"And by "other electronic resources" you're talking about …?" Luna wanted to know.

Before Bench could answer, Tanis blurted out,

"Security tape of what was going on in the club. Upstairs, downstairs—did you know that I heard Sparky had the balls to make the stripper pole look like a totem pole?! So how much is something like that worth?"

"Uh, Mrs. Sparks, I would suggest not to talk about "worth," in terms of Ms. Nightcrow's..."

Tanis glared at Bench. ""Worth," as in getting whatever sentence I'm going to get reduced. *Geesh*: With what I'm paying this guy, you'd think he'd get where I'm coming from!"

"If you're hoping for a deal or plea bargain, that's up to the district attorney's office," Luna forewarned Tanis. "They apparently have enough evidence to charge you with murder or being an accomplice. Whether it goes to trial is up to you.

"Technically, I can subpoena your cellphone and Sparky's security footage. But volunteering what you have would save me a lot a paperwork and make me seriously consider saying you went out of your way to be helpful to my investigation."

With the chance of returning to her cell empty-handed looming, Tanis had to pull out her last stop. And why not, especially if what Luna said about Sparky was true? "Sparky also applied for some of those coronavirus business loans," Tanis claimed. "You know, the ones companies going under could get if they didn't fire their workers?"

"Paycheck Protection Program, or PPP, Loans," Luna named them.

"That's them! Sparky reported me as an employee at the electronics shop. He had me cleaning it the week he put in for the loans, but I don't know the first thing about fixing electronics and never got paid for doing anything. That's got to be fraud and right up your alley, Nightcrow."

"I am very busy with the houseboat case now, Mrs. Sparks. But as with many fraudulent loans, the penalty may be that the borrower has to pay fines, be imprisoned, or both. And if they don't have the money, they may have to surrender assets to cover it. Perhaps a car, your house ..."

Tanis hadn't thought about that. "I-I don't know that I..."

Bench patted his client's hand. "Mrs. Sparks, you've provided Ms. Nightcrow with plenty to think on," he counselled.

"For now, it sounds like you're unsure of what was on the alleged PPP loan and just asked my opinion if whatever it was could be dishonest. But an FBI field office is the place to report white collar crime," Luna recommended.

Beaten, Tanis moaned, "Sounds like I'm not getting a damned thing!"

Luna couldn't resist taking another dig. "I wouldn't say that, Mrs. Sparks. You got out of your cell for a while. And if confession is good for the soul, then you're getting a clear conscience."

On her way out, Luna heard Tanis call out, "And Luna: I'm sorry about what happened at the house."

Luna's bruise may have faded, but not the lasting sting of Tanis's insults. Luna thought about Tanis's parents, though, and the pain they endured far longer. So she apologized, "I shouldn't have sat in your chair," and then left.

CHAPTER 33

A Wider Net

The Juneau Police Department finally released Freddie Burns's true identity to the press. It stirred up both sides in *The Burning Desire* mess. Those who hated the club were more convinced than ever that Sparky was an arsonist and murderer while those in favor had no doubts it was all a setup.

Lieutenant Salmon Lunker responded to knock on his office door.

Detective Sergeant Garrett Fisher's entered. "Good Monday morning, Lieutenant," he said.

"Let's hope so," Lunker cautiously replied.

"I know what you mean with the press release. Doing it over the weekend softened the blow; most people are too busy planning to get away from it all on Saturday and Sunday to care."

"Sparks declined the offer to put a police car outside his house and the electronics repair shop," Lunker announced.

Fisher couldn't help but to laugh, "He barely gets by as a fix-it guy and probably doesn't want us to scare off the few customers he has."

"Anyway, G, I called you in because I have breaking news on the Brutus Chekoff case."

"You mean you got him to confess when the rest of us couldn't, Lieutenant?"

"No such luck. But it looks like we collared a very wanted man in Chekoff."

"*Oh?* In what state?"

"Poland."

"Now I have to get used to saying, "The Lower 49," Lieutenant?"

"No: "State," as in nation-state," Lunker chuckled.

"Brutus isn't Polish, is he?" Fisher asked.

"The Poles say he's Russian, but they want him for multiple murder-for-hires and can link him to others throughout Eastern Europe."

Fisher knew what that meant. "Don't tell me: They want him back," he groaned.

"The Polish embassy talked to The U.S. State Department; State to The U.S. Attorney in Anchorage; she to the chief; he to me; me to…"

"I get it, Lieutenant. In the big picture, Poland is an important ally. While a stripper and an arsonist being popped by Chekoff stateside are small potatoes."

"*Purportedly popped, G.*"

"Innocent until proven guilty, I know. Though I doubt Chekoff will sue for slander."

"Of course not. Taking a shot at you for such a slur is more his style."

Fisher grinned. "Good thing we've got Chekoff's gun, which doesn't match any models from retail or military databases. It is apparently a custom-built job or what they call nowadays a ghost gun. Largely plastic and probably crafted by a 3D printer, it looks like a toy that's been jerry-rigged with an oil filter suppressor. And the bullets left in the magazine match those the coroner pulled out of Sunny Ignacio and Freddie Burns."

"A 5.56 NATO round, no less. Lighter than our SWAT's .308 caliber," Lunker read from the coroner's report.

"Travelling at probably three thousand feet per second—the speed of sound being one thousand one hundred feet per second—that smaller bullet was plenty enough nasty. Neither probably heard the shot, much less knew what hit them."

"I tried to question one of the area's biggest ghost gun manufacturers until he shot back, *"Talk to my lawyer!"*"

"No surprise there," Lunker remarked. "But at least we know who killed Ignacio and Burns, and that he was an assassin overseas. Maybe Chekoff made a killing at it stateside, too."

"*Maybe?* So even though Burns and Ignacio had ties to the houseboat, you don't think that Chekoff acted alone? That he wasn't just a rejected Romeo or lone wolf radical who might have got even with the two, Lieutenant?"

"If it was just the dancer, I see your point. But why would he bump off Burns, too? Besides, you saw all the customers we questioned about the fire; they were scared to death of being arrested for just visiting the club." Lunker then reviewed Fisher's report: "From Chekoff's few Alaska employment records you found, he was a blue collar temp type who wasn't opposed to working for anyone who paid cash.

"Now here's something you found that made me think Chekoff wasn't acting alone. Even though *The Burning Desire's* employees and Sparks didn't see him onboard, when Chekoff was asked by a few co-workers if he wanted to go, he allegedly said, 'No, I would not waste money on a pretender.'"

"So Chekoff didn't go to the houseboat but wasn't against going to a *real* strip joint," Fisher replied. "Maybe both sides saw a glass half full kind of guy who, when they found out about his military skills, could be filled up with their houseboat beliefs and used to their advantage."

"Right," Lunker agreed. "I also acted on a tip from that insurance investigator Nightcrow and rounded up some of Reverend Herald's group. The sketch artist did renderings of Chekoff and IT did a computer composite. Both match their descriptions of a mysterious man who was present during several of their protests. Sounds as though he was shopping both sides for the best deal."

Fisher thought he understood. "And so Chekoff settled on the anti-houseboat side, by killing 2 on the pro side."

"Or maybe he had it both ways," Lunker said. "Chekoff collects from the anti-gentleman's club crowd for 2 murders that they hope to use as a reason to never allow another strip club in town. Meanwhile, he doesn't touch the houseboat owner, making the pro-club set hopeful that Sparks will collect an insurance payout and pick up business where it left off, only with a better houseboat."

"So you want me to find out if one side, the other, or both hired Chekoff," Fisher said.

Lunker nodded. "If nothing else, this will help quiet down conspiracy theories that we wrote off it all off as the work of an angry immigrant."

"Yeah, we weren't getting anywhere by grilling a man who the Poles will probably fry anyway. So how do I start, Lieutenant?"

Lunker directed him to, "Look into any unusual purchases of burner-type cellphones. Not just in Juneau and the cruise ship circuit but in Anchorage and Fairbanks, too. They are a hot item on almost every criminal's Christmas list because they are a cheap, disposable, and hard to track method of communication.

"If you pick up on any odd purchases or store

employee reports, write up a warrant to seize surveillance footage of the act. It might turn up familiar faces on both sides of the spat."

Fisher added that, "The Anchorage PD has CARP (Cellphone Actualization Recognition Projection) access. So maybe they picked up unusual cell activity up there. Because if they're physically following someone and pick up and examine the RF energy from their device, it doesn't require a warrant since scanning the area for cellular signals doesn't expose anything that isn't already open to the public.

"A lot of departments keep it on the low because it pretends to be a cell tower and redirects calls, texts, and online traffic. Even though most of the time, 90 percent of the information gathered isn't related to the target and isn't examined."

Lunker sounded pleased, telling Fisher, "Now you're getting it."

Fisher asked, "Do you want to add Luna Nightcrow and Kelly Day to the team? Afterall, that was a clutch play Nightcrow made to help bag Chekoff and then getting Reverend Herald's followers to ID him hanging around."

Lunker advised against it. "They're still civilians. That Evil Knievel stunt Nightcrow pulled got results but put lives in danger, including her own; a fact I reminded her of. And what's to keep them from leaking info if we use CARP? The press will poke its nose into whether or not it's legal and create another ruckus."

"In their defense, Lieutenant, they didn't leak Burns's identity," Fisher noted.

Lunker heaved a sigh. "Okay," he recanted on excluding the independent investigators. "When they ask about CARP, it's not a stretch to say that we don't have it here. But if they know Anchorage has it, tell them it's out of our jurisdiction. Let them in on Chekoff's extradition before it hits the news; then, the ballistics report that links his rifle to the dancer and the arsonist homicides; and also our look into the possibility, mind you, that someone hired him. If they want more, tell them that their focus is on the insurance angle which they still haven't solved from what I hear."

Fisher nodded and left. Lunker then dialed his Anchorage PD counterpart about CARP.

CHAPTER 34

Tested by Fire

By Monday afternoon, the physical scars from Luna's weekend healed. But inside, at her core, her conscience kept pushing her to do more. "They're asking for donations for Sunny's funeral," Luna told Kelly over the phone. "I am going to foot the whole bill."

"Luna..," Kelly began to say.

"I can't find any relatives yet," Luna continued, "and I don't know much about her lover upstate."

"I was going to say that you don't have to go it alone, Luna; I'll chip in," Kelly finally got a word in edgewise. "But just remember that rule about not making an investigation personal."

"Too personal, you mean?" Luna asked. "Because I learned over the years that we aren't computers. We are gathering information for others to use but sometimes, you can't simply erase it from your memory and move on."

Kelly disagreed. "I let go of Burns' death."

"Easy to do when it's a bad guy you hoped would be stopped one way or the other," Luna argued.

"True, but who knows what we might still find out about Sunny? No one's perfect; she could have helped to burn down the houseboat, for all we know."

"Why is it that you sound like the wise old veteran investigator, Kelly, and me like the rookie partner?"

"All I meant was that before this thing is through, Luna, there may be another body or two to bury on both sides."

Luna sighed, "You're right. And you're not exactly a rookie."

"And you're not "old," at all," Kelly reassured her partner. "We have both been tested by fire, as the "Good Book" says, and remained pretty honest."

After Luna's laughter let up, she remembered something. "I almost forgot to tell you that it's movie night…my suite."

"*Lovely!* What's on?" Kelly asked.

"*The Burning Desire Dupe*," Luna answered.

"Sounds like a porno, given everything we've found out so far," Kelly said.

"Maybe," Luna warned. "I can watch and report back, if it crosses your spiritual line."

"Don't worry. I will be by for my latest trial by fire," Kelly promised.

··◆··

Luna returned to the hotel with plenty of Chinese food and 3 boxes of old-style video cassette tapes taken from Sparky's home by subpoena. The surviving tapes contained hours of security camera footage from inside and outside *The Burning Desire*. Luna set up a couple of tape and video disc combo units and turned on the flat screen TV. She opened the first box of tapes to load but had to first answer the knock on her door.

Kelly stopped by with a six-pack. Luna immediately recognized the contents by their tawny tone. "Frappe and cappuccino…how nice," she commented.

Kelly elbowed Luna and giggled, "This feels like high school again!"

But Luna recalled, "It was bottled iced tea that was "in" back then, not bottled blended coffee."

"I was talking about the old video cassettes we used to watch," Kelly laughed. "By the way, the GC/MS tests show no direct evidence of arson."

"Tight Ship is sure to love that," Luna snorted.

"I know the bad news a payout represents."

"Not just a payout, but it's politically explosive, too. How did Bernila take to your findings?"

"I haven't sent them and didn't tell them about the specific tests at our meeting. Without more proof, I said I wasn't totally sold on arson for scientific reasons and was looking into other causes. The state fire marshal's special agent agrees with Bernila that it's a torch job. But the presence of a Bureau of Alcohol, Tobacco, and Firearms suit kept them from twisting my arm until I cried arson."

"Well, without further ado," Luna announced the start of the main event of the evening, as she finally popped a tape into the player.

Anyone looking for Playboy Channel from The Panhandle was out of luck. True, the women watched anxiously for a man who himself could pass for an exotic dancer. However, it was for confirmation of his ability to bring the houseboat down not figuratively, with his smoke show build, but literally (with fire). And for the first couple of hours of footage, only clothed customers and their easy-going entertainers (whose brassy, neon bikinis teased the Northern Lights) drank, chatted, or danced peaceably. No signs of crimes showed even in V.I.P.

After the first tape ended without a black customer sighted, Kelly asked, "Are you sure Sunny *really* saw Freddie Burns in the club?"

Luna rubbed her eyes and stretched her arms. "That's what she said," the insurance investigator yawned.

Kelly reviewed the interview notes. "None of the other dancers did."

"And if they're wrong, I can hear the excuse, Kelly: Blacks all look alike. Mistaken identity: Ground we've already covered."

Kelly grinned. "Is that what they say about American Indians too: That if you've seen one, you've seen them all?" she asked her fellow minority.

Luna was still making amends. "I hate to say

it, but my partner on the San Francisco car insurance case and I thought Freddie Burns was Casper Duppy."

Kelly forgave Luna. "I get a lot of mileage out of dressing and speaking well. But when the suits and makeup come off and sweats or shorts are on, I'm mistaken for a mad black woman or black woman with a mad black man to avoid."

Luna shared her skin color story. "I had a boyfriend once who liked that I was "ambiguously brown.""

"*What?!*" Kelly gasped.

"He said I looked Mexican or Filipina at times, but not "Indian." It sounded like he thought all Native Americans are supposed to look the same; and that usually means the way "we" are in bad Westerns. Usually, I hear "Indians are all the same" when it comes to tribal membership. In The Lower 48, I'm either Sioux or Apache, like there aren't other nations. Here, Reverend Herald thought I was an Alaska Native. Then, Sparky mixed me up with some Alaska Native dancer wannabe named "Connie"; and later, with a dead Italian actress."

"No offense, but the part about looking like a different race would make for a great spy or private eye skillset," Kelly said.

"I actually went with it on that San Francisco case," Luna told the truth. "Freddie Burns took me for a Latina gal from SoCal! I got a lot of great undercover footage, though it was of an arsonist and not the car insurance con artist I was after. Nice transition back to the problem at hand, huh?"

Kelly smiled and nodded. "So, Sunny told you Burns sat in the corner the only night she saw him. Like a lot of bars, though, these videos are dim in spots. So maybe she really *thought* she saw Burns, but in a darkened room..?"

"Or in a place with plenty of liquor, Kelly, maybe the other dancers really can't recall seeing Burns, especially if they drank the night away."

"Touché," the fire investigator said. She then changed topics. "What about those threatening phone calls? Any ideas who made them?"

"Sunny thought the other dancers received calls too. While they opened up to me about club conditions, mum's the word about threatening calls. Sunny described hers as always a male voice with maybe a Canadian accent. She never said how long the calls lasted but described them as warning her to keep quiet and could have come from either side of the spat."

"We could subpoena the dancers' phones to search for suspicious numbers," Kelly suggested.

Luna cautioned against it. "We want to keep them agreeable. Let's get a court order only if we have to, like if we can't find anything on these tapes," she said.

The evening dragged on until suddenly, things

finally began to pick up. First, the investigators discovered a couple of lengthy gaps in recent camera coverage. Both knew though that the remanence decay of the magnetic charge in most video cassettes causes streaking, fading, blackouts, and a complete loss of recordings over time.

Kelly added, "And since video cassettes are hard to find nowadays, Sparky probably reused his."

Luna was more skeptical. "Or Sparky used video tapes exactly because they don't last long, unless kept in climate-controlled storage. And his damp basement wasn't that. Most security cameras these days use servers or the cloud to file video footage—*evidence perhaps*—that lasts way longer. It is also convenient that the missing footage covers a couple of days before the fire."

"Which could have been the time Freddie visited the club," Kelly replied.

Luna sighed, "Sunny said that Burns supposedly exceeded the 1 hour stay without pay limit and didn't get called on it. But it will be Sunny's word that she saw him against those of Sparky and the house who say they didn't. And if these gaps are like that infamous 18-minute break or so in the Watergate tapes, we'll never know for sure what they showed."

Kelly then picked up on a recurring customer in multiple videos. "Who's the old guy in the captain's hat? He doesn't seem to care who he picks up."

"As long as they're female and nearly naked, you mean," Luna added.

Kelly chuckled, "Of course. But if he's a regular, he's probably seen or heard things that, even in passing, could be useful."

CHAPTER 35

Anchors Aweigh

The first round of examining security camera footage lasted until close to midnight. And it took a couple more evening sessions to complete the task. Luna made several screenshots of the mysterious repeat customer in the captain's hat from numerous security camera frames. On Thursday morning, she contacted a few dancers who were willing to talk and then dialed Sparky.

Kelly asked later, "Any luck with finding out who "the captain" is?"

Luna shook her head. "No," she said. "Sparky didn't answer his phone. And the dancers I got didn't get a name, only that he blathered about working on ships."

"*On:* Like fixing them? Or aboard, as in being a part of the crew?" Kelly sought clarification.

"From the sounds of it, "aboard": Like navy

vessels, cargo ships, and pleasure boats. But I couldn't get his name."

Kelly groaned, "Then who knows if that was beer talk or straight talk? And with all the ships coming and going, we could be asking around for info on a guy who may already be out to sea and never to return."

Luna's eyes lit up. "If this were a bigger town, yes. But we have Juneau's small, comfy confines working for us," she shared the beginning of her sudden idea with Kelly.

"So in that case..?"

"In that case, Kelly, it's anchors aweigh, as they say."

That afternoon, the investigators visited Juneau's prime maritime spots. Luna took the harbor, and Kelly, the private marina circuit. Both showed "the captain" screenshots around and eventually, a number of people identified the man as Jonah Schipper: A long-time marine surveyor who inspected either their vessels or others' over the years. Luna returned to her car and placed a call to Tight Ship Assurance in Seattle for more information. When done, she briefed Kelly.

·· ◆ ··

Kelly found who she was looking for and approached. *"Ahoy!"* she called out.

"I knew it was just a matter of time before

somebody showed up," was Jonah Schipper's resigned reaction to Kelly Day's formal presence at the gangway of his 40-foot sports boat. "With that red business suit, Miss, you're either here to ask about *The Burning Desire* or you've come for my soul."

Kelly smiled and edged up the incline. "I'm the former," she said, showing Jonah her credentials. "Permission to come aboard, captain?"

Jonah gave a salute and said, "Welcome aboard, admiral."

Kelly declined the offer of a drink or smoke but accepted a seat on one of the deck chairs in the stern. She plunged straight into business, "My partner talked with Tight Ship about the terms of Sparky's insurance policy."

Jonah lit an unfiltered cigarette. After a puff, he said, "And I know what they probably told you: The company backed *The Burning Desire* with the understanding that since Sparky is a qualified electrician, he would replace its old-style Knob-and-Tube wiring. Sparky told them he fixed it, and the houseboat could now be verified by Tight Ship Assurance staff, meaning me."

Kelly nodded. "But the modifications are estimated to cost tens of thousands of dollars," she added.

"And that doesn't even cover the haul out."

"Haul out, sir?"

"Oh, yeah. It's not just enough to inspect everything above the waterline. You have to also go underwater and inspect the hull. If there's any damage that can't be fixed down there, you have to lift the whole boat out of the water for repair."

"If what I remember from TV and movies is right, that sounds like a drydock."

"You have been watching the right movies, Ms. Day," Jonah laughed, then coughed. "In drydock, you check the hull and other parts and repair any damage. And with the size of *The Burning Desire*, it was going to cost Sparky a pretty penny to get the right equipment to haul her out. One trailer wasn't going to cut it."

"When was the inspection due?" Kelly asked.

Jonah took a drag. "Next year," he answered.

"Would you have done them, too?"

"*Oh, no!* Not in my shape. Plus, I don't have the hauling equipment. I handled the Knob-and-Tube and topside check due this year."

"What if Sparky didn't have that kind of money at the time? Or would you say he had it but found a way not to pay it?"

"It's more the second choice. It was only going to take about an hour, 2 at most, not days like the big cargo ships. But Sparky told me that if I said everything was shipshape, "his houseboat was my houseboat." I got free drinks and dances for looking the other way on the inspection."

"And you'll swear that Sparky bribed you under oath?" Kelly still had to ask.

"Yeah, but my word is all I have; Sparky and I didn't put anything in writing," Jonah warned.

Uh-oh! Kelly groaned silently.

"But I'll testify. After all, the captain is supposed to go down with the ship or, in my case, the life raft because that's pretty much all I am good for to most folks: Being used for one thing or the other. But I knew what I was doing and that it would catch up to me someday. So, I have enough stashed away to not worry about my torpedoed job prospects and can sell my boat to stay afloat. And being 79, I'm near the 8th bell of life and will be boarding "The Old Ship of Zion" any day."

"Have you taken bribes before from other customers, sir?"

"No. But this—well, you wait until you get my age. I am a loser: My hair and my health are gone. The memory is taking on water in spots. No woman is going to court me unless I have upfront money or put her in my will. It was nice to have those houseboat beauties eat up my seafaring stories. I felt like admiralty."

Jonah's repentance was refreshing for Kelly, a woman used to filtering not just rubble but rubbish, to hear. But her heart sank at seeing him rotting to skin and bones and baldness (explaining the conspicuous captain's hat that gave him away). Yeah, Kelly sighed inside, the average woman would throw

Jonah back. Only the sharks and leeches aboard *The Burning Desire* would consider him a prize catch.

More cigarette smoke being blown by her host snapped Kelly out of sympathy and back into neutral questioning. "If Sparky was capable of bribery, do you think he could commit arson, too?" she asked.

"There's an old saying: A Marine is a rifleman by default; a sailor, a fireman. Out at sea, if there's a fire aboard, you have to put it out. I am not saying that I have your level of firefighting expertise, Ms. Day. But having put out a fire or two aboard active duty warships, I don't think *this* was arson. It was because Sparky is as stubborn as a cabezon."

"Cabezon, sir?"

"Sorry, Ms. Day. The cabezon is a fish with a big mouth and head who is content on the coastline's crusty bottom. When they get old, they settle down in rock pools just offshore and dine on a steady meal of barnacles, starfish, and shellfish. But they can be lured out by fisherman, and are an acquired taste, or so I hear. Anyway, the last owner warned Sparky of how much time and money it would take to maintain a houseboat the size of *The Burning Desire,* but Sparky acted like he was exaggerating or defending his asking price."

Kelly took down the previous owner's information.

Meanwhile, Jonah reflected on Sparky's sentiments. "It's just a boat; it's supposed to float," he mocked. "So what if the wiring was as old as Sparky and could lead to a power outage aboard? Just stick sails on it, fire up a generator, and it's as good as new! And as long as it didn't spring a big leak and sink, it just sits along the shore in shallow water."

Kelly's cabezon curiosity was piqued, leading her to punch up more information on her smartphone. "*Cabezon* is Spanish for 'arrogant,'" she read aloud from an online source. "That seems to fit Sparky's attitude towards ships."

In between coughs, Jonah agreed. "Sparky knew he had to follow all the city and state codes, even if they seemed extreme. He loved the money the club made but not what it cost for its upkeep. So burning her down wasn't going to stop maintenance requirements on a new boat. Hell, inspecting and fixing a new boat would probably cost him double the money. So in my view, it made more sense to simply keep *The Burning Desire* and fake an inspection when the time came."

Kelly then pulled a photo from her purse and handed it to Jonah. "You were a houseboat regular. So did you ever see this guy?"

Jonah studied the photo of Freddie Burns but wasn't sure. "I never really noticed anybody else, except for the drinks and dancers."

Kelly then reached across and patted Jonah's hand. "Thank you, sir. I wish there was more I could do for you."

"Those dancers already did enough. But as an old

navy petty officer, thanks for the field commission to "captain." Fair winds and following seas, Ms. Day."

"Thanks for your service now and then, sir." As she started down the gangplank for the parking lot, the sight of her car brought a sudden question to mind. "Captain," she turned and asked, "what were you doing the day you weren't inspecting *The Burning Desire?*"

"I drove to a bar to wait for the club to open," Jonah replied.

"You drove your car?" Kelly asked for more detail.

Jonah wheezed, then said, "No, the company car; I drive it to surveys."

"Thanks again," Kelly said. That put a spring in her step, as she disembarked.

CHAPTER 36

Risky Business

It was close to sunset when Luna approached The Sparks Residence again. She couldn't park in the driveway because another car was there. While awaiting a ways off, Luna saw the lodge door open; a woman walked through, but not alone. Sparky was with her. Luna grabbed her ever ready binoculars. They captured the woman and Sparky hugging; then, her license plate number (which Luna scribbled down). Sparky escorted the woman to the parked car. Luna scrunched down into hiding as the car started up and sailed by. It was now time for her go at Sparky again; Luna finally drove in.

Sparky responded the knock on his front door with a broad grin. *"Why it's the unmatched Ms. Nightcrow! Come right on in."*

Luna passed through the foyer and the intensity of cheap perfume from Sparky's previous visitor to the living room. Inside, the fireplace crackled. "Want something to drink?" Sparky asked.

"No thank you," Luna declined.

Sparky headed into the kitchen to fix his idea of a nightcap: Root beer. He poured himself a frosty Mason Jar full, returned to the living room, and then plopped down in his favorite recliner. Luna recounted the arson allegations made by his wife. Sparky didn't have trouble saying, "Maybe jail's the best place for Tanis, Ms. Nightcrow. Her folks ponied up a pretty penny for one of the best law firms in the state to represent her; so it's not like she's going to do hard time anyway.

"I mean, Tanis hit you. Next, she will probably have her lawyer summon my club's security camera recordings. And now, cooked up some cock-and-bull story that I'm an arsonist. All of it stirred up by her drinking like a fish all day. So, let her dry out."

"Or perhaps be hung out to dry?" Luna asked intentionally.

Sparky was adamant in his denial. "I wasn't so stupid as to have my wife hire some Frisco firebug to burn up the houseboat I was making money from. Tanis was right: I had a hankering for a bigger, better houseboat and I still do. As you know that houseboat could only hold about 26 customers and staff."

"So I guess size mattered, Sparky?"

"You're oh so good with the hidden meaning jokes, Ms. Nightcrow."

"Double-entendres, you mean."

"I reckon."

"We watched your security camera recordings from the club, and there was some missing footage," Luna revealed.

"What are you trying to say? That I erased the part that hides a visit from the arsonist that I didn't hire in the first place?"

"Well..?"

"Nope, Ms. Nightcrow."

"To erasing the tapes or having Freddie Burns aboard, Sparky?"

"No to both. Tanis is the one that had the hots for him and is who they caught with him."

"She's not the only one who saw Burns."

"Oh, yeah?"

"Sunny Ignacio, a.k.a. Ember, remember?"

"Now there's lovely way to burn, Ms. Nightcrow!"

"She also said Burns was a club customer and not even a paying one."

"Then she was wrong."

Luna asked, "Do you think someone hired Brutus Chekoff to kill her simply for 'being wrong?'"

Sparky sipped some root beer and said with a sneer, "I didn't know that solving killings was your line, Ms. Nightcrow. You working the cops' side of the street now?"

"I prefer the cleaner expression of "one hand

washes the other," instead of the hooker comparison," Luna replied.

"Sure enough. Just thought I'd try one of those double intentions myself. My apologies for stepping on your toes." Sparky swigged more root beer. "No, I didn't have Ember snuffed out; she was the best of the best dancers. I used to kid her that if she wasn't showing, things weren't smooth-going.

"Sure, Ember bellyached about me making her work holidays and having to playact Italian, Indian, or German. But she had "the look," we used to call it. Or what your generation calls–*what the hell's that song the disc jockey plays?*—oh yeah, "I'm Every Woman." That summed up Ember. She packed out the house with a line outside waiting to spend dough; so, I let her whining go."

"Need I ask if Brutus Chekoff ever stopped by the club?"

"Save your breath, Ms. Nightcrow, because the cops say that commie, not me, did away with Ember. Why he did it, who knows? But it sure cost me a lot of dough. I don't reckon I'll ever find me one like Ember again." Sparky glanced at his wristwatch. "Well, it's about time we both punch out."

Luna stood. "Yes," she agreed. "I wouldn't want to keep your next guest waiting."

"*Next guest?*" Sparky asked.

"Probably another vanity plate like the one I saw leave earlier. Miss IAMA34-28-32."

"I guess all you private eyes are voyeurs at heart. But I will thank you kindly to get your field glasses fixed, Ms. Nightcrow. That young lady used to dance at the club but moved out of town. She was back in Juneau for business and stopped by to say hello."

"As in *talking* about the good old days or staging a re-enactment?"

"Chatting, Ms. Nightcrow," Sparky interrupted. "But there's no convincing you unless I pile on what you want to hear. Is she still good looking? *Hell, yeah!* Did thoughts about the good old G-string days come to mind? Of course. Did she dance here near naked tonight? No."

"You do know how it will look having her here, with Tanis in jail," Luna cautioned.

"The same way having you here looked to Tanis before she was in jail," Sparky said sourly. "And you know, maybe you are the one putting on for show. It could be all your trips up here are to pad your expense account when you already know who set the fire. Or maybe you are into that dominatrix stuff and enjoy pulling my chain."

"These aren't social calls, Sparky. Everything you've said or not said has been most useful in figuring out who set the fire."

"Glad to hear it," Luna's host said, slurping the rest of his root beer. "I bet my bottom dollar that it was Tanis and her Left Coast Mr. Right."

"Nice to finally hear how you think this will play out," Luna replied.

"Speaking of 'out,'" Sparky asked, as he opened the front door, "any need for me to walk you to your car?"

"Not if you're expecting a great big hug in return," was Luna's way of saying no. She walked outside but spun around when the porchlight came on. She saw Sparky standing in the doorway, as if ready to defy her request not to be accompanied to her car. But he didn't.

"It won't get dark until the wee hours," Sparky explained. "But I turned on the light for whoever is out yonder that you came with to see that we are closing up shop on the warmest of terms. I wouldn't want you to say trip and fall in the dark, maybe on purpose, to stir up a hornet's nest of trouble for me."

What?! I didn't bring anyone, Luna thought. Sparky slammed the door and doused the light, leaving Luna alone in what was now full-on dusk. She turned to see the car mentioned. It was parked behind hers with perhaps untold occupants lying in wait. But waiting for Luna or Sparky?

Forewarned, Luna crouched down, then crawled towards the car behind hers. From a side view, she could see the front license plate wasn't that of the woman she saw before. Luna paused briefly, reached into her purse, and pulled out her smartphone discreetly. With her finger poised to pop into action the pincers of the 60,000 volt stun gun concealed in its protector, Luna at last reached the passenger's side door, Then like a lioness, she leaped up to see at the wheel …

"*Mr. Yéil!*"

Sparky's father-in-law was as shocked to see Luna. "Ms. Nightcrow," he said, rolling down the window, "out late aren't you?"

Luna put away her smartphone and dusted herself off. "Sorry about that," she apologized. "I had to get more information from Sparky, regarding the case."

"Can't your job also be done by simply calling him up with your questions?"

"That's what my partner told me, too. But sometimes, you discover things in person that you can't over the phone. What is your business with Sparky that can't be done over the phone, by the way?"

"I did call him tonight, anonymously, but thought I heard a woman laughing in the background, as Sparky hung up. Was it you, Ms. Nightcrow?"

"Must have been. I've been here for a while but didn't see another woman inside."

"So, what information did you find funny, Ms. Nightcrow?"

"When Sparky wished me "warmest regards." Funny, coming from a coldhearted bastard."

Mr. Yéil nodded. "I suppose I would laugh, too," he admitted.

Luna became serious. "Please don't do something foolish, Mr. Yéil. If something bad happened to Sparky tonight…"

"Then we would both be suspects," Mr. Yéil reminded Luna.

Luna grinned. "I guess we're both involved in risky business then."

"But because I personally despise Sparky, the police would blame me," Mr. Yéil said.

"I know. Tanis told me you and your wife were both questioned for the murder of Freddie Burns, for example," Luna added.

"Since you are a thoughtful woman, Ms. Nightcrow, I will leave Sparky to what was probably just the laughter coming from an adult movie he was watching earlier. But if Tanis were your daughter, you would be here on more than insurance business." Mr. Yéil angrily put the car in reverse, turned around, and drove away.

"I know," Luna sighed, as she got in her car and left too, although not empty-handed like Mr. Yéil. She had a few more valuable clues.

CHAPTER 37

Critical Test

The next morning, Kelly drove the winding highway lengths to the Panhandle School of Polytechnic Research on the northern outskirts of town. Once on campus, she unpacked her toolkit and walked to the engineering department where the supervising engineering professor waited.

"Ms. Day, meet my 2 brightest students: Ammar and Nasira from Dubai," the professor proudly announced.

"And fraternal twins," Nasira added.

"Yes, I see the resemblance," Kelly noted.

"If we were identical, Professor Bridges might suspect one of us was sitting in for the other on occasion," Ammar joked.

The professor chuckled, "Fortunately, you are both smart and grasp the coursework in such a masterly way that either would get an "A." Well, I'll let you get to work."

According to plan, the Gen-Z aged duo showed Kelly the 3 models of *The Burning Desire's* wooden roof built to her specifications. "Good job," Kelly praised their quality work. She then removed from her toolkit a sample of the type of wiring found in the roof that ran down to the dancers' dressing room and the outlet near the stairwell leading to VIP. It was cracked and exposed the copper below.

The engineering students studied the sample before and showed Kelly the version they re-created for the test. The two wires looked identical. "Perfect," the fire investigator indorsed their skillfulness. "Okay, let's goggle up."

Once safety eyewear was in place, Kelly took a piece of roofing insulation from the club and spread it along the wooden surface of one of the models. Next, she laid the exposed wiring over it and took out an eyedropper. "This represents raindrops," Kelly described its contents.. "Nasira, start soaking the pile please."

Nasira nodded and the squeezed off drops until Kelly instructed her to stop. She then produced something that the students found fascinating. *"Wow, a handheld camcorder!"* they marveled aloud.

"Yeah, it's an antique from the museum," Kelly teased the two.

"I get it: We're too young to remember how things used to be!" Nasira remarked.

"We know what it is, Ms. Day. It's just that I,

anyway, hadn't seen a camcorder so small," Ammar added. "The ones on TV and even in the department are big or mounted on a tripod. You must have one strong battery."

"Roger that: That's why I still keep her around," Kelly confirmed. "And because cellphone cameras aren't really designed for precise video recording. It's just one feature that usually doesn't offer the same high resolution and image stability. And this test will need the best quality photography."

"*Her?*" Ammar asked about the oddity of Kelly's camera having a gender. "So you have a name for your camera, too? Like when they name a ship?"

Kelly hadn't thought of that. "Yes," she said, and then christened the camcorder as "Cammy."

Kelly finally began filming. After a few minutes, the wires suddenly sparked. Kelly excitedly zoomed in. While wood doesn't conduct electricity, the carbon from the burnt wiring did. So it wasn't long before whitish smoke rose from a burning hole in the wooden surface below. As Kelly suspected, the moisture absorbed into the carbon tracks and created a conductive path. Everyone repeated the experiment multiple times; the results were the same.

Kelly then tried a different experiment on the second model roof. Ammar handed her wiring of the same design that was instead intact rather than damaged as before. Kelly added dry, not wet, insulation made with fire resistant material such as that aboard *The Burning Desire*. When the pile was lit multiple times, there was no spark nor combustion.

For the final test, the group used undamaged wiring and the same type of insulation. Only this time, the insulation without the fire resistant material was moistened. While the wire itself didn't spark and catch fire immediately, the insulation did. And when the temperature was raised, the wiring eventually sparked, intensifying the burning of the third model roof.

"Does this help you, Ms. Day?" Nasira asked nervously.

"Yes, thank you both so much!" she answered.

CHAPTER 38

Shedding More Light

The next day was sun-drenched and therefore fitting, beyond the metaphorical sense that came to Luna's mind, for holding the funeral of Sunny Ignacio. Kelly and she joined mostly ex-dancers from *The Burning Desire* and her coworkers from The Mount Roberts Eatery, as condolences were paid and the artist's cremated remains scattered over the mountaintop area she was inspired by. Luna noticed a bouquet of roses from Sparky, though she couldn't blame him for not showing up personally.

When they returned to the hotel, Kelly returned the call of the prior owner of *The Burning Desire*. He confirmed Jonah Schipper's information about the houseboat maintenance costs and Sparky's reactions. Afterwards, the rest of Kelly's day was spent organizing all the interviews and engineering and scientific data to date into a clear cause of the fire.

Meanwhile, Luna received a call from Detective Sergeant Fisher. "I am looking into the possibility that Ms. Sunny Ignacio's death was a contract killing and not a random act of violence," he told her.

Luna jumped at the opportunity to share her thoughts. "Someone hired Chekoff to kill Sunny, but it wasn't Mr. Sparks, given her value to the club. He had more affection for her than his wife it always sounded like. Although Sunny didn't return the love."

"I see your point," Fisher replied. "If not him, then who?"

"The Yéils…"

"Yes, the Yéils have motives but also solid alibis," Fisher interrupted. "We have their daughter in custody on conspiracy to commit arson but not the dancer's murder. Reverend Herald's group helped identify Chekoff but we still can't finger any of them for hiring him to kill anyone. And, we also can't question every business owner who lost money because of the popularity of *The Burning Desire*."

Luna finally revealed the one suspect she held for this moment. "Perhaps Sunny's lesbian lover, Ursa, had reason to have her killed." "Perhaps Sunny's lesbian lover, Ursa, had reason to have her killed. Long distance love affairs can be rough, although Sunny planned to finally move to Anchorage to be with her. Sunny also danced with many other pretty women; that could have made Ursa jealous."

"Was there anything to this "Ursa's" fears? Were any of the other dancers lesbians, Ms. Nightcrow?"

"Not that I know about. Sunny said none of them knew she was. I got the feeling Sunny may have told some people she worked her day job with though; they thought I was Ursa."

"Did Ms. Ignacio mention a special customer she had trouble with?" Fisher asked.

"I know where you're going with that, and the answer is no," Luna responded emphatically. "Yes, it isn't beneath some dancers to go out with customers after work for extra money and then get stalked by the guy who feels jilted when she reminds him it was just a part of the show for extra dough."

"What if Ms. Ignacio wasn't above going out with a lesbian customer? What if it was the gal who felt jilted after being told they weren't an item?"

"Sunny made the most money at the club, held down that daytime job at the restaurant, and was devoted to pyrography. So I still can't see any need to date customers, gay or straight."

"Okay, Ms. Nightcrow. Now about this "Ursa": Is that her real name, nickname, or maybe a fake name? You don't by chance have a way to reach her, or do you? We haven't found any contact information in Ms. Ignacio's apartment, just a lot of woodworking equipment, carvings…"

"It is called pyrography," Luna kindly informed Fisher.

"Sorry. My only dabble with arts was high school shop class: What we called "industrial arts,"" he disclosed.

Luna laughed softly.

"Anyway," Fisher continued, "Ms. Ignacio's apartment was her studio more than a living area. All the flammable materials we found probably would have given the landlord fits. No emergency contacts were on file with the leasing office. And as you know, her purse and phone were missing from the crime scene."

Luna nodded. "Both stolen during the commotion. And the phone no doubt wiped for reuse by whoever—*wait a minute!* Sunny mentioned having a storage unit for the things she couldn't fit in her apartment."

Fisher asked if she gave the name of the business.

"No," Luna sighed, then excused herself from the call to find the location.

The ensuing online search quickly netted a dozen self-rental unit companies in Juneau. It wasn't until the 5th call that Luna found Sunny's choice of self-rental companies. But that was the easy part. Luna then did a crash course in storage unit law.

Most property laws hold that if a tenant dies and no one claims the contents of their storage unit, they can be sold at a foreclosure auction, Luna moaned to herself. And Sunny had no will—*what healthy 25 year-old would?!* And the only "family" that Luna knew of was the shadowy Ursa. But what if Ursa (now a murder suspect) gained access to vital evidence in the shed and destroyed it? *One way or another, I've got to find out what's in Sunny's shed!* Luna vowed. But after speaking with the storage company owner over the phone, it wasn't going to be easy.

The owner and manager of Stacking Stuff Storage, Ben Stackhouse looked every bit as gruff as he sounded over the phone. Weather-beaten with gray hair receding, the sexagenarian stood six feet tall and immovable against illegal infiltration of his rental properties. "I've been in this business for nearly a decade and know that breaking rental law also means breaking my neck," was how he rebutted Luna's petition to gain access to Sunny's shed.

"And I'm not asking you to," Luna insisted.

"I also know about *U.S. v. DeTurbiville*: A tenant gave a friend the key and code to the unit, and the judge said it was okay for the friend to allow others to open it and go in. But you don't have the code nor does talking to Sunny about working at the titty bar make you her bosom buddy and free to look in her shed for lord knows what? I was born at night, but not last night, Ms. Nightcrow."

"You could open it to one of Sunny's family, Mr. Stackhouse."

"Are you telling me you two are sisters now?

Sunny didn't have any "family" I know of and didn't act like a dancer either when she came around. Probably because she was paying me instead of me paying her. Just in with the monthly fee and out. A fee which she didn't pay, by the way, for this month."

Luna snorted, "I am sure Sunny would have paid up if she was around."

That softened Stackhouse's that's life attitude a little. "Yeah," he sighed. "She was on time; I'll give her credit for that. And her private life was none of my business. But when you work where she did, you're asking for trouble."

"I take it you didn't like *The Burning Desire*?"

Stackhouse shook his finger and warned, "Oh, no, Ms. Nightcrow. We're not going down that road. Live and let live: That's what I say. I may be Alaska Creole—white father and Tlingit mother—like that Reverend, but I'm not a member of his bunch who probably had a hand in burning the bar to the ground."

"Thanks for your thoughts in my investigation. But the cops will still ask you a lot of questions. Not the least of which will be your feelings about where Sunny worked. And that if you didn't care for the club, was it maybe grounds for hiring someone to kill its star performer and, incidentally, your renter? And with that in mind, will you volunteer to open her shed for the cops, if not me?"

"Do you want me to have a heart attack on the spot?!" Stackhouse gasped.

"Don't worry, I know CPR," Luna tried to assure him.

Stackhouse scoffed, "Now you're a doctor *and* an insurance investigator? What is there you can't do, except get into that shed?"

"Think of it this way, Mr. Stackhouse: We are both connected to Sunny. She worked for Bernie Sparks, who I'm investigating, and you rented storage space to her. It's only a matter of time before the cops show up with a search warrant and lots of questions for you, too. But if you volunteer, like I did with information, you're in their good graces and less likely to be tagged a suspect or with obstructing justice. Do you know how much trouble getting a search warrant can be for a cop?"

"Yeah, but it keeps them looking at specific stuff, not everything."

"You could move anything suspicious before they arrived couldn't you? I mean, if Sunny hasn't any family or friends, you'll need to take inventory of anything valuable that can be auctioned off."

"With your help, of course."

"Only if you asked me."

Stackhouse declined. "Nice try to get in again, Ms. Nightcrow, but the answer is still no. If you nab Bernie for arson, who knows what you might get me on, too? Safety violations that could cause me to lose my license? Finding something illegal that Sunny may have dabbled in and try to connect me to it?"

"That's not how it works, Mr. Stackhouse. Had Sunny not been murdered, I doubt we'd be having this conversation. The cops caught the shooter but are looking into whether or not he was hired by someone. If they can't find anyone, the case is closed."

Stackhouse began putting the pieces together and saw where he fit in the big picture. "So your connection is strictly whether or not insurance fraud was committed in that fire," Stackhouse sought to make sure.

"*Exactly!* The faster I can clear that up, the faster I can leave town and you alone," Luna answered.

"Well let's not go our separate ways so soon," Stackhouse began to change his tune. "There's this problem with Sunny's unpaid rent. I ..."

"How much is it, Mr. Stackhouse?"

He told Luna and she offered to go to an ATM and withdraw the cash. "And letting the cops have free run of a unit is risky," Stackhouse added.

Luna raised the stakes. "*Very* risky," she agreed. She then sweetened the developing deal. "But not only would the cops owe you one for being agreeable, but so would I."

Stackhouse thought he was dreaming. "And you're an insurance investigator, you say?"

"Only when I'm working."

"And when you're not?"

Luna looked at her blazer dress and said, "I'm certainly not dressed like this."

You've got her where you want her, Ben, Stackhouse told himself. "Your IOU grabs me most," he finally admitted.

You've got him where you want him, Luna prided herself, as she stepped into Stackhouse's private space and asked, "Where does it grab you?"

CHAPTER 39

Back Pay

After an hour or so, Fisher answered his cellphone again. "You found the storage unit?" he sought to confirm Luna's claim.

"Bingo," she reaffirmed.

"How did you do it so quickly, Ms. Nightcrow?"

"Deduction, Detective Sergeant," she laughed. "Alaska has the third fewest storage units of any state and Juneau has 12 of them. They didn't take long to call."

"Did you visit the location and ask anyone to unlock the shed for you?"

"Yes, I did," Luna confessed. "And to his credit, Mr. Stackhouse refused. But he couldn't deny common sense. I told him it would only be a matter of time before he's embroiled in this hot mess but that cooperating with the law has its rewards."

"So Mr. Stackhouse knows we'll be by?" Fisher asked.

Luna answered, "Yes, and without a warrant."

"That saved me a lot of paperwork."

"I do have a license plate number that I saw around town, if you could..."

"Scratch that saved paperwork remark," Fisher groaned.

"Sorry."

"Just kidding, Ms. Nightcrow. It's a simple check. Thanks, and I'll be in touch."

Luna's line dropped in time for another call to come through. "Luna Nightcrow, speaking," she answered.

"Luna, it's Ben," a chipper voice announced. "How does 8 grab you for that date?"

"Great," Luna answered. She laughed to herself, *Talk about turning over a new leaf!* But she would too, in order to properly honor that IOU.

··◆··

Ben Stackhouse was amazed when Luna arrived at the shoreline restaturant he'd picked to meet up at in a black cocktail dress. It was as smooth and luxurious as laquer and highlighted her hourglass attributes—features Luna had hoped would be witnessed by Adonis's eyes only but were now on full display as informant back pay.

Luna strolled over to the table and took a seat across from Ben. "The afterhours Ms. Nightcrow," he said. "You look like a million bucks."

"Try nine hundred ninety-nine thousand, eight hundred after this," she said, opening her purse. Luna then removed a white envelope and conspicuously pushed it across the table.

Ben opened it and thumbed through its cash contents. "Sunny's storage fee to the T."

"*Happy?*" Luna asked pointedly.

"Aren't you, Ms. Nightcrow?"

Luna remembered her end of the bargain and began playing the role expected. With a grin, she replied, "Well, your wool blazer and ducktail hairdo are breaking the ice quite nice, enough to forgo the formality of Ms. Nighcrow. Call me Luna."

"*And who said women are hard to find in Alaska?!*"

"Finding is one thing, Ben, but keeping is another."

"It's a good thing I have something that will keep you glued to your chair."

"Like the untold contents of Sunny's shed?" Luna guessed.

Ben looked stunned and a bit hurt that Luna knew.

"Sorry: Just my insurance investigator intuition kicking in. The cops didn't tell me what they found."

"So I still have me a kept woman, in a manner of speaking?"

"Until Juneau PD comes clean."

"Then, I'll never see you again."

"Not like this. But in a fishbowl like Juneau, you'll see me around," Luna promised.

Ben sobered up to what he had agreed to. "It figures," he laughed.

The waiter arrived, which finally signaled the dinner portion of the date was about to begin. Ben chose local delicacies and put the order in. He then returned to Luna and said, "I made the switch to self-storage at the right time. I was too old to move people's stuff long distances but not over the hill enough to help move stuff from their offices into storage, as they made room for their work-from-home jobs. And with most of Juneau's economy depending on pencil pushing..."

And so went the evening: Listening to the ins and outs of the self-storage business. *Sunny, I feel you!* Luna said to herself. Night after night of listening to tripe and pretending to be fascinated with it. All the while understanding the bottom line: To walk the tightrope of keeping the money flowing and not fall for the customer. To know that the night must end with an until we open again but never a shared happily ever after.

An hour later, Luna and Ben strolled onto the deck for a spectacular, though windy, view of the indigo-hued highlands afar. But things heated up, as Luna felt the sudden warmth of Ben's wool blazer over her shoulders. "Thanks," she said.

Luna's return smile had the effect of an electric blanket on Ben, making the evening breeze sufferable. "Do you know the last time I went out on a date was 20 years ago?"

Luna tried to guess the reason. "She was that beyond compare?" she asked.

"No, that forgettable," Ben replied. "So when I found out you could just about find anything on the Internet, I spent my money staying plugged into it. And ever since then, I get any women of age I want, when I want. Beats wasting cash for an hour or two on a boat full of gold diggers."

"I would say you need to get out more, Ben. But you've probably seen everything there is to see here. And when you have to fly or sail hundreds of miles away for something different, I see why you prefer porn."

"It got me through the COVID mess just fine, while everybody else who was single and locked down were losing their minds."

"The virus couldn't stop fraud. There was an increase in medical, unemployment—I guess I was too busy a beaver to take much of a break."

"Well, Luna, everybody needs a vacation now and then. That's why I chose this as the IOU. You see the sights—a beautiful one I'm beholding, by the way—but then, you go back where you came from. I figure you feel about the same; you dressed up but seem clocked in even when you've clocked out. You're real love is finding out what it's all about."

"That is a charming segue into my unyielding

interest in what the cops took from Sunny's shed," Luna said.

Ben finally let her have it. "I saw them take artwork and a notebook: One of those old, spiral wire jobs with about 100 double ruled pages left."

Luna wanted to know what questions the police asked.

Ben shrugged. "Nothing I could answer about Sunny personally. They wanted to know if I knew she was an artist. No. I asked if she made the art they took or if she stole it. The lead detective didn't seem to say one way or the other. But I told him the same as you: Sunny wasn't a Chatty Patty. She just paid her monthly fee in cash and then left."

"Alright, Ben. I appreciate everything you've done," Luna replied.

"I'm not done yet," Ben announced. "Look inside my coat pocket."

Luna did and felt the frayed edge of a piece of rolled paper. After taking it out, she realized it was torn from a spiral notebook. There was still enough twilight for Luna to make out inked phone numbers.

"From the notebook, *my notebook*," Ben confirmed the source. "I took your advice, turned off the camera, and went through the shed to make sure there wasn't anything suspicious before the cops came. I didn't want to get charged with withholding evidence; so I thumbed through Sunny's notebook and found a page with phone numbers on it and wrote them down. The rest looked like a diary. I thought kids nowadays kept stuff like that on their phones."

Carefully, Luna folded the find into a small square that fitted neatly in her bra.

"Women do that in real life, huh?" Ben asked.

"We also do this…for the right guy." Luna moved closer and looked Ben in the eye. She then guided his calloused hands around her abundant bust and looped her arms around his neck.

"You sure you want to do this, kid?"

"Don't tell me you haven't seen it done all the time online?"

"But in *real* time, you know I'm not getting any younger," Ben warned.

"That makes two of us," Luna added. "This is just a vacation, right?"

"Perfect. Now where were we?"

"Seeing the sights." Luna felt safe in Ben's embrace. She closed her eyes and gave him what he only dreamed to get from this: A warm, slow kiss.

When it ended, Ben looked satisfied and said, "You weren't fooling, Luna."

"About what?" she asked.

"Knowing CPR: You sure put the wind back in my sails!" Ben confessed.

CHAPTER 40

Ursa

The next day, a stout, young Inuit woman sweated as she finally removed the battery from the back of her normal cellphone. Then, she fiddled with components of a small green cellphone and waited for it to ring. It did, on schedule, and she answered calmly, "I picked up the SIM card and switched out mine."

The voice on the other line said, "Good. Such a shame what happened to your...*friend*."

Once she stopped crying, the woman asked, "Do they know for sure who did it?"

"You didn't hear? The accused will not stand trial."

The woman nodded. "They let him go back to Europe," she answered.

"He was only sent to prevent another fire that an "ember" might cause."

"Who sent him?"

There was a hint of pleasure in the caller's otherwise even tone. "It is good you burn with a desire to know."

The revelation hit the young woman like an electric shock. She knew what had to be done and was encouraged by the voice when it said: "Only you can prevent fires."

The line suddenly dropped. The young woman sat frozen on her bed, forming a plan her head. She took out a hammer, smashed the small cellphone to bits, and dumped it in the trashcan. She then reassembled her personal phone just in time for it to ring. The young woman didn't recognize the caller named…

"Luna Nightcrow?"

Luna looked at one of the phone numbers Ben provided. "Is this Ursa Denali?"

"Who are you?!" the young woman demanded to know first.

"I am an insurance fraud investigator working on *The Burning Desire* fire in Juneau."

"I-I already know about the fire."

"I also knew your friend, Sunny Ignacio."

"Oh, really?!" Ursa grunted.

"Sorry. I didn't mean we were close friends," Luna explained. "She was just helping me with the case."

"I know all about Sunny dancing on the houseboat if that's what you're talking about. But I wanted her to move up here with me."

"To pursue her passion, pyrography," Luna added.

Ursa choked back tears. "I-I have a desire to come back down there."

Ursa's wording sounded strange. *"A desire?"* Luna asked.

"I mean, I want to pick up some of her things and pay off any bills."

"When you get here, Ursa, can we meet?"

"What for?"

"To talk more about…"

"I don't want to talk about how she died!" Ursa shouted. "The guy who shot Sunny got a freebie back to Europe. Talking to you won't change that. You're not a Fed, just some insurance agent."

The last thing Luna heard was the line drop.

CHAPTER 41

Flying the Coop

Ursa crammed some things into a duffel bag, quickly locked her apartment door, and hurried outside. She was in such a rush that she didn't notice the dark sedan near the back of her apartment complex's crowded parking lot. And that was just the way its two occupants wanted it. The young Mexican passenger with a suede jacket that conveyed an urbane vein and an Inuit driver whose craggy complexion indicated a tougher road hoed watched as Ursa gave away which car was hers.

The passenger nudged the driver. "Hey-hey," he whispered.

The driver saw Ursa get in. He then took out a nickel-plated piece and swung out its cylinder. "Six," he counted the bullets tucked snugly inside.

The passenger asked, "Overkill, isn't it?"

"That is one brickhouse of a girl! Six might not be

enough for pushing that cushion, if it comes to it," the driver warned.

Inside her car, Ursa checked the weather report for Juneau. Foggy and windy conditions, her app read. She thought about it for a moment; then, about the SIM card phone call that seemed to reveal Sunny's killer. Her fingers nervously tapped the steering wheel. *I have to go through with it,* Ursa finally convinced herself. She started the car, a lavender coupe. It wouldn't be hard to follow, which was the order also given to the occupants of the dark sedan.

"Showtime," the dark sedan driver said, turning the key.

Ursa was lost in thought, driven only by retribution for the murder of her lover. Twenty minutes later, Ursa reached her destination. The ensuing dark sedan suddenly pumped its brakes, allowing the coupe to continue on.

"This is Code 5. She's flying the coop, over," the tough-looking driver, a detective, radioed dispatch.

"Roger, Code 5. Return to base, over," the dispatcher instructed.

"Ten-four, out." The detective looked at his passenger, an IT officer with Anchorage PD. *"What about it?"*

The tech officer switched off his equipment, removed his earbuds and smiled. "Whatever all that stuff the guy said to her means, detective, we sure got it!" he confirmed.

The detective gave the tech a thumbs-up and gave up pursuit of Ursa's coupe.

CHAPTER 42

Paid Off

"That tip about Sunny Ignacio's lover and the storage unit paid off," Detective Sergeant Fisher told Luna, as they watched from the Juneau Airport concourse for the afternoon arrival of Anchorage Flight 102. "We at least got an idea of what this Ursa Denali looks like."

Luna accepted copies of Sunny's pyrographic portraits of Ursa. They were breathtaking in their granular detail. Some looked like wood-burned portraits; others, illustrations etched into gourds, leather, and other materials. "Thanks," Luna said. "Did you find anything else?"

"As I'm sure Mr. Stackhouse told you, we also found a diary that seems to confirm there was a thing going on between Ms. Denali and Ms. Ignacio. Unless she made it all up."

"The amount of detail in this artwork says to me it was real," Luna replied. "As for Mr. Stackhouse…"

"Yes," Fisher replied in a knowing tone, "he wouldn't let you into the unit. But you convinced Stackhouse to cooperate with us in exchange for a dinner date and probably intel on what we took."

"Nothing illegal about barter, is there, Detective Sergeant?" Luna defended herself. "One party gives something in return for something from the other."

"Barter is done all the time in the bush. But this wasn't that, Ms. Nightcrow."

"You mean it was quid pro quo?"

"The thought had occurred."

"As long as you don't pay to look the other way, all's good. All we got out of it was peace of mind that neither is obstructing justice and a dinner which, I have to admit, had an excellent roasted elk and braised Romanesco main course."

"About that 'dinner,' Ms. Nightcrow: A few diners called to ask if you were auditioning as a dancer, with your taste in evening wear. No indecent exposure charge, but there was concern that the restaurant was changing its format to a gentleman's club."

Unflustered, Luna asked, "Disturbing the peace, was I?"

"Depends on which side of the debate you're on. Among the electorate, it was fifty-fifty. My tiebreak coin flip came up in favor of no harm no foul.

"Now, I'm coming at this from a hardnosed homicide angle again. Was there anything sexual or combative between Mr. Stackhouse and Ms. Ignacio that you might have picked up on?"

"No. He said it was all about the bills and keeping them paid which, by the way, I did for Sunny."

"Okay. I checked the Mount Roberts Eatery. Her co-workers claimed they didn't know she was gay. That Ms. Ignacio only described this Ursa as a "life-long friend.""

Great! I may have just made things worse by outing Sunny, even if after her death, Luna blamed herself.

"And that license plate number you gave me? It checked out to one of the ex-dancers at *The Burning Desire:* A Ms. Connie Akin, aka "Frisky Fathoms,"" Fisher added. "She moved up to Anchorage a little over a year ago and became an accountant. She was in town on business though and participated in questioning about the fire. But like everyone else at the time, Ms. Akin didn't add much."

Looks like Sparky was right about his evening visitor, Luna sighed. "Sparky confused me with her and, given Juneau's size, I guess I unintentionally bumped into her."

"A fender-bender?"

"*Oh, no!* I mean "bumped into," as in saw her out and about. Since you mentioned questioning, though, did CARP come up with anything that you could call Ursa in for?"

"I can only stick my neck so far, as a cop, Ms. Nightcrow."

"Good thing I'm not. My small fry civilian standing helped me finger Freddie Burns, catch Chekoff, and give you the Ursa Denali heads-up. All of it freeing you up to work what I'm sure are many other important cases."

"Amen to that last count, though you're anything but insignificant, Ms. Nightcrow. You have the most guts of any outside investigator I've worked with."

"My partner, Kelly Day, might have something to say about that."

"You both have been aces. So here's what I know about CARP. Yes it is real, but out of our jurisdiction."

Obviously, given Juneau's size! Luna laughed to herself. "I thought Juneau has CARP because it's the capital," she feigned ignorance.

"*The Burning Desire* was a hot button subject statewide, as it brought in customers from all over. So when you mentioned Ms. Denali's connection to one of its dancers, Anchorage PD offered us a hand by way of an old-fashioned stakeout of her place for anything shady, à la Brutus Chekoff types. When she left, they tailed her. Had it been to the gas station, grocery store, or just the bathroom, they'd have simply reported that. It so happened she went to the airport.

"Your tip, not CARP, got us Ms. Denali's information from the storage unit. And your call picked up on something suspicious in a plan to come to Juneau. That's why we're here, Ms. Nightcrow."

"Then it's all me."

"To a degree, Ms. Nightcrow."

Luna mentally unpacked what she heard and began separating fact from fiction. Despite what Fisher said, Juneau PD got the okay from Anchorage to borrow CARP. But I bet the deal was that if Anchorage overheard any local criminal activity involving Ursa, they would get first crack at her. That would suit swamped Juneau authorities fine. Actually, I guess I wouldn't mind either. But Ursa must have been big city clean. But Fisher was frank on one account: As usual, it will be up to me to find any criminality before he can act.

All that assumed Ursa would arrive.

CHAPTER 43

Getting in Gear

There are some airports that because of bad weather and rough landscape are tough for passenger planes to land in successfully. Juneau International Airport is one. Located on a stretch of land on the fringe of town, it is surrounded by rugged mountains thousands of feet high and glaciers. Today, the heavy fog was lifting, but the shifting and gusting winds bounced off the mountains and still swirled dangerously.

The 737 from Anchorage that the local stakeout squad saw take off without a hitch now prepared to land in the misty, gray wind tunnel that was Juneau. Confident of their abilities, the veteran pilots prepared for landing and flight attendants dutifully reassured worried passengers. Suddenly, onboard sensors screamed as an intense blast of cold air smacked the jetliner. It banked 30 degrees to the right, causing a sideways roll.

Luna was shocked to see the plane bolt like aluminum-sided lightning towards the tarmac. She couldn't bear to look but was nonetheless shaken by a thunderous *BOOM!* that implied the loss of Flight 102.

The crash immediately pressed Garrett Fisher into first responder service, leaving Luna to reflect on what she did right and wrong. Sparky was right, it seemed, about him not being an arsonist and involved in killing Sunny. But did I get Sunny and probably Ursa killed? No, Luna told herself. Ursa was coming down anyway. Sunny came to me for a heart-to-heart and I caught her killer. As for *The Burning Desire*, Tanis confessed to conspiring with Freddie Burns to commit arson.

Luna began to feel better and then great, when she saw a familiar face fighting her way through the crowd. *"Kelly!"* she called out.

The women finally met and hugged. "Luna, are you okay?"

"Yeah, I'll live," she finally answered. "But—"

"Oh, no!" Kelly moaned intuitively, "Sunny's lover is —"

Luna nodded. "— dead. Anchorage PD saw her take off."

"But did they see her board the plane, Luna?"

"It's a longshot she didn't but let me see." Luna pulled out her smartphone and dialed Ursa's number.

The automated voice droned, "You have reached a number that has been disconnected or is no longer in service."

Luna reported the message.

Kelly said, "Come on. There's nothing more you can do here." As they left, a couple of familiar faces approached. "Bernila, Akashi," Kelly greeted the Juneau fire marshal and the state fire marshal's special agent.

Both stopped. "Hi, Kelly, Ms. Nightcrow. What brought you two out?" Akashi Hono wanted to know.

"Awaiting an arrival from out of town," Kelly answered.

Bernila Lluvia asked about the crash. "Is it as bad as we heard?"

Kelly held out hope. "Looks like a total loss, but who knows? I thought everyone in that roof collapse last week were goners."

Mentally, Luna was elsewhere, absorbed in analyzing Ursa's automated cell phone message. "Disconnected and no longer in service — *bingo*!" she shouted.

Startled, Hono asked, "Excuse me?"

"Me too," Lluvia added.

Luna described what she was thinking. "What if," she asked, "the key to the deaths of Sunny and Burns is in the way Brutus Chekoff was contacted? If someone hired Chekoff to pop both, how did they make contact? Face to face? Nah. Too much risk of being seen in a small town like this. But what about using a go-between?"

"What are you talking about, Luna?" Lluvia

interrupted. "I thought you are helping us with the fraud side of *The Burning Desire*."

"I still am, ma'am," Luna assured her. She paced back and forth while piecing together a line of logic. "The go-between could relay the orders to Chekoff by burner cellphones or prepaid SIM cards. They're cheap, hard to trace, and disposable. Prepaid SIMs also don't need credit checks, long-term contracts, or activation fees. I wonder how much luggage survived that crash?"

Lluvia cleared her throat. "How about how many *people* survived first, Luna?"

Luna grunted, "Don't worry, Bernila. The fire still burns; you'll get your turn."

Lluvia fired back, "Yeah, my turn to do my job and not someone else's like you want to!"

Kelly stepped in between the two. "Ladies, this isn't easy for any of us," she said.

Luna and Lluvia backed away from each other but not their stubbornness.

"I will do my job: Examining fires," Lluvia swore. "And remember this: The Federal Aviation Administration, The National Transportation Safety Board, and state will have priority over the crash site pickings; then, me."

"Get in line, in other words," Kelly said.

"Or get it in gear," Lluvia answered, looking at Luna. The senior fire investigation leaders then hurried on to the crash scene.

Kelly whispered, "I wouldn't read too much into the way they acted, Luna. They're headed into a world of hurt back there. Besides, Berlina's got a point: We're not homicide cops."

"So said Garrett Fisher, his boss, and Sparky, too," was Luna's jaded replied. "But contrary to popular belief, I don't pretend to carry a badge. Not being a cop gives me latitude, which I'm not afraid to use."

CHAPTER 44

A Hot Time

Kelly and Luna headed to the car. As they waited inside for several emergency vehicles to pass, Luna asked, "What's your take on Lluvia and Hono? You work with them more than me."

Kelly grinned. "You know they're convinced this is all arson. Enough said."

"That's not what I'm asking."

"Then what, Luna?!"

She finally came out with it. "Do you think they are thorough?"

"Yes, even though we all aired our opinions openly during our meeting," Kelly answered. "Bernila had no problem spouting off about public enemy number one's peccadillos, mentioning the high number or rapes and sexual assaults up here and the negative image of women that the club spreads. Add to that, her comments about the houseboat and sympathies for Tanis when we first arrived. Akashi was more business-like, agreeing with Bernila that it was arson but not having as much of a cow about Sparky."

"Thanks for the backstage pass," Luna said. "So Lluvia and Hono are professionals who, unlike Jonah, are actually on the job. But their methodology is narrow-minded and ... lazy. Once an arsonist, always an arsonist. If Burns was present, he must have set the fire even though Tanis called him but didn't tell Sparky. You can see why skeptics might think they've found a convenient way to do away with Sparky and the whole idea of strip clubs."

"*Come on, Luna!* They are still full-time public safety servants; their time and money are limited. That is why they called us in: To offer other possibilities."

"But if one of them isn't arson, it means a better than ever houseboat is in the cards, *The Burning Desire 2.0*," Luna argued.

Kelly chuckled, "I am sure you have something up your sleeve that they could use just as nicely to put Sparky away and the idea of strip clubs to rest. Like this whole conspiracy to commit murder."

"The cops brought it up, but Sparky didn't set it up. Tanis, The Yéils, and Eleanor Fjord all have reasons for wanting it to look like he did, though," Luna replied. "The cops cleared The Yéils of Burns's killing but not Sunny's, who they might see as

Sparky's lover. It was a lucky break that Mr. Yéil didn't catch that dancer I saw leaving Sparky's place last week. And The Yéils have enough to hire the best defense for Tanis. So why not Chekoff too? Or, Tanis could have talked them into it.

"As for Eleanor Fjord, she's so obsessed with losing business to Sparky that she wouldn't let Sunny enter the pyrography exhibit. Yet she sees the profitability in adult nudity and cleverly allows some nude exhibits."

"Maybe they all worked together like a task force. One paid for the hit and the others, the intimidation calls," Kelly conceived.

"Good thinking but no. I don't think they would trust each other not to blabbermouth if the plot went south. One of them called all the shots, literally."

"And that call from Ursa makes you think the Yéils or Fjord manipulated her into coming back to kill Sparky?"

"Not with Sunny dead. She plans to get rid of everyone involved."

"Are you going to warn The Yéils and Fjord, Luna?"

"If they'll listen. But I'll definitely let the police in on it. Maybe they can offer them protection."

As the last ambulance whizzed by, Kelly started the car for the return to the Chichagof. "I hope my final report will make both sides happy," she said.

"If not, as the song goes, '…there will be a hot time in the old town…'"

"Well, at least Mrs. O'Leary's cow won't be on the hotseat for it," Luna laughed.

CHAPTER 45

Knob-and-Tube

Back at the hotel, Luna met in Kelly's suite to hear her final fire investigation analysis and to help prepare for its presentation.

"I don't believe it was arson or an accident, but was willful negligence made worse by weather effects on the property," Kelly finally announced. "Each year, arcing flaws start more than twenty-eight thousand home fires that kill and injure hundreds of people and cause over seven hundred million bucks in property damage. Some come from outlets that are no longer grounded due to daily wear and tear. It is also possible that wiring behind a damaged outlet can short-circuit and cause a fire. And the college kids found *The Burning Desire* wiring to be at least forty years old and of the Knob-and-Tube design."

"*Knob-and-Tube?*" Luna asked. "Sounds like it's either outdated equipment or some cheap knockoff that is prone to easily catch fire."

"More the first than the last," Kelly remarked. "Knob-and-Tube was commonly used electrical wiring until the 1950's. It contains insulated copper conductors routed through stud drill holes by way of porcelain insulating tubing. The wires are then reinforced by fastened-down porcelain knobs. It is obsolete now and yes, poses a significant fire hazard by reacting with copper."

"Since many insurance companies won't insure Knob-and-Tube wired properties without assurances, Jonah Schipper's importance is easy to see," Luna said.

"Add to that, the insulation was made with paint and fibers that are at risk of wear and tear. The twisting of Knob-and-Tube may have caused the insulation to flake or break off. The wiring was also meant to disperse heat into open air, but building insulation doesn't allow that. Insulation around these type of wires will cause overheating; so the greater the risk of a fire starting is. On whole, this system doesn't have a grounding conductor to lower the risk of electrical fire and damage."

"So where does the rain come in? I would think that water puts out fire, no?" Luna asked.

"It can, but not in the case of electrical fires," Kelly replied. "Electricity conducts water; so, firefighters can be electrocuted. They can use something as common as baking soda or as swish as a carbon dioxide extinguisher to put out electrical fires. Juneau's rainy climate causes things like mud-slides and floods, resulting in rain damage. Lightning probably caused the fire, not matches, paper, or alcohol-based accelerants that most arsonists use."

Luna couldn't help but marvel. *"Great job!"*

"With any luck, this will clear things up," Kelly hoped.

It should...*on the insurance fraud front, anyway,* Luna thought. But she still worried about another storm brewing; this one, called Ursa. And if Kelly and Luna looked like they got Sparky off the hook, they too were now targets of her wrath.

CHAPTER 46

The Burning Desire Dupe

After almost a month of exhaustive analysis, additional clinical tests, intense witness interviews, and even a citizen's arrest, Kelly and Luna combined their efforts into one official report that also criticized the state and local findings in *The Burning Desire* matter. The following Monday, they presented it to the Juneau district attorney and then Bernila Lluvia's office. Monday night and into Tuesday was filled with fine-tuning for the big presentation.

On Wednesday, it was lights, cameras, and action, as Kelly and Luna conducted a prime time press conference at the SOB (State Office Building). They publicly laid out the evidence in PowerPoint fashion to a captivated audience that included Bernila Lluvia, Akashi Hono, Garrett Fisher, and other state and local officials mingled in with members of the press.

"Having been retained by insurer Tight Ship Assurance of Seattle, Washington and asked to consult with The Office of The Juneau Fire Marshal's investigation of a fire aboard the 65-foot houseboat turned gentleman's club, known as *The Burning Desire*, fellow investigator Ms. Luna Nightcrow and I have reached a conclusion about the cause of said fire," Kelly announced from the podium. "First, I will review the findings and conclusions of The Juneau Fire Marshal and The Special Agent of the Alaska State Fire Marshal's Office. Both believe arson is the cause of fire because of the following reasons:

1. The presence of a V-shaped pattern along the bottom of the corner nearest the stairwell leading to the attic, or "VIP section" of the club. This pattern normally shows an area where something flammable causes a fire.
2. The incidence of a bar in close proximity to the V-shaped pattern provided ample accelerants, in the form of alcoholic beverages, to set fire to the houseboat.
3. The verified presence and death of a fugitive arsonist, Mr. Freddie Burns, in Juneau and the testimony of Mrs. Tanis Sparks, wife of *The Burning Desire* owner Mr. Bernie Sparks, that she asked a specific Tlingit Alaskan

Native contact in San Francisco to refer said arsonist.

4. And before her death, an employee of *The Burning Desire*, Ms. Sunny Ignacio (a.k.a., "Ember"), allegedly saw Mr. Burns onboard and in the vicinity of the fire's origin.

"While there are uncontestable elements of truth in many of these findings, there are also parts that, when more thoroughly examined, suggest that *The Burning Desire* wasn't destroyed by arson. That it instead fell victim to weather effects on willfully neglected property despite claims from Mr. Sparks."

A veteran of many press conferences, Kelly paused to let the stunned catch their breaths; the photographers refocus and load more film; and reporters flip their notepads to continue notation. She then chronicled the history and liabilities of the houseboat's Knob-and-Tube wiring system. When finished, Kelly formally introduced Luna.

The insurance fraud investigator stepped forward and said, "Tight Ship Assurance of Seattle, Washington insured "The Burning Desire" with the understanding that its owner, Mr. Sparks, is a qualified journeyman electrician and would make the necessary modifications to the Knob-and-Tube wiring infrastructure. Documentation signed by Mr. Sparks states that such modifications would be made and could be inspected for implementation by Tight Ship Assurance personnel. Said modifications came at a cost estimated to be in the tens of thousands of dollars which, according to business records, may have been difficult for Mr. Sparks to obtain because he also owns a small electronics repair business that was near bankruptcy on multiple occasions."

"Thank you, Ms. Nightcrow," Kelly said. She then dimmed the conference room lights and typed commands into her laptop that brought the big screen to hi-definition life. "Surviving evidence from *The Burning Desire* indicates, however, that building insulation surrounding the upper deck wiring wasn't removed. There was also evidence of surviving wiring having been cracked and not replaced. This represents wear and tear and incorrect Knob-and-Tube maintenance.

"While Mr. Sparks is a certified electrician, his documented interviews on other aspects of property maintenance and repair, as they relate to the upper deck, indicate he is not a professional carpenter or roofer. Nor is there evidence that he hired either to adequately protect the houseboat from a host of disasters, including fire."

Samples of the insulation that Kelly tested flashed in succession on the screen. She explained that, "Samples of surviving attic insulation were also studied by The Engineering Department at The Panhandle School of Polytechnic Research-Juneau. Their chemical and electrical laboratory analysis found the insulation to be so out of date as to lack necessary fire-resistant chemicals, leaving ineffective material."

Luna added that, "Various employees of the gentleman's club provided photos of water damage to the top deck ceiling, showing the roof leaked water or other liquids into the establishment's VIP section: That is, the portion of the club that provided interactions of a more intimate, private nature between dancers and customers."

The audience chuckled at Luna's tactful description.

"Furthermore," she continued, "Mr. Jonah Schipper, a contract marine surveyor for 15 years and currently employed by Tight Ship Assurance, testified that he was bribed with unlimited entertainment gratuities from Mr. Sparks to certify that all Knob-and-Tube modifications were made as promised and not to accurately report the condition of the houseboat since its initial survey. Surveillance footage Ms. Day and I watched also confirms Mr. Schipper's repeated presence in the club."

Kelly nodded and changed from photos to a datapoint presentation. "The cause of the fire was arcing from 2 probable sources: One, lightning and two, weakened wiring.

1. Weather service information shows lightning strikes in the Juneau area before and during the rain event on the night of the fire.
2. And certain employees of the establishment, namely dancers, reported failed attempts to

start a space heater in a bottom deck dressing room during business hours the evening before the fire. The Knob-and-Tube-wired roof connected to the dressing room outlet too. And in interviews with Ms. Nightcrow, certain dancers claimed to be unaware of the dangers of connecting appliances to outlets not designed to carry specific electrical loads. The appliance in question, a space heater, was two thousand watts, but the outlet carried only a thirty watt load.

"The old copper wiring in VIP that led to the dressing room was permanently corroded by moisture from a roof weakened by unrepaired rain damage. Since the space heater was turned off before the club closed, it is likely that lightning instead arced with carbon insulation that lacked fire-protective chemicals. The damaged wooden roof then burned very quickly, causing flames to fall onto the top deck, burn through it to the bottom deck, and eventually lead to a blaze that was intensified by the presence of alcoholic beverages in the bar area."

The screen then displayed the video footage from Kelly's simulations performed at Panhandle School of Polytechnic Research that illustrated the idea.

"Please note that if properly protected wiring and insulation were used," Kelly said, "it is less likely that a fire would have started versus examples of when damaged wiring, impotent insulation, and moisture increased the likelihood of a fire."

The room slowly brightened, and Luna stepped to the podium again. "An interview I conducted with Mrs. Tanis Sparks, in the presence of her legal defense counsel, indicates that she believed her husband intended to commit arson because he suggested she search for new or used houseboats. Mister Sparks later told me in separate interviews that the purpose of the request was not to willfully destroy *The Burning Desire* but to search for a bigger houseboat to accommodate more than its limit of 26 people. Mrs. Sparks believed otherwise and enlisted the help of a contact in the San Francisco Bay Area Tlingit community to find an arsonist.

"Although Mrs. Sparks talked with Mr. Burns about arson, there is no documented testimony that Mr. Bernie Sparks was informed of the act and approved it. Nor is there video evidence of the arsonist onboard *The Burning Desire*, despite testimony of 1 employee that he was. There is missing surveillance footage that could be the reason but could also have been erased for practical reasons."

Kelly added, "And finally, there was no premeditated hydrocarbon (as in gasoline or oil) accelerant found in the vicinity of the V-shaped pattern nor in GC/MS analyses of debris in that area which, if found, would indicate arson as a strong probability.

So we believe that arson cannot be conclusively proven as what destroyed *The Burning Desire*."

Luna concluded by saying, "Regarding whether an accident caused the fire and can be the basis for filing an insurance claim, Ms. Day's evidence indicates that the former owner of *The Burning Desire* informed Mr. Sparks of the amount of repairs it required. Mister Sparks promised to renovate outdated equipment but neglected to do so. Mister Jonah Schipper's testimony goes so far as to suggest it was faked under the direction of Mr. Sparks but without the knowledge of the insurer.

"Therefore any accident claim for insurance compensation submitted to Tight Ship Assurance of Seattle, Washington is not required to be paid per the terms of the policy. A copy of these findings will be made available to all interested parties."

"And now, we'll take questions," Kelly said. A sea of hands surfaced from the conference room crowd, and Kelly pointed to one. "Yes, go ahead please."

The chosen one stood. He looked to be in his 20s—probably a cub reporter—and introduced himself as "Jason Nary of *The Juneau Jabber*" before asking, "So even if Bernie Sparks won't collect insurance money from this, there is the confession of his wife and two murders connected to the club. So how likely is it that he does time?"

Kelly answered, "As far as we know, the man responsible for the murders has been extradited to

Poland. And yes, there is still the testimony of Mrs. Tanis Sparks to consider. As an independent fire investigator and a former fire marshal, I can say that it's possible to be charged with conspiracy to commit arson without starting the fire because "conspiracy" relates to agreeing to do it, not whether it was carried out."

Nery persisted. "Considering conspiracy to commit arson then, have you made a criminal referral to the Juneau district attorney?"

"Ms. Nightcrow and I have kept the district attorney's office informed of our investigation, but no decisions have been made. Nor have any been made by the law enforcement and public safety personnel we worked with. Remember we presented many of our findings as consultants. Others will use them as they see fit."

"The insurance side of the matter will be decided quicker, I would imagine, than any possible criminal actions," Luna added.

It was time for another question and this time, Kelly chose a suave-looking interrogator. *Hmmm, a big city newsman!* she thought from his strong jaw and thick hairdo. But it only turned out to be local TV newshawk Ted Hack.

"About how many hours of security cam footage would you say was reviewed by Ms. Nightcrow and you…ballpark figure?" he asked.

"Probably 18 to 20 hours over a weeknight

stretch with lots of great local cuisine," Kelly guessed, and then shamelessly plugged several restaurants.

Hack stepped up his pursuit. "Did you see anyone of note aboard the houseboat?"

"Like many bars, the lighting was dim in many spots."

"But still enough to see maybe...someone important?"

"Important to our investigation, yes: Marine surveyor Mr. Jonah Schipper was spotted, as I mentioned earlier."

"And thanks for that exposé, Ms. Day. But News Team 1 is conducting our own ongoing look at *The Burning Desire*. So, I was just curious if you may have seen someone well-known aboard?"

Kelly asked in her best journalist tone, "Locally well-known, nationally well-known, internationally well-known?"

Hack narrowed it down. "Locally."

Kelly shrugged. "I didn't see you."

The room erupted in laughter, some of it from Ted Hack. "Good one, Ms. Day," he approved.

Kelly enjoyed the back-and-forth but had to cut Hack's dogged pursuit of a scandalous scoop short. "Let me break it to you this way," she wrapped things up. "What we looked for was definite proof that the houseboat was intentionally set on fire. We concluded there was none, based in part on *some* of what we saw in the security videos. Additional scientific evidence, like that shown today, led us to believe that it is more likely Mr. Sparks so badly wanted to keep the club open that he ignored safety rules and asked others to do the same."

Without being chosen, an unidentified male voice clamored, "What about this marine surveyor? What can you say about him, his believability?"

Luna answered, "His background will be released as part of our findings. But if you want to know about the profession in general, I'm unaware of specific state licensing for it. There are many accepted associations that issue credentials for those who pass training. But in other cases, all it takes is the confidence to print up a business card and buy some surveyor for hire ads. The "expert" surveyors know more than just ships and their marine environment; they also know human nature and how to deal with owners who don't want to pay to have their ships rated badly."

Many hands rose again as did voices wanting to be heard. It was Luna's turn to choose; she decided to be poked and prodded by what appeared to be a fellow Native American. "Arnaq Page, *The Athabascan Ask of Fairbanks*," the reporter identified herself as.

"*A foreign correspondent!*" Luna kidded her.

That got many laughs from the crowd.

Page played along. "You might say that, given our long distance from Juneau and relatively different view of gentleman's clubs," she said.

"I don't know about your views being that different, Ms. Page. Anchorage, Fairbanks, and now Juneau—your 3 largest cities—allow gentleman's clubs," Luna debated a bit. "And from my short time here, Alaska strikes me as more purple than red in its sensibilities. Not as red as say Oklahoma, where I am from, but not as blue as California."

"Interesting observation. So what exactly are your views of gentlemen's clubs, Ms. Nightcrow? And what effect did they have, if any, on your investigation?"

Sunny came to mind, as Luna replied, "I interviewed employees of *The Burning Desire* and found that dancing was, bottom line, a job. For some, their only income; others, part-time pay. Some liked it, others didn't." Then, Luna thought about Sparky. "And I would be lying if I said there aren't those for who the club provided someone to talk to, if not spend the rest of their lives with. But was spending a lot of money on what boils down to providing expensive fantasies worth it to everyone involved?"

"I guess that's what I'm asking, Ms. Nightcrow," Ms. Page said.

"Juneau must have thought so, since it allowed the gentleman's club to be built after many years without one. And its economic boost was undeniable. Maybe the community hoped that all things in moderation would apply here," Luna answered. "But everything in life has a price, including keeping *The Burning Desire* up to code. Unfortunately, it wasn't paid and could have cost the community—no *did* cost it—dearly, both haters and supporters.

"So all I can say, Ms. Page, is that what Ms. Day and I found is now Juneau's to consider. Will it change how such establishments are run in the future or help ban them completely? Either way, there will always be a "burning desire" to connect with someone special. The question is will the community provide opportunities for it and if so, will its members think it's enough?

CHAPTER 47

Budding Business?

In Anchorage, not many cared about 2 capital city killings and the broadcasted end to that silly, old squabble between Panhandle prudes and the rube from The Outside whose wannabe gentleman's club burned down. Gabriel Palaver, or "Gab" to his friends, was one of the few who had a rooting interest.

Suddenly, there was a knock on Palaver's apartment door. He prayed, *Please let it be what I've been waiting for!* Cautiously, the kid opened the entrance to a crack and spied what looked like a deliveryman holding a package. Palaver undid the door chain. The nondescript courier pushed the package forward; Palaver took it without delay. The carrier turned on his heels as the door closed. The only words Palaver heard him say from beyond was an accented farewell. *"Do svidaniya."*

The package's "fragile: handle with care" label went unnoticed, as Palaver tore open the cardboard box. After clearing away the equally burdensome bubble wrapping, a miniature totem pole (about a foot in length) appeared. Palaver removed it and noticed the crowing crow head was actually a twist cap. He unscrewed it. Inside the engraved Tlingit icon was stuffed with tightly rolled bundles of cash. Palaver looked up and gave thanks for safe arrival of his payment for his part in the "J-Town topless joint tussle," as he dubbed *The Burning Desire* dispute. But with the boat burnt, this was his last payment unless he moved to Juneau and took his employer's job offer.

Chickenfeed! Palaver scoffed at the proposal. I got something better. A group with pouches of crystals, powders, and grasses prized by the masses needed "salespeople." And from his part in the J-Town topless club tussle, Palaver thought he qualified. So did the group.

Palaver checked over his stash. Ready for launch, he thought. With the drugs cleverly concealed in his puffer jacket, Palaver proceeded to bury the houseboat job cash in his mattress. He dragged out his commuter bicycle, locked up his apartment, and then pedaled to where the deal was to happen. About fifteen minutes later, he arrived at what passed for a suburban park: A scummy pond, surrounded by a thicket, with a couple of plastic public outhouses.

Except for the rundown car Palaver once saw the buyer drive, the parking lot was empty.

The first sign of human life besides the peddler finally appeared from the ladies outhouse. It was a twitchy African American woman who looked to be one of Palaver's Gen Z peers. Palaver remained mounted, as she approached.

"Thought you weren't going to show," the woman griped.

"All that drive-time traffic, don't you know," Palaver laughed.

The woman just folded her arms and tapped her foot impatiently.

Junkies: No sense of humor! Palaver laughed to himself. Confident of his surroundings, Palaver calmly unzipped his pocket and removed one of the larger pouches. "One hundred percent *purp,* as we call it back in T-Dot. How does it look, Milli?"

The woman named Milli took the heavy pouch that contained well over the legal limit of marijuana allowed and eyed it suspiciously. "Better not be bunk, Canuck!" she warned. "This isn't Toronto. Anchorage is a burg; you won't be hard to find, especially with that announcer voice of yours."

Palaver laughed at the comparison. "My alter ego, but not for long," he said. "What budding business wants to remain under wraps? Now where's the pay?"

Milli said, "Okay," and reached into her jacket. Only it wasn't money she drew but a gleaming symbol of her alter ego: A badge. *"Drug Enforcement Administration, you're under arrest!"*

Palaver seemed to surrender. "You got me," he sighed.

But as Milli reached for Palaver's wrist to apply handcuffs, he jerked away, pulled out another pouch, and ripped it open. A white, powdery cloud erupted. Milli covered her face and staggered backwards.

My chance to escape! Palaver thought. But as he turned his bike, the ratty car in the lot suddenly roared to life. Palaver started up but the driver rose from hiding and cut in front of his path. The bike struck the front fender, dumping Palaver hard onto the hood. He rolled off and now fueled by a flight-not-fight instinct, started to run. But it wouldn't be far.

Milli recovered and readied what looked like a rifle. She took steady aim and fired at Palaver. But it wasn't a bullet that brought him down; it was a projectile that burst into an entangling net. The driver and a trunk passenger (both Milli's fellow agents) finally jumped out with real guns and proceeded with Palaver's formal arrest.

CHAPTER 48

Lynchpin or Liar?

On Tuesday, Detective Sergeant Fisher visited the office of Special Operations Officer Lunker again. This time, Lunker had a guest by way of video conference call: Nana Graham, the Drug Enforcement Administration Task Force Agent for Alaska HIDTA (High-Intensity Drug Trafficking Area) who busted Gab Palaver. Polished by business attire and makeup, she bore little resemblance to her undercover persona "Milli." After introductions, a briefing began.

"Looks like Sparky won't be collecting any insurance money to re-open another strip club, if that's what he had in mind. The D.A. plans to charge his wife with conspiracy to commit arson and left us with two homicides to further investigate," Fisher reported.

"Sounds like something for everyone," Graham replied.

"As far as Ursa Denali, she didn't board Flight 102 but entered the airport parking lot. So, she could be here or anywhere in the world," Fisher added. "And so far, no cellphones were recovered in the Flight 102 wreckage. If any are found, though, everyone from the FAA to Homeland Security will be examining them first."

Lunker then announced, "Anchorage PD's Information Technology Squad analyzed the CARP data taken from surveillance of Denali's apartment."

This is what Fisher had been waiting for. *And Lieutenant..?*" he wanted to know.

"Denali was informed—some might even say brainwashed given the cinematic metaphors that were pretty easy to cut through—on the murder of Sunny Ignacio."

"Brainwashed, Lieutenant?!"

"The caller tempted Denali to return to Juneau and punish the murderer of girlfriend Ignacio. That murderer, she was told figuratively, is Bernie Sparks who hired Brutus Chekoff to pull the trigger. But sources in Sitka haven't spotted her coming south through the ferry nor airfield there. And we have no proof that she's in Juneau. So it doesn't look like Denali took the caller up on it.

"The call to Denali came from a prepaid SIM card she picked up at a local cellphone store. Anchorage PD canvassed all the stores up there and store staffs reported selling many such SIMs but no burner phones. But DEA picked up on something important."

The Juneau officers heard Graham reveal that, "Gabriel Palaver, a Métis or mixed European and Indian descent émigré from Toronto, Ontario whose voice got him lots of work in telemarketing until COVID closed the big call center in Anchorage, was busted for possession of not just marijuana that was over the legal possession limit, but also meth, LSD, and a thousand grams of a synthetic drug with an estimated street value of around seventy-five thousand. For now, he's charged on eight total counts: Four for misconduct involving a controlled substance in the third degree, then four charges in the fifth degree. He is probably looking at another felony count on the synthetic drugs, once they're identified, and another for resisting arrest.

"What is of interest to your investigation is that Palaver also bought a large number of prepaid SIM cards from a couple of stores with cash. A clerk at one of the stores recognized him and said Palaver also left a SIM at the counter to help those in need with a freebie. At first, we thought it was just for his distribution network."

"Instead, Ursa Denali needed a SIM and picked it up instead," Fisher figured.

"That too," Graham said.

"There's more," Lunker whet Fisher's appetite.

"A lot more," Graham added. "Palaver told his public defender that he bought the SIMs at someone's direction to use for "a big job in J-Town," but won't elaborate unless he scores a get out of jail free card on the drug bust."

"Sounds like the kid's been using too much of what he pushes; it's dulled his common sense," Fisher said. "We're all assuming that Palaver's big part in this is his speaking skills. So if CARP can verify it's his voice luring Denali, threatening strippers, or maybe even giving Chekoff instructions, then he's in deeper than he thinks."

"Maybe not," Lunker cautioned his fellow cop. "Palaver's probably got it figured out. With no prior arrests or criminal records stateside, he knows he has a degree of leverage if he gives us whatever we want, whether it's the SIM cards, his phone, and whoever hired him and/or Brutus Chekoff."

"I agree, Lieutenant," Graham said. "If Palaver confesses to trying to recruit Ursa, you can use that testimony instead of controversial Anchorage CARP data. And if he gives DEA the crown jewels, that is his narcotics supplier and knowledge of the network, then Palaver is maybe even looking at further deals. And I'm not talking about drug deals, but possibly from some prosecution."

"I see," Fisher replied. "So this kid is either a lynchpin in a bigger plan or a liar trying to put one over on everybody with pieces taken from a publicized murder or two and a long-time houseboat feud."

Lunker nodded. "The Juneau D.A. will be interested

in these developments. Thanks again, Agent Graham; it's always good working with The Administration."

Nana Graham bid good-bye, and the line dropped.

Before Lunker could phone the district attorney, Fisher reminded him, "Since this all involves the dead stripper, her lover, and Sparky, you can bet that Nightcrow and Day will probably still be snooping around."

"Unless we prove Denali's in town, don't waste time with Sparks."

"Do you mean as in questioning or police protection, Lieutenant?"

"Both. You already spoke to him about the houseboat and got nothing. As far as what CARP picked up, Sparks may be the motivation for Denali's alleged trip but wasn't named specifically. And he didn't want protection when there were serious concerns for his safety and probably won't for what is still just speculation. As for Nightcrow and Day, they got their insurer off the hook for the houseboat loss and should be on a boat or plane out of town."

"They were pretty helpful all around, Lieutenant."

"Does your wife know you're so obliging to those two, G?"

Fisher grinned. "Does yours?"

"As long as obliging means "considerate" then Lucy would approve of what I'm about to do: Ask for a BOLO (Be On The Lookout) for Denali, but not an APB (All Points Bulletin) without more to go on. I will talk with the brass about it."

CHAPTER 49

Forewarned

The sun shone brightly for the first time in nearly two weeks and was expected to continue for at least Wednesday before another front moved in. And how was Luna celebrating it? By seeing the sights, of course, even if that meant returning to a gloomy one: The Yéil residence.

"If Tanis doesn't go through with a trial, our daughter's lawyer says the fire marshal and district attorney recommend she go to prison for a year for conspiring to commit arson," Mrs. Yéil told Luna.

"While Sparky is free to start another strip club probably!" Mr. Yéil huffed.

Luna replied, "Your daughter was very helpful. She turned over a lot of evidence, including testimony about the Tlingit contact in California who referred Freddie Burns. It will help in some open arson cases down there. And she has other financial information that might be useful elsewhere."

"We appreciate everything you did to work with them to lower the sentence from 20 years in prison," Mrs. Yéil thanked Luna.

"My partner, Kelly Day, had the most influence," Luna replied.

Mister Yéil grunted and left the women in the living room.

"The reason I came by is to ask if you heard anything from a young woman from Anchorage named Ursa Denali?" Luna asked.

Mrs. Yéil said, "No."

"I checked the downed Flight 102 passenger list, and she wasn't aboard. When I called her before, Ursa planned to come back to Juneau to pay off her girlfriend's debts," Luna said.

"What does that have to do with us, Ms. Nightcrow?"

"Ursa's girlfriend was the murdered dancer from *The Burning Desire*, Mrs. Yéil."

It didn't take long for Mrs. Yéil to make the connection. "And because Tanis is Sparky's wife, this girl holds us guilty by association, even though we feel the same way about Sparky as she probably does."

Mister Yéil entered the living room again. "Ms. Nightcrow..," he called out.

Luna turned directly into the sights of his .38 caliber Colt revolver.

"*Rhys!*" Mrs. Nita Yéil gasped, grabbing her chest.

Luna raised her hands in defense. "Please don't do anything silly. Your daughter needs you especially now," she said calmly.

"Consider us forewarned was all I meant," Mr. Yéil said, tucking the revolver into the waistband of his trousers. "So what does this "Ursa" look like?"

"She is Inuit," Luna answered, handing Mr. Yéil a copy of the pyrography likeness.

Mr. Yéil looked it over and nodded. "I hope you see why so many hate *The Burning Desire*. Two people are dead, and now our lives endangered by some woman with a score to settle."

Luna reached into her purse for a business card and gave it to Mrs. Yéil. "Please let me know if Ursa Denali contacts either of you or if you see her around," she asked.

The Yéils agreed they would.

CHAPTER 50

Quite the Questioning

It was an important day for Eleanor Fjord. Your countrified curator clothing won't do. *Show those bumpkins who is boss!* she told herself. After preening her feathery hair and lashes with care, Fjord donned a dark blue skirtsuit with gold pinstripes and a South Seas pearl necklace. Once designer heels were in place, Fjord checked her face and saw a portrait of power in the mirror. The director of the capital's premier center for the arts was ready to take on ... The Juneau Police Department.

Detective Sergeant Garrett Fisher was the specific reason for Fjord's fortification: He called her in for questioning. But his wife briefed him on what to expect from her social dealings with Fjord through a ladies poker club.

"She'll be holding all the cards," Mrs. Bridgid Fisher warned.

"No doubt she'll be holding them close to her vest," Fisher tried to convince his wife.

"I don't know about that. She always seems to have a winning hand at the ladies poker club. And she doesn't mind showing off all her other high cards in life: A thriving business, a PhD, super model looks..."

"Like any decent husband, I hadn't noticed how she looks. And as a cop, I have to obey one of our basic rules: Keep your eyes on the road."

Bridgid patted her husband's knee. "Good boy," she teased.

"But today, Fjord will be front and center. So..."

"So, it means upping your dressing game, Sir G, so you look worthy enough to breathe the same air as 'Her Excellency.' That's assuming she doesn't suck it out of the room."

"No bluffing her with my gun and a glare, I guess?"

Fisher saw Bridgid signal no, therefore knotted a black knit tie around his red flannel shirt and topped it off with a tan corduroy sportscoat.

Bridgid was pleased. "Perfect," she approved. "You look like a brawnier version of Robert Redford's Bob Woodward in *All The President's Men*."

"May our investigation have the same luck," Fisher wished, as he headed out the door.

·· ◆ ··

Eleanor Fjord lawyered up with Amicus, Bench, & Associates (the same high-powered Anchorage firm representing Tanis Sparks). Her attorney and she arrived at the police station, checked in, and received their visitor credentials. Meanwhile, Fisher let them settle into the interrogation room before making his formal entrance. "Thank you both for coming. I'm Detective Sergeant Garrett Fisher."

"A pleasure to finally meet you, detective," Fjord said. "I know of you through certain social circles your wife frequents. She is on her best behavior."

"Thank you for letting me know," Fisher politely replied. "Now, Dr. Fjord, about this matter."

Fjord maintained her cool, as Fisher started in. "*Gab Palaver?* Yes I know him, although as Mr. Gabriel Palaver," was how the doctor answered her connection to the convict. "He worked as the coordinator of our pyrography fundraising drive. Mister Palaver's vocal talents were used by other telemarketing firms throughout Alaska and in Toronto, Ontario, or so his resume read. Therefore, it seemed sensible to employ him."

"He also claims that you promised him a better job, working in your public relations department," Fisher added.

"*If*," Fjord stressed, "he carried out his job properly and successfully."

"Properly: As in buying several prepaid SIM cards, correct?"

"Correct, detective. Mr. Palaver asked me how to best carry out the assignment, as it required use of his own equipment. But he wasn't limited to that method, detective."

"Mister Palaver also said you mentioned SIMs as a 'discreet way to contact the people on the donor list.'"

Without blinking, Fjord replied, "Yes: He was provided with a list prepared by my office, however, not me."

"After the list was done, was it read, approved, and then given to Mr. Palaver by you?" Fisher asked.

"I would, of course, ask to see the list Mr. Palaver showed you, so as to guarantee it was indeed prepared by my office and then approved by me," Fjord answered.

"And just to be clear, your instructions for interacting with potential donors, according to Mr. Palaver, was 'not to coerce them,' right doctor?"

"Yes, detective. To approach subjects with the utmost tact."

Fisher pushed on. "Did you advise Mr. Palaver to also use multiple cellphones to call on?"

"His initial interview was conducted via cellphone, using mine and presumably his. And as Mr. Palaver wasn't in a formal call center environment, this assignment required him to use his own equipment. But to ensure his safety, if using only his phone for outbound contact, I did suggest purchasing cheap cellphones that could be disposed of after a certain time."

"Ensuring his safety, doctor, when he's calling on behalf of your business?"

"Some dislike unwanted solicitation to the degree of finding the caller's identity to complain or perhaps do worse to them. Again, detective, suggesting a manner in which to carry out a job doesn't make my office or me accountable for, dare I say, any misdeeds that may have been committed by someone with ulterior motives."

Misdeeds: Fjord slipped up! Fisher tried to follow up, saying, "Misdeeds is an interesting word, doctor. What kind do you think Mr. Palaver may have committed, regarding..?"

At that point, Fjord's attorney Bethel Amicus of the Yup'ik Tribe made her entrance. "Before we start assigning blame for misdeeds as yet unproven, my understanding, detective, is that Mr. Palaver was recently arrested and detained for violation of marijuana laws and for illicit drug trafficking, correct?" she asked.

Fisher nodded.

"So, are questions about pre-paid SIMs, hypothetical cellphones, and advice on how to use them related to his Anchorage arrest? And if so, are you implying that my client, Dr. Fjord, had some involvement in *that* matter?"

"No."

"Then what matter, detective?"

Fisher came out with it: "Mister Palaver claims that the arts donation drive was a front planned by Dr. Fjord to intimidate employees of *The Burning Desire* gentleman's club not to release any information that could clear its owner of arson. He was also told, allegedly by Dr. Fjord, to use a hard to trace system of disposable SIMs and burner cellphones to do the job."

"We are aware said establishment grew in popularity among some tourists and citizens of Juneau," Amicus acknowledged. "But my client hasn't anything to fear from *The Burning Desire*."

"As in *now* Dr. Fjord doesn't have anything to fear because the houseboat's gone. But was she afraid of the waves it was making before?"

"My client still maintains a reputable business that thrived economically during COVID shutdowns, detective."

Fisher moved on. "We also found an interesting phone number on the donations list. It belonged to Mr. Brutus Chekoff. Do you know Mr. Chekoff?"

Amicus nodded. "He held legitimate jobs, if largely temporary in nature, throughout the state, which may have placed his name on the fundraising list you mentioned. But to answer what sounds like your *real* question, certainly we know of Chekoff's most publicized occupation: That of a self-employed contract killer...*in Europe, however.* We also know that he was charged, though not proven to be in that capacity, with 2 Juneau slayings whose victims seem more related to *The Burning Desire* matter than anything having to do with my client's fundraising."

"Has your client ever visited Russia?"

"Really, detective! Are you suggesting that..?"

Eleanor Fjord stepped back into the fray. "It's okay, Ms. Amicus. As the sister-state agreement between Alaska and Khabarovsk is legal, yes: Many, including me, have visited Russia and that particular city."

"And was your visit for business or pleasure, doctor?" Fisher asked.

"It was certainly a pleasure to visit such a beautiful city. But my business there was to arrange for the temporary display of a rendering of a classic piece of art at the center," was how Fjord chose to answer the Russia question.

Fisher then pulled a photograph from his jacket pocket and placed it on the table. "Does this piece of art look familiar?" he asked his guests.

Fjord recognized it immediately and said indifferently, "It is a replica totem pole or *Kootéeyaa.* Surely you know that Alaska has many kinds."

"But this isn't one of them," Fisher said. "In fact, doctor, State Crime Lab analysis says it is made of

East Siberian Fir: A tree native to the Khabarovsk area."

Fjord shrugged. "Countless replicas of American art are made in foreign countries and exported to the U.S. for sale, exhibition, or other purposes."

"Did you, by chance, buy it during your business trip?"

"No, detective, I did not."

"So what does this replica have to do with my client's fundraising activities, detective?" Amicus wanted to know.

"According to Mr. Palaver, a deliveryman who said good-bye in Russian (or *Do svidaniya*) dropped the replica by his place. Inside was final payment for his part in 'fundraising activities' which amounted to five thousand dollars. If Mr. Palaver is on the fundraising payroll and paid by direct deposit, as he claims, then why would that amount of cash be suddenly sent via an unknown deliveryman and not through more reliable postal or banking services?"

"Hypothetically speaking, detective," Amicus prefaced her defense, "if cash must replace electronic payment because of some technical or other difficulty, then it is understandable and legal. And I don't suppose Mr. Palaver objected, as long as he was paid. As for concerns of sending cash by courier, how much more reliable is sending five thousand in cash through a postal system that is known to misdirect how much mail per year? And as for this

"Russian speaking" courier: I don't have to tell you the importance of verifying his existence, in light of Mr. Palaver's confirmed misuse of marijuana and trafficking illicit narcotics.

"So as it stands, detective, I do not see evidence of a connection between my client and Mr. Chekoff's activities, whether committed on a local or international scale. Nor do I put much confidence in Mr. Palaver's accusations to date."

Fjord looked directly at Fisher and asked, "Am I being detained, detective?"

Unflinching, he simply said, "No."

Amicus stood. "Then thank you, Detective Fisher. We'll take all you said into consideration."

Fisher moved to the door and opened it. "Thank you, ladies, for taking time to come by," he said.

On her way out, Fjord turned and smirked at Fisher. As she left the station, her perfumed wake also turned a few heads. One belonged to junior detective Eddie Lansky. He went up to Fisher. "When you get a chance, sarge, we have a new lead on that commuter boat mugging," Then the conversation turned to the results of "the interrogation of the year," as it was referred to around the station. "Well, how did it go?" Lansky was dying to know.

"It turned out to be quite the questioning. Fjord stayed cool under fire and distanced herself from *The Buring Desire*. Even when I had a shot at her, counsel stepped up and gave it to me with both barrels," he answered.

"Tag team bout," Lansky gathered.

"It always is when an attorney's present, and even more so when she's an ex-Army JAG (Judge Advocate General) like Beth Amicus," Fisher chuckled.

"You still got your jabs in, sarge, even if the only knockout was Fjord. Damn, what a waste if she's guilty, huh?"

"She's all yours, Eddie. I'm a married man, so Fjord's the forbidden fruit. Speaking of my card-sharp wife, Brigid would say that Fjord overplayed her hand. She gave me the kind of look that only a crook who's beat the rap in court gives."

Lansky grinned. "Rookie mistake."

"More like beginner's luck...*this round,*" Fisher conceded. "But the game ain't over. Stay tuned. Now, about that mugging..?"

BOLO

Luna gave a number that had been busy all day one last dial. To her delight,
the voice she wanted to hear answered.

"Detective Sergeant Garrett Fisher, Juneau PD: How can I help you?"

"Detective Sergeant, thanks for taking my call."

"Sorry I couldn't earlier, Ms. Nightcrow. It's been a busy day."

"You've probably been catching up on other cases and thought my partner and I would be on our way out of town."

"Catching up on other cases, always. But I know you wouldn't let the Denali thing go. So I went to the Lieutenant earlier; he got the all systems go on a BOLO for her."

"BOLO?"

"A Be On The Lookout. It's for specific cases that aren't necessarily life-threatening."

"Not to sound ungrateful, but why not an APB (All Points Bulletin)?" Luna asked.

"An APB is for escaped convicts, known killers, and the like and involves issuing arrest orders, notifying the media, and pulling in more resources," Fisher explained. "And Ursa Denali doesn't fit any of those conditions."

"But what about her direct connection to Sunny? And what Ursa told me sounded like circumstantial evidence of a veiled threat to kill Sparky, Eleanor Fjord, Tanis Sparks, and The Yéils."

"I remember the phrase "I'll be back" from the "The Terminator" and what it led to. But in real life, Ms. Nightcrow, "a desire to come back" doesn't mean Ms. Denali plans to commit a crime if she comes to town."

"Then can a patrol car kind of *cruise by* their homes? Not protection, but..?"

Fisher was patient with Luna's persistence. "Even if we offered Dr. Fjord, let's say, protective detail, she could call it off without probable cause. For what it's worth, Bernie Sparks turned it down. For anything more, brass will want proof that Denali is here."

Luna sighed, "Need I ask if an old-fashioned stop-and-frisk dragnet of Juneau is out of the question?"

Fisher chuckled, "Back to reality, Ms. Nightcrow: Is there anything else?"

"No, it all makes sense, Detective Sergeant. Thanks. I'll be on the lookout for Ursa, too."

··◆··

Kelly Day finished shopping for groceries at Fresh Findings for her crack at cooking dinner. After nearly a month, Luna and she exhausted the menus of every restaurant in Juneau, including the Chichagof's. After loading up the car, Kelly's phone buzzed. It was Luna. "What's up?" the fire investigator asked.

"The cops did as much as they could," Luna said.

Kelly groaned, "So that means no home cooking?"

"Probably not," Luna managed to laugh.

"Then what couldn't the cops do that we'll need to?" Kelly asked.

Luna answered, "They can't issue an APB or assign protective detail on a hunch that Ursa's in town. I told the Yéils to watch for Ursa. Mister Yéil has a gun handy, but I couldn't reach Eleanor Fjord. Can you head over to her house and watch for anything suspicious outside?"

"*Stakeout?*" Kelly wanted to know.

"Let's just say neighborhood watch." Luna put it more diplomatically.

"And if the neighbors start watching me instead?"

"Then maybe, Kelly, they will call…"

"…the police, who will then watch Fjord's place for sure," Kelly responded. "And I thought I was paying *you* to take this crap! Okay, what's the address?"

Luna gave it.

"Oh, Luna..?" The line dropped off before Kelly could ask where Luna was going.

The insurance investigator returned to frantically redialing another phone number.

Foreign Currency

Eleanor Fjord left the police station satisfied with every cent she spent on Bethel Amicus's firm defense. But she worried with good reason about Gab Palaver's sniveling surrender to police pressure in Anchorage.

"If only Brutus Chekoff wasn't deported; I could have sent him to take care of Palaver. *Damn that nag Nightcrow!*" Fjord groused aloud as she drove. "But with Palaver in custody, doing away with him will be a dicey proposition."

Fjord then remembered something: *Maybe Georgy can help me again!* Contacting him might be risky, too. Are the police tracking my cellphone now with Georgy's payoff-in-a-totem-pole to Palaver? I mean, I like how it was probably an attempt to point to the Yéils as Palaver's employers instead. But it helped put that police dog Fisher on my trail.

Fjord drove downtown, but not to the arts center.

Her next move had to be careful. But not so secretive
as to park in the woods and maybe have someone
assault me or my car breakdown and start rumors
as to why I was alone in the first place, the doctor
pondered, as she planned where to call Georgy from.

Finally, Fjord settled on the busy Franklin Street
area; its hundreds of tourists wouldn't pay her much,
if any, attention as they went about their business.
But it had plenty of safety if things turned bad. The
doctor parked, turned off her regular phone, and
opened its back panel. The battery popped out and
into her hand. Fjord delicately wrapped it in alu-
minum foil, hoping to make it hard for cell towers to
lock on the battery's embedded chip and her location. Next, Fjord took a giftbox from Georgy out
of her shoulder bag. It contained what looked like
simple earrings. She replaced her noticeably gold
hoops with them.

Fjord then got out and unlocked the trunk. She
swaddled the dismantled phone within her emergency blanket and, with the raised lid shielding
her, slipped into a raincoat, a pair of oversized
sunglasses, and tied a scarf around her head. Good
thing this isn't the 1960s, Fjord thought. I would
be mistaken for Audrey Hepburn or Jackie O.! I still
might still be, what with Juneau's decidedly aged
population. She left her shoulder bag in the trunk
and finally waded into the stream of shoppers and
sightseers to become submerged in anonymity.

Fjord reached into her raincoat pocket for a satellite burner phone. She activated its encrypted voice scrambling system, taking no chances that the police may have recruited military assets to spy on her from Joint Base Elmendorf-Richardson upstate. After punching in the desired number, Fjord moved towards a storefront (as if to window shop).

"*Hello?*" a male with a heavy accent answered.

Through the earrings, which were cleverly fashioned earbuds, Fjord asked how he was. "*Как дела?*"

"I am well," was the man's response. He always appreciated Fjord's attempt to learn Russian, so forgave her occasional mispronunciations. "*Как вы, мой дорогой?*"

"I too am well. Thank you for asking," Fjord answered the man's concern for her comfort. "I am doing some shopping and could use a bit of advice. Someone was paid for his job but now wants more than what was agreed to."

"*Hmmm..,*" the male on the other end though aloud.

"Greed can be bad for business," Fjord added. "So what do you suggest this person be told?"

"Yes. If this person has already been paid but wants more, he must be reminded of what he agreed to and what happens when such agreements are broken."

"He is aware of the costs of doing business but is not in town to remind."

The man on the other end was curious to know, "Where is he?"

Fjord realized she had been standing still too long—the police might triangulate on the call—and walked toward another busy establishment to confuse cell signals. "The man is in Anchorage," she answered.

"Ah, yes. He is the guest of some very questioning people, or so I hear."

That told Fjord the man knew of Gab Palaver's arrest.

"Love, you hired this man. If only I had known of his displeasure before, I could have had my courier pay his trust and also his betrayal.'"

Fjord's heart raced. "So there is no more counsel you can give?"

"If only there wasn't such a great distance between us, then maybe..."

Fjord rushed to close the gap. "I-I have a most pleasing way to bring us closer. I mean, I have never given you my full ability. Just business."

The man agreed. "Yes, life is too short for you to always work. What do you do for pleasure...shopping, as you are now?"

Shopping? Fjord forgot her cover story. "Yes, shopping," she confirmed.

The man asked, "For whom, as you have no spouse?"

"With you in mind," Fjord lied because she

cringed at the thought of the man in another sense than strictly business. With his gargoyle-like face, bald head, and bushy eyebrows, the man could pass for that movie vampire Nosferatu. But Fjord had to cash in the one chip every woman has when all else fails. "I-I am looking at something that I thought about changing into sometime after work."

The man had the beautiful American eating from his financial hand for years. Now, he had her on her knees with the chance to get more than money.

Fjord's fertile imagination (that which convinced her she was the end-all-be-all of the Alaska arts scene) now toiled to turn a cut rate furniture store display into burner phone foreplay. She intensified every syllable into an arousing picture that she hoped Georgy would see of her trying on "something lacy, hot—red-hot—and racy."

Fjord's captive audience sighed, *"Ты согреваешь мою душу."*

Fjord let her false affection flow. "I am pleased I 'warm your soul,'" she echoed the sentiment. "Imagine how you will feel when it is truly cold and you see me —"

"*Enough!* Do not 'spoil it for me,' as you say. And do not worry. The other man shall never lay eyes on you nor do business with you again. Until I shall see you, love, remain well, in contact, and, most importantly, in business."

The line dropped and Fjord's spirits picked up. It was one of her easiest, if sleaziest, transactions: Exchanging the promise of sex (a currency not foreign to Fjord but whose use she abhorred) for the elimination of Gab Palaver by Khabarovsk tycoon and self-proclaimed patron the arts Georgy Mogulinski.

As she walked back to her car, Fjord tossed her burner phone into a sewer vent but forgot to remove the earbud earrings. Once behind the wheel again, she restored her regular cellphone, scrapped the spy wear, and started up.

Not So Well-heeled

The long day's haze finally faded, and a pink and orange glow descended on Juneau as Eleanor Fjord's E-Class Mercedes cruised the upper channel shoreline to the affluent Back Loop Neighborhood. She parked and then trudged into what passed for a luxury home. The living room felt cold, even though Fjord knew she left the heat on. Before she could check the thermostat, Fjord heard her smartphone vibrating in her purse and instinctively pulled it out. But she stopped at the sound of a throat that wasn't hers clearing.

Fjord turned and froze at the sight of the uninvited guest who got her attention. It was a young Inuit woman who the doctor didn't immediately recognize but whose intent was clear, by the .22 caliber pistol she aimed her way. Fjord didn't break a sweat when she said, "We're closed. Can you please call back tomorrow, Miss..?"

"*I'm not one of your customers!*" the young woman sitting on the black leather sectional growled. "And just drop the effing phone."

It fell to the floor with a thud rather than a crack. Fjord was at least happy that her high-end smartphone protector sounded like it did its job.

The young woman faked a smile. "I bet it's been a long day. Why don't you chill for a while?"

"The temperature feels right for it," Fjord said, if sarcastically.

"Sorry about breaking your window to get in," the young woman lied. "But you can get it fixed again. Although I'd get it burglar alarmed or something."

Fjord walked to the chair on the other side of the coffee table and sat. She removed her shoulder bag and carefully pushed it across the tabletop to the young woman. "Take my bag. It's easily worth a thousand dollars. If it and its contents are not enough, I can get you more. You must know I am a well-heeled businesswoman."

"Yeah, I know all about your gallery with its pretty little pictures. A friend of mine wanted to have her engravings there. But someone believed she was a ho; so her artwork had to go. That strip club was trash, not Sunny!"

Fjord's stomach flipped, followed by a tingle down her spine that wasn't from the wind gusting through the broken window blinds. It was the frightening identification of her visitor. "You are not alone in your disdain for *The Burning Desire*; many people felt it was rubbish. So, I devised a plan to rid us all of its proprietor permanently," Fjord tried to talk her way out of trouble.

"Rid us of what?!" Ursa asked.

"Bernie Sparks: The owner. Did you not receive a prepaid SIM card and then a call from a convincing young man.., Ms. Denali?"

"You had him call?"

Fjord nodded. "I told him to tell you that I need your help to stub out Mr. Sparks."

Ursa was rightfully suspicious. "Then why didn't you call yourself?"

Fjord tried to convince her that, "This is a group undertaking. If everyone does their part, we can stop Mr. Sparks and any plans he has to rekindle *The Burning Desire* without going to jail."

"Bullshit!" Ursa snapped. "Without *you* going to jail, you mean!"

"Surely you know the saying "the enemy of my enemy is my friend." If so, can't we agree this is Mr. Sparks's fault, Ms. Denali?" Fjord asked.

"It's not only *his* fault," Ursa snarled and clicked the safety off her pistol. "If you had let Sunny show her art, which wasn't even naked like that actor on the paddle you let in, she would have quit the club sooner and not been killed by Sparky's hitman!"

Fjord's hostage negotiations now circled the drain. She stammered, "I-I had no choice. I am heavily in debt to someone to keep the arts center open. *The Burning Desire* was...putting me out of business."

"You don't look like you're broke," Ursa grunted.

Fjord tittered, "Oh, you mean this outfit? I had to dress for an important meeting today."

"You are home now. So why not take it all off?" Ursa asked.

"Take my clothes..?"

"*...off!*"

Fjord baited Georgy earlier but had time to build herself up to bare it all. But now she trembled as cruelty, not arousal, consumed Ursa and strengthened what was always deadly intent. The doctor swallowed hard and struggled for air. "Disrobe...now, Ms. Denali?" she gasped for perhaps the last time.

Ursa aimed the gun with both hands like a pro. "*YEAH, STRIP!* Like Sunny had to!" she shouted,

No one was coming to Eleanor Fjord's rescue this time. Not her lawyer, Gab Palaver, Brutus Chekoff, nor Georgy Mogulinski. It seemed she was at death's door. She hoped her late boyfriend, Lieutenant Colonel Chad Armstrong, would be on the other side. But suddenly, in that reverie, Fjord thought of something he once said: "Having a gun doesn't mean you know how to shoot it. The trigger pull on some makes getting off multiple quick shots hard."

Has the gun lulled this girl into complacency? Fjord wondered, Is it real? Can she even shoot? So the doctor began to undress, but now with a plan of escape in mind.

Ursa watched with feline fascination, as Fjord's impeccably manicured fingers unfastened and slid her posh pearl necklace across the table. Next, Fjord went for her heels, first prying one off with the toe of the other. Carefully, she leaned over to remove the other heel with her hand. As it came off, Fjord clutched it firmly and finally put her plan into play.

The sizeable shoe flew straight for Ursa's face. But the sound of it striking the back wall meant it missed. Undeterred, Fjord raised the other heel, shrieked, and lunged at her abductor. Only instead, she collided with a single burst from Ursa's very real, as it turned out, pistol. Fjord grabbed her chest and fell onto the glass-topped coffee table, crashing face-first through and onto its shards.

Ursa stood, stuffed the pistol in her parka, and then looked down at Fjord. "They won't have to dress you for your funeral. You already look...*smashing!*"

Ursa stepped over the mess of bloodied body, carpet, and shattered glass. She pulled the hood over her head and prepared for a furtive front door departure when what sounded like a motor running stopped her in her tracks. Ursa dropped to the floor, then crawled to the window. She crouched, rose, and peeled back a sliver of curtain. A sigh of relief ensued. *Whew! That's not a police car across the street.* Then came second thoughts. *Wait a minute!* Ursa fretted. *Is the black chick at the wheel a Fed?* Ursa couldn't take the chance. *The jury might just buy my try to even the score for Sunny, but not for shooting a government agent while trying to escape.*

So Ursa crept back into the living room, stopping at the sight of Fjord's smartphone. The screen was black, but was it broken or just turned off? Ursa left Fjord's phone. *The lost phone tracking service will find me,* she reasoned to herself. This touched off another litany of uncertainties.

"Don't touch the phone...*fingerprints!* Just shoot it or smash—*wait a minute!* The Fed outside might hear it! *Hear*: Did the neighbors overhear the art gallery owner's scream and the gunshot? Sure they did; they called the Feds and that black chick is waiting for police backup. I-I've got to get out of here!"

Ursa finally came to her senses and hurried into the kitchen. She grabbed a napkin from the table and headed for the backdoor. Draping the napkin over the knob, she opened the door and fled into the woods.

Meanwhile, from the car, Kelly saw concerned neighbors on their porches with eyes directed towards Eleanor Fjord's luxury home. *Something must have happened inside!* Kelly left her car and joined an elderly couple in Fjord's driveway. Other neighbors soon arrived. Kelly flashed her independent fire investigator ID, putting those who wondered if she was part of the problem at ease.

A couple of beefy males battered and finally broke down the front door. One ran back out. *"Call an ambulance!"* he shouted.

Kelly grabbed her smartphone.

CHAPTER 53

The Wrong Stop

Luna called earlier to warn Eleanor Fjord about Ursa Denali. On the second try, Fjord picked up. But Luna only heard her answer, "We're closed. Can you please come back tomorrow, Miss..?" Then, a *thud* and no reply. When no one answered Luna's frantic hellos, she hung up.

"We're closed," Luna mouthed Fjord's message. "That sounds like she didn't get home yet."

Luna hurried to the arts center to find it open. But a check with her top administrative assistant inside revealed that Eleanor Fjord was "out of the office on undisclosed business and wouldn't return today." *Dammit!* I got off at the wrong stop, Luna cussed her miscalculation.

Ever-thinking, though, she focused on the rest of Fjord's message, specifically the word "Miss." Was the doctor going to say "Miss Nightcrow?" No, she was too precise; Fjord knew it was proper to refer to women as "Ms." in professional settings.

"*Miss...*" Was it Kelly? No, it can't be. She's outside, not inside, the house. Just the same, Luna speed-dialed Kelly's smartphone. A busy signal beeped. Another try, another beep. So, Luna's train of thought rolled.

This time, the insurance investigator tracked Fjord's tone. It sounded as though she asked "Miss," as in whom? Then it struck her, like a 60,000 volt jolt from her Stinger smartphone stun gun case. *"Eleanor Fjord already ran into Ursa Denali!"*

Luna ran back to her car then, at equally break-neck speed, raced to …

CHAPTER 54

Where It All Began

Sparky went back to where it all began: His electronics fix-it shop. It took a little while getting reacquainted with the daily smell of oil, whiffs of ozone, and the clutter of parts and equipment around the store. Sparky had been intoxicated by the perfumed aromas of the dancers and their exotic vapes wafting off the verandas. But the presence of a beloved Bettie Page pinup on the wall kept Sparky company and brought back memories of good ole Nevada days. And lonely-hearts, hen-pecked husbands, and Don Juan wannabes kept Sparky busy restoring toasters, ham radios, video tape players, and other old technology in greater quantity. It didn't make him as much as the club, but Sparky was strengthened by what seemed like their silent show of solidarity.

A radio tuned to AM still kept Sparky rooted in reality though. One station broadcasted news updates on the 2 murders; another turn of the dial brought Reverend Sebastian Herald's sermon about how Juneau was going to hell in a handbasket; and a final tuning piped through leftwingers proposing that more diverse Anchorage should replace it as the state capital. Sparky told the bearers of bad news to *"Blow it out your nose!"* and switched to FM music instead.

Suddenly, the old-fashioned bell above the front door jingled. Sparky jumped like Pavlov's dog at the prospect of more business. But when he saw the customer was female, his creative juices flowed from electronics to thinking of a new way to get *The Burning Desire* back in Juneau.

Elvis belted out "Surrender" in the background, as Sparky walked to the front counter. "Howdy, Miss. Are you here for Sparky to brighten your day with his electronics cachet?" he asked.

The young woman pulled the hood from over her head and stretched her lips into a big smile. Sparky took mental notes. Not bad, he judged her facial assets to himself. She can draw a guy in but I can't tell much else with that big coat on.

"Sparky!" the young woman squealed. "You're the owner of *The Burning Desire*?"

Sparky gleamed. "Yep, that's me," he said proudly.

"I hitchhiked to your house, but nobody was there."

"...to my house?! How do you know...?"

"A friend of mine who used to dance at the club

told me. She was the one who said I should try out, and that she made a lot of extra money by you."

"I see. Didn't you hear that it burned down? No more dancing for now."

The young woman's smile vanished. She whipped a .22 caliber pistol from her parka pocket and pointed it with both hands at Sparky. *"Yeah, that's what Ember told me!"* Ursa Denali snarled.

"Quite the quickdraw, I see," Sparky complimented Ursa's gun handling.

"I missed Sunny's funeral because I didn't have enough money for a plane ticket. Do you know what I did to get here? I let a fishing boat crew have their way with me. But stripping you of what little manhood you have will make it worth it. *Get away from the counter!*"

Sparky moved and then raised his hands in the air at Ursa's command. "Now wait just a cotton-picking..," he began.

"NO, YOU WAIT! That art gallery owner should have killed you herself. But now that I'm here, you are going to pay for all the things you made Sunny do and for having your hitman kill her so she wouldn't tell what she knew!"

"Why now that's just not true. I had nothing to do with Ember's passing. Hell, I even sprang for a nice bouquet at her funeral."

"He's right," another voice deadpanned from behind.

Enraged, Ursa Denali spun and fired her gun. *"LIARS!"* she shouted.

But Luna Nightcrow dodged the shot, dove for Ursa's legs, and tackled her. The women fought. Luna gained the advantage, straddling Ursa and pounding her shooting hand against the floor until the pistol finally flew free and across the room. Ursa's parka protected her from Luna's bombardment of body blows, though. And she shoved the insurance investigator off her chest and hard onto her back. Luna was down, but Ursa made sure it wasn't for the count. She yanked Luna by the hair back into battle.

With both fists dug into Luna's hair and pulling hard, as if to control a bucking bronco, Ursa left herself open to attack. And Luna took advantage. She felt skin with her next punch: A penetrating uppercut that was intended for her jaw but still connected to Ursa's neck. Luna heard a grunt and felt her hair fall free. But Ursa's youth and surging adrenaline allowed for a quick recovery. She wound up for what would hopefully be a knockout, round-house slap. But in the seconds it took for Ursa's hand to come around, Luna drew her ace-in-the-hole: The Stinger smartphone stun gun.

With pincers locked into place, Luna reached up and jabbed Ursa. She shrieked, as if touching a hot stove, as 60,000 volts bit hard into her sweaty palm. It gave Luna the break needed; she seized it, driving her boot into Ursa's crotch. She flew backwards, smacking her head against the bottom of the counter. This time, the feisty young woman hurt too much to think about returning fire. It was over.

Luna wobbled to her knees and knelt there for a moment, panting and perhaps giving thanks for the hard fought victory. Once she caught her breath, Luna reached into her jeans pocket for a couple of tissues and wiped the sweat from her brow and blood from her lip. But before she could get up, a collection of cable ties, compliments of Sparky, dropped in front of her to fetter her foe. Luna couldn't believe Sparky's spectator status during the row. "You could've made it easy on me with a little gallantry!" she let him know.

Sparky told her, "When a man's roughing up a woman, it's a sin to not jump in. But a catfight is a fair fight. And the best woman won. By the way, where did you lay hold of that stun gun?"

Luna was too tired and angry to answer. She bound Ursa's hands. Then, she switched off the crackling stun gun case protector and returned the smartphone to its normal function, which she used to call the police.

"Why are you working with him?" Ursa whimpered. "He killed Sunny, can't you see?!"

Luna cradled the trembling young woman, knowing that she couldn't change her mind.

Sparky leaned over the front counter. "You know,

Ms. Nightcrow, I owe you one for saving my bacon," he said.

"*Really?!* Then how about turning yourself in for insurance fraud and saving the taxpayers the money for your trial?" Luna suggested.

Sparky's manner suddenly soured. "You know darned well that I haven't been found guilty of any..."

"...fraud, Sparky?" Luna begged to differ.

Sparky thought he had an answer. "I saw you and your firewoman friend on TV. You both said it wasn't arson, and I never even filed a claim," he explained.

But the explanation wasn't to Luna's satisfaction. She stood and looked Sparky in the eye. "You falsified that second marine survey to stay insured and in business," she asserted, then laid down the law. "If you intentionally own a forged certificate of insurance or other document relating to insurance, in this case Jonah Schipper's falsified second certification of *The Buring Desire's* electrical wiring, it is still a fraudulent act, not conspiracy to commit, and is worth up to 10 years behind bars. And with willful negligence and punitive damages likely, face it, Sparky: The only dancing you'll be doing is to 'The Jailhouse Rock.'"

"I thought you were a smart bird, Ms. Nightcrow. But 'you ain't nothing but a hound dog.' Trouble is though, you're barking up the wrong tree, trying to get me on a felony."

"Is that so, Sparky?"

"Folks tried to frame me before. You tell ole Jonah to let her rip because with nothing on paper about a payoff, he's got zip. Like y'all said on TV, I sure as hell got him on tape at the club, painting the town red every night."

"Every good investigator knows not to tell everything you know until it's been proven. Well, Sparky, I have a surprise for you: Jonah's GPS data doesn't place him in a part of town you claimed has was."

"Come again, Ms. Nightcrow?"

"Jonah uses a company truck when doing surveys that is equipped with GPS tracking, to prevent theft. It also keeps tabs on him—whether he's working or, like on the day of the marine survey, *not* working. He wasn't aboard *The Burning Desire* when you claimed the second survey happened. What will be interesting to see is, when your cellphone tracking data is subpoenaed, where you were, Sparky."

Sparky didn't have time to reply, as 3 police cars roared up outside. And moments later, their officers finally took Ursa Denali into custody. Luna didn't have to introduce herself, as one officer announced, "Ms. Nightcrow…"

"I know, I know," Luna said, as she surrendered, "you need the blow-by-blow."

A female officer remained to take a statement from Sparky while a crime scene crew moved in and secured Ursa's gun, spent casing, and a customer's ghetto blaster that absorbed the gunshot.

"Here's my card, in case you remember anything else," the officer eventually told Sparky and left.

Well, that's one way to get a woman's name and number! Sparky laughed hysterically to himself. But then another thought occurred, perhaps a money-making one.

Sparky heard that patrol officers didn't make a lot of money in most of the Lower 48, considering the tremendous risks they undertook. Alaska was different, being one of the highest paying states for patrol officers. Nevertheless, Sparky wondered if the blonde policewoman who just took his statement (probably still be in her thirties and not bad looking) might one day retire or just be down on her luck and become open to make herself and him lots of bucks.

I could even offer her more for the names of undercover cops posing as customers or dancers. A list of names—*I got it: Why not try an escort service next time?!* No boat. No upkeep. No insurance, so to speak. Just a list of eligible women to hook guys up with for a fee. *Sparky, you're a genius!* he flattered himself.

Sparky tapped the officer's card thoughtfully against his palm. Then he filed it away for future refence in his incurable quest to re-ignite *The Burning Desire*.

CHAPTER 55

A Big Help

"*Sergeant, how is she?*" Kelly Day asked Garrett Fisher, as he appeared from Héen Hospital surgery where Eleanor Fjord was rushed to.

"It is too early to tell. Doctor Fjord has a team of surgeons working on her now," Fisher reported.

"I saw lots of cuts and scratches, as the paramedics brought her out of the house," was all Kelly could add.

"The shell casing from the scene suggests Dr. Fjord took a single bullet, .22 caliber, to the chest," Fisher verified.

"Did the ole airbags absorb any of the blow?" Kelly asked.

Fisher grinned. "I'm glad you're asking that indelicate question."

"Just a sincere anatomical inquiry, Detective Sergeant. And one I'm qualified to ask, I might add."

"One more reason to have you and Ms. Night-crow on the case?"

"Variety is the spice of life."

"I do know that Fjord fell on the glass table in her living room which caused the injuries you saw, Ms. Day."

"When Luna is done with questioning, I will let her know. Thanks for the update."

"Doctor Fjord is one tough lady, but your being on the scene was a big help."

"Well, thank Luna; she asked me to watch over the place."

"It could make a difference, if Fjord pulls through."

"*Difference:* As in her living carefree or to be held accountable for 2 homicides, Detective Sergeant?"

Fisher would only say, "Stay tuned, Ms. Day."

"I know," Kelly said, "these things take time."

"Policework isn't as easy as it is on TV. And this isn't San Francisco: We have to deal with domestic abuse, robberies, drunk driving, and other daily crimes with far less manpower and budget. And now with that jet crash..."

"We appreciate everything you did, Detective Sergeant," Kelly assured the detective.

Fisher nodded. "Want some coffee?"

"No thanks," Kelly declined. "I have had my fill of hot, cold, cappuccino, and frappe cappuccino blends. But if there's a can of cola that needs a home..."

"One cola on me, coming up," Fisher replied. Before stepping into the elevator for the ride down to the cafeteria, he looked over his shoulder. "You know, if you two get tired of fraud in the Lower 48, maybe you will consider setting up shop up here."

Kelly declined again. "What's that old saying from the westerns? This town ain't big enough for the three of us," she laughed.

CHAPTER 56

Real Deep Ditch

Sparky worried that if someone knocked on his door after midnight, it meant trouble. Who would be out that late but thieves? So whoever was knocking on his door at 8 am wasn't a big deal. It was probably their job: Selling something that, if Sparky didn't need, he could ignore. No need to grab his shotgun; after a while, they would go away. But after 10 minutes, this morning's knocks didn't end.

So, Sparky rolled out of bed, into slippers, and a dingy bathrobe. He grumbled as he plodded like a zombie to the front door and opened it. Two men in dark suits appeared.

Damned bible-thumpers again! Sparky moaned to himself. "Morning, brethren," Sparky yawned. "You are too late: My houseboat met a fiery fate. There is nothing to save."

"Mr. Bernie Sparks?" asked the first man in a

dark suit and tie with a plain face but a badge that denoted FBI.

Sparky's fingers tried to comb his unruly bed hair into some respectability, as he answered, "Yep, that's me."

"Mister Sparks, we'd like to speak with you about allegations of misuse of COVID-19 PPP loans you received," the second agent announced and folded his I.D..

"May we come in, sir, please?" the first agent asked ceremonially.

Sparky thought, Tanis, you stupid bitch. *You just put us both in a real deep ditch!* But as usual, he managed a grin and told his visitors, "Yeah, come on in. You boys want some root beer, by the way? It's one surefire way to take the edge off what feels like another hell of a day."

CHAPTER 57

Heading Out

Two weeks later marked a month's stay in Juneau for Luna. She returned to the downtown docks where it was cloudy and cool, leading her to breakout the trench coat. As she leaned over the railing overlooking the harbor, another inbound cruise ship appeared in the distance. Luna turned away at the sound of a car pulling up. The driver parked, got out, and walked over with luggage that Luna asked for.

"Heading out?" Kelly asked.

Luna nodded and accepted her rolling duffel bag and suitcase.

"Well, sailor, where are you bound for?" Kelly wanted to know.

"Points south, where I hope to pick up where I left off: Peacefully exploring Inner Passage ports before summer ends and cold weather sets in," Luna answered.

"I thought you said you had enough of Alaska?"

"*Juneau:* Enough of Juneau."

Kelly chuckled, *"I feel you!* We can't go anywhere without being hailed as heroines for cleaning up this town."

"Or hated for killing the big city creature comforts of *The Burning Desire*," Luna said about the flipside of fame. "But it's not like either side got off Scot-free. The biggest murder-for-hire trial this state's ever seen kicks off once Eleanor Fjord pulls through her injuries."

Kelly nodded. "Too bad she answered your call about Ursa and left the phone on. The cops confiscated her cell and snazzy earbud earrings from the crime scene and heard her admit just about everything. Without the recording, Fjord could have pled she made it up to keep Ursa from killing her."

"She still might, but it will be a hard sell," Luna added. "Ursa will probably plead the heat of passion made her do it, while Palaver plays whatever cards he's got. And then, there's Fjord's Russian connections."

"The houseboat haters are happy that Sparky pled guilty to one count of staging a fraudulent/criminal insurance act, based on Jonah's GPS evidence," Kelly said.

Luna added, "Some of them think he got a slap on the wrist, with just a few months in jail and a twenty thousand dollars fine. But they don't know about the brewing investigation of those PPP loans he applied for and probably misused to buy the houseboat with. So I didn't just save Sparky's life but gave the Feds a shot at him, too. He may wish Ursa pulled the trigger, considering the mess he's in when he gets out."

Kelly shook her head at the degree of debauchery. "And who would have thought that all of this happened in Juneau: A place you go to get away from it all."

"Sleepy little communities are sometimes where the weirdest, sleaziest stuff goes on. Stepford, Amityville, Peyton Place..," Luna listed some cinematic examples. "It wouldn't surprise me if the local chamber of commerce is drooling over the publicity the trial will bring. Lots of money spent on hotels, car rentals, and restaurants by the national and international media and ordinary looky-loos. All in Juneau, not Anchorage, for a change."

"The trial reminds me: The D.A. offered to pay for my extended stay at The Chichagof, in case they need me as an expert witness," Kelly announced.

"And will you be extending your stay, Ms. Day?" Luna asked.

"Nah," Kelly declined. "I can catch a quick flight back from anywhere on the West Coast.

"Staying someplace warm until then, I trust?"

"As a fire investigator, I wouldn't have it any other way. I will check out that naughty museum paddle before I skedaddle though," Kelly answered with a mischievous grin.

"Look but don't touch. If this case has strengthened anything I already believe it's that Mark Twain was right: 'The more things are forbidden, the more popular they become.'"

"Alright, no hanky-panky paddle play. I will let you know my thoughts about it."

"*Oh no you don't!* Not this time." Luna drew her smartphone and tossed it into the harbor.

Kelly rolled her eyes. "Who are you fooling? The last I recall, that wonder phone of yours is also waterproof!"

"Then it will be the perfect catch for some fish in need," Luna laughed.

"With your hard-earned fee, you can buy another when the time comes." Kelly suddenly thought of something. "Did you know that an electrical fire can smell like fish?"

"*Great!*" Luna groaned. "I will never look at pan-fried catfish the same again."

The two women finally hugged good-bye.

Kelly's voice quivered. "Take care."

"Later," Luna replied teary-eyed.

Epilogue

The perfect catch for some fish in need, Luna laughed at her sunken smartphone deed. But that "generosity" was rewarded by the cruise ship that finally arrived, giving the forlorn insurance investigator the vacation she craved.

Once onboard, Luna learned *The Glacier Goddess* was docked for shore leave and wouldn't leave Gastineau Channel for another 8 hours. Relax, she thought, there's plenty of ship to get reacquainted with.

Luna made it to her stateroom and opened the door to warmth that spread over her like a blanket. No need for the trench coat, she breathed a sigh of relief and tossed it aside. Her eye then caught a bouquet of pink and blue forget-me-nots on the dining room table. Luna moved closer but dismissed it as "probably complimentary; forget-me-nots are the state flower, after all." Upon closer inspection of the table setting, however, a crystal carafe of her favorite iced espresso and 2 gold-rimmed Martini glasses signaled this wasn't just a first-class benefit but was prepared by someone whose knowledge of Luna was far more intimate.

"Shall we pick up where we left off?" a masculine voice asked.

Luna turned to see a dream come true, charming her anew in fitted jeans and a white Oxford shirt. Luna put her hands on her hips and chuckled, "*Well aren't you just what the doctor ordered!*"

Luna ached for dinner date Adonis Healy's passionate embrace and fell effortlessly into his waiting arms. Adonis was again enchanted by Luna's delicate scent and felt her shiver as his fingers swam through her river of dark hair.

"I tried to text you that one of the interior villages needed a doctor during shore leave," Adonis explained. "It only had what's called a community health aide, but she took ill herself. And to make matters worse, the village was accessible only by charter plane—*imagine being seventy miles from the nearest grocery store!* I tried to text a couple of times en route and on the ground, but the signal must not have gone through. After that, I just became busy and from what I read coming back, so did you: Defending "The Last Frontier" from what some called the onset of the world's oldest profession."

"I believe you," Luna said. "And thanks for considering my mess. I should have been as understanding of yours."

"You are welcome, and I'm glad I passed your lie detector test," Adonis replied.

"Well…I am still curious about something," Luna wondered aloud.

"Uh, oh."

"How much did you pay the purser to get into my stateroom?"

"I didn't." Adonis then explained, "I told the purser we missed our stopovers, hadn't seen each other in a month, and were frantic to catch up—all true. Once she checked the original passenger logs, it was clear we were onboard, registered for the recreational volleyball competition, and began what was a wonderful dinner. But in case the purser didn't buy all that, I convinced her how crazy we are for each other with one of your texts that finally got through."

For a moment, Luna panicked. *"Which one?!"*

Adonis assured her that memories of her disco dream danced only his head. "Not that one," he said.

"Whew! Okay, no more questions," Luna said.

"Sorry, but now I have one," Adonis apologized. "With plenty of time before we shove off, what will we do?"

"What we intended to: Explore the Inner Passage, of course."

"What do you mean, Luna? We have already seen Juneau."

"Not Juneau; I mean *this* inner passage."

Luna cradled the back of Adonis's neck and guided him towards lips that longed for more than a peck. His gladly met hers and appeased the need for affection, as both made the connection through a passionate kiss.

After he came up for air, Adonis breathed, "Oh *that* inner passage."

Luna nodded. "And the rest we'll explore later."

"As in Ketchikan and points in between?" Adonis asked.

"Especially the 'points in between,'" Luna guaranteed.

Adonis got into the act, wanting to know if that even meant "penetrating the bush country?"

Luna tipped her head back and giggled dreamily, *"Who writes this stuff?!"*

Adonis said, "For all we've been through, whoever it is better have a happy ending in store."

But Luna asked for more. "No, a happily ever after because I don't want it to end this time," she insisted.

After another kiss, Luna poured two iced espressos. Her glass raised to meet Adonis', then both clinked. And after her smooth drink, Luna felt at least the beginning of an unforgettable cruise was on the brink.

··◆··

Also by Amy Knupp

<u>Single Dads of Dragonfly Lake</u>

Singled Out

Single All the Way

<u>Henry Brothers Series</u>

Untold (prequel)

Unraveled

Unsung

Undone

Unexpected

Or binge the Henry Brothers in audio:

Henry Brothers Audiobooks

<u>North Brothers Series</u>

True North

True Colors

True Blue

True Harmony

True Hero

North Brothers Box Sets:

North Brothers Books 1-3

North Brothers Books 4-5

North Brothers: The Complete Series

Or binge the North Brothers in audio:
North Brothers Audiobooks

<u>Hale Street Series</u>:

Sweet Spot

Sweet Dreams

Soft Spot

One and Only

Last First Kiss

Heartstrings

<u>Hale Street Box Sets</u>:

Meet Me at Clayborne's

Clayborne's After Hours

It Happened on Hale Street

<u>Island Fire Series</u>:

Playing with Fire

Heat of the Night

Fully Involved

Firestorm

Afterburn

Up in Flames

Flash Point

Fire Within

Impulse